THE INNOCENT HOUR

Vietnam veteran Charlie Alderfer hires Ben, an 18-year-old hard-working student, whom teachers, coaches, classmates, and their parents adore. But when his adoptive parents accuse him of a crime he didn't commit and police terrorize him into pleading guilty *to something*, Ben believes them and confesses *to make the charges go away.*

Outraged, Charlie takes Ben to a polygraph expert who confirms his innocence, but his accusers refuse to back down. Charlie hires a lawyer who withdraws the guilty plea, but Ben's only defense is his word against a little girl's.

Incensed by the impending miscarriage of justice, Charlie risks his own life to uncover the truth. Everyone lies—except Ben. Charlie's digging exposes them both to an ongoing criminal enterprise.

OTHER BOOKS BY NANCY A. HUGHES

The Dying Hour

A Matter of Trust

Redeeming Trust

Vanished: A Trust Mystery

ACKNOWLEDGMENTS

I owe heartfelt thanks and deepest appreciation to so many people who have made my novels a reality. My publisher, Black Opal Books, brought my novels to life. Lauri Wellington, newly retired, tops my list. Artist Jack Jackson, did another killer job by nailing the essence of The Innocent Hour for my cover. My editor, Faith C, continues to diligently make my work better. I wish I could personally thank the whole team for their behind-the-scenes miracles that ensure our books are beautifully produced to the highest standards, marketed, and shipped on time. In the past year alone, they endured impossible weather and landslides, epidemic flu, and technical failure. Thank you—for your perseverance so that we can keep our readers up at night.

While my mystery novels are works of fiction, crime writers can't just make it all up. I am indebted to the legal and law enforcement professionals in Berks, Lebanon, and Lancaster County PA who shared their knowledge, opinions, and corrected my misconceptions to help me get the facts straight. They prefer to remain anonymous. My undying appreciation goes to our dedicated first responders who run toward danger every day to protect us.

Words can't express my gratitude to my readers, who invite me into their imagination and give me encouragement, feedback, and invitations to their book clubs, library, and community events. Special thanks to the BOLD authors group for sharing their creative insights, especially Troy Rauenzahn of Roughtooth Photography, Mary Ann Hayes, and Pam Gockley for their technical expertise.

THE INNOCENT HOUR

Nancy A. Hughes

A Black Opal Books Publication

GENRE: MYSTERY

This is a work of fiction. Names, places, characters and incidents are either the product of the author's imagination or are used fictitiously, and any resemblance to any actual persons, living or dead, businesses, organizations, events or locales is entirely coincidental. All trademarks, service marks, registered trademarks, and registered service marks are the property of their respective owners and are used herein for identification purposes only. The publisher does not have any control over or assume any responsibility for author or third-party websites or their contents.

THE INNOCENT HOUR
Copyright © 2019 by Nancy A. Hughes
Cover Design by Name:
Cover photos used with permission
All cover art copyright © 2019
All Rights Reserved
Print ISBN: 978-1-64437-208-1

First Publication: NOVEMBER 2019

All rights reserved under the International and Pan-American Copyright Conventions. No part of this book may be reproduced or transmitted in any form or by any means, electronic or mechanical, including photocopying, recording, or by any information storage and retrieval system, without permission in writing from the publisher.

WARNING: The unauthorized reproduction or distribution of this copyrighted work is illegal. Criminal copyright infringement, including infringement without monetary gain, is investigated by the FBI and is punishable by up to 5 years in federal prison and a fine of $250,000. Anyone pirating our eBooks will be prosecuted to the fullest extent of the law and may be liable for each individual download resulting therefrom.

ABOUT THE PRINT VERSION: If you purchased a print version of this book without a cover, you should be aware that the book is stolen property. It was reported as "unsold and destroyed" to the publisher, and neither the author nor the publisher has received any payment for this "stripped book."

IF YOU FIND AN EBOOK OR PRINT VERSION OF THIS BOOK BEING SOLD OR SHARED ILLEGALLY, PLEASE REPORT IT TO:
lpn@blackopalbooks.com

Published by Black Opal Books **http://www.blackopalbooks.com**

DEDICATION

In loving memory of my Godparents Milton and Dorothy Shannon Henriquez

Prologue

June

Had Charlie Alderfer grasped how an overheard conversation would impact his life one year later, he would have paid more attention. He would have interrupted and asked a few questions, especially their names. Still learning the fundamentals of healthy cooking, he had been scrutinizing a peculiar squash nestled among its brethren. Two women's exchange piqued his interest while he was puzzling over the label *spaghetti*.

"My daughter heard that the police dragged a junior out of the cafeteria and hauled him to jail," a woman's voice said.

Charlie dared a glance beyond the grocery's vegetable bins. The pair, about the right age to have high school children, were engaged in what sounded like serious gossip. He replaced the spaghetti squash and pretended to consider a zucchini, unable to stop himself from eavesdropping. Not that his life was that dull—he just had an innate fascination with people and their inevitable drama.

"That's not what I heard. It wasn't a boy—it was some foster girl who was nothing but trouble," the other woman said.

"Did your daughter know what it was about?"

"She said that the girl was bragging about getting her

foster family's son in big trouble with the police. That she'd done it before. How she'd laughed! Thought it was hilarious. I'm guessing she's been bounced around and learned that malice was entertaining. The kids were stunned. Hung on her every word, which I'm guessing was her motivation—to shock them. I mean, this is a conservative rural community. Stuff like that just doesn't happen around here."

"Which was…"

"Story goes, she waited until she and their son—he's a junior weight lifter—were alone in the house, supposedly supervising the younger foster kids. She comes on to the son. He tells her no—that it's 'inappropriate,' and the son thinks that's it. The next day she tells the guidance counselor that the son committed—"

A blaring announcement about a bakery special in aisle ten drowned out the rest of her sentence. Charlie continued scrutinizing the zucchini as if looking for imperfections, hoping she would continue.

"The story's all over the school. Bet it was the dinner topic at every table in the district. Not just what she did, but what she brazenly admitted to a table full of kids. We just don't have foster kids like that around here. We're too far from the city."

Before the speaker could finish her story, she spotted him. "Hey Charlie! I didn't see you at first."

Busted! Charlie jerked to attention, having feigned preoccupation with an acorn squash. He set it in his basket.

As a matter of explanation, the mother began volunteering some background to her friend. "Charlie Alderfer spent ages helping me choose my appliances. I had no idea what I wanted, and my contractor was apoplectic about my indecision. Charlie walked me through every detail and answered all my stupid questions." She grinned her appreciation. "I can't thank you enough."

"I loved my job. It's easy when a salesman believes in what he sells and the store stands behind the products." Charlie took a chance and guessed. "How did that stove work out for you?"

"Love it. Went back for the fridge, washer, and dryer you recommended."

Charlie dredged his mind for the woman's name but hadn't a clue. She didn't supply one—if only he'd asked.

"Gotta go," she said, having snapped a glance at her watch. "Hope you're enjoying your well-earned retirement." The pair rolled away, any embellishment to their story fading with their departure.

Later that day tragedy struck, the chance conversation forgotten among events that changed Charlie's life. Having found a recipe to bake that acorn squash in his Emma's worn red plaid cookbook, Charlie feasted on it for dinner. After tidying the kitchen, he went outside to watch an ordinary day fade into a glorious evening.

The week had been dry. He had watered Emma's roses, turned off the soaker hose, and tucked the wand under his arm. He would remember swinging his arm as he strode toward the faucet to shut off the gush. Satisfied, he sank into his favorite old lawn chair, his gaze drinking in a perfect June evening.

Emma's beloved garden—the scent of the ox eye daisies, roses, and verbena, their profusion glowing in the gathering dusk. Beyond the garden stretched fragrant, crisply mowed grass. Charlie valued such peaceful moments. He had overcome crushing challenges—the Vietnam war, surgery for his wounds, the transition to civilian life, Emma's illness and death, the empty nest, but he chose to live thankfully—for his marriage, their two amazing daughters. The grandkids.

If only...

He remembered Emma's last admonition as her health

faded: "You must dance at our daughters' weddings." The way that she stated it left no opportunity to argue.

"We. *We* will dance…"

But that wasn't to be. Fifteen years—where had it gone? A soft breeze carried the scent of cut grass, flowers and, could it be? His neighbor had mucked out his barn.

As Charlie waited for that first heavenly jewel, just as his family, his parents, and siblings had done, he heard the kitchen phone ring. Nearly tripped by the chair's collapsible frame, he chastised himself. If it weren't for his nasty habit of leaving the cordless out in the rain he wouldn't have to tear into the house. And that answering machine only gave him five rings. Breathing hard, he yanked open the screen door and stumbled into the kitchen. Before he could traverse the half dozen steps, a searing pain overwhelmed him.

Ripping!

Crushing!

Tearing!

Like nothing he had ever experienced, not even when he was shot. With ultimate effort he grabbed at the phone, which clattered from its bracket onto the floor, landing several feet from where he collapsed. Pain ratcheted even as his strength plummeted. In excruciating pain, he snagged the handset.

"Help me! Help," he gasped as horrific pain inflamed every nerve in his body. "Wallet! On. Kitchen. Counter! Call—daughters…" He whispered his pleas, praying his failing voice had connected with someone.

Sirens. An ER's blazing lights. Aggregate people who staccatoed clipped instructions. Voices that barked, equipment that bleeped, and hands—lots of hands that worked with cold stuff. Then he was airborne. Blades thump-thump-thumping and lights flickering like an old black and white movie. A jumble of impressions sluicing in disjointed snatches. Blackness cocooned him. Then there was nothing.

Charlie's catastrophe—a ruptured aneurism—was followed by weeks in the VA's hospice. They expected he'd die any moment. But he had defied them, relishing his victory over nearly succumbing. Struggling to regain his health, he *graduated* from hospice. How grateful he was to be home, knitting together his disjointed life, flying to visit his daughters, and enjoying simple pleasures like grocery shopping.

His daughters, however, warned him to be on his guard. That made him smile. They were concerned, not just about his health, but about predatory single women, trying to seduce him with casseroles and cleavage. And his dear friend and neighbor, Old Mr. Greer, would get him into trouble. That Charlie's kindhearted nature would rekindle his passion for getting involved, drawing him into new battles. Charlie had smiled—a lot—and indulged his girls with promises to thwart their long-range worrying. Funny how nearly dying—twice—had awakened his spirit for adventure.

Chapter 1
The Following Fall:

The nip in the air and the maple's crimson leaves spurred Charlie into action. With judicious pruning and deadheading, he might coax some flowers to bloom a bit longer, and depending upon the timing of the first killing frost, postpone the inevitable until Halloween. His Emma would say, "It's summer as long as there's one flower in the garden." And she would add, "A clean garden is a happy garden." How grateful he was that his neighbors had tended his yard during his lost summer in the VA's hospice.

Roxie appeared to be sleeping, but her ears were perked for the big yellow bus that would bring her six-year-old master home. Another timely ritual was unfolding across the street, as Old Mr. Greer tested his two webbed chairs for stability. Shortly he'd amble into his garage and emerge holding two eight-ounce cans of Miller beer. That was Charlie's invitation to join him.

As Charlie crossed the two-lane rural road, Roxie herded his progress in spirited circles, stopping at Mr. Greer's outstretched hand to lick a few drops of forbidden beer. At Charlie's raised eyebrow, the little Sheltie planted her butt between the two chairs.

"How's your little guy liking first grade?" Mr. Greer asked.

"Loves it!" I'd worried a bit about his missing

kindergarten and having no playmates—living in isolation with his mother, grandfather, and an invalid grandmother. When I first met Jonathan, visiting his grandfather in the VA's hospice ward with his mom, he was mute. Obviously deeply troubled. Now his teacher can't shut him up. Marks *N—Needs Improving* beside "works quietly" on her reports home.

"I remember when you and Emma built your house over thirty years ago. Who would have thought that the in-law suite would end up housing Jonathan and his mom? How's she doing in school?"

"Gobbling up life science courses; planning to transfer to premed. I didn't think I was lonely, living on my own, but having their company and assistance if need be in exchange for that useless apartment is such a blessing. That is, if I ever do need help."

"Speaking of which…"

Oh dear, here it comes again, Charlie thought.

"You're going to need help with those leaves. I know—don't say it. The doc says, 'you're as good as expected for sixty-seven, as long as you stay out of trouble.' Have you noticed my fine young man over here? Mowing, pruning, tilling my garden? Shoveling my driveway? Six-two, skinny as a rail? Strong as an ox. He never stops moving."

"I did. And your yard's picture perfect."

"As long as I have help—and he'll even wash windows. He's offered to clean house if it comes to that so I can stay in my home. Gonna die here, later than sooner."

Mr. Greer paused. Charlie took a sip of his beer, letting the old gentleman plan the segue to his next point, as was their custom. "I mentioned to Ben that you might need help too. I hope that was all right."

Not a real question.

"He's a hard worker. Earns every dollar. Keeps a killer schedule, what with school, fast-food jobs, and the swim team. He's never at home. Doesn't smoke, drink, or do drugs. Comes from a huge family with little money who adopted him when he was four. You'd be doing both him and yourself a favor by hiring him."

"I'll give it some thought." His girls had been hinting—no, nagging—that he should have help with the house, at the very least someone on yoo-hoo standby. He had told them flat out that he would not be warehoused in a retirement community, no matter how fancy. And he would never live on the fringe of their lives. He'd rather live in a shelter or under a bridge. In spite of their twenty-five-year difference in age, he and Old Mr. Greer were like-minded spirits.

Suddenly Roxie leapt, all four feet hitting the ground simultaneously. She ran toward the street, skidding to a stop where the grass met the asphalt. Looking left and then right, she bolted toward Charlie's driveway, all wiggles and waggles in anticipation of the big yellow bus turning onto their street. Depositing the two empty beer cans into a small bag of recyclables, Charlie shook Old Mr. Greer's hand, as was their custom, and carried the bag across the street. Mr. Greer's few recyclables hardly warranted the trash hauler's monthly fee.

By the time he had crossed, Jonathan and Roxie were rolling on the grass, a joyful chorus of yips and squeals, a tangle of black and white fur and blonde hair. Backpack flopping, arms extended, Jonathan leapt into Charlie's outstretched arms. He chattered nonstop about his day—harvest season, what story they'd been reading, which kid broke what rule, and whose mommy sent yummy cupcakes with no nuts 'cuz some kids can't eat peanuts and tree nuts and what's a tree nut?

Together the threesome entered Charlie's kitchen via the garage and laundry room doors. Jonathan toed off his shoes, aligning them carefully on his personal spot, and hung his jacket on his special hook. Inside, he sprinted into the powder room. Charlie could hear his little stool being scraped into position, the running water orchestrating the child's sweet rendition of *happy birthday*, having mastered the lathering time needed to kill those nasty school germs. Jade was such a good mother!

Charlie motioned him toward the kitchen table, the cookie jar, and a glass of milk. "Mom says two cookies—but they're big ones." He pointed to Jonathan's backpack, which the child had dropped by the laundry room door. "May I?" With Jonathan's nod of consent, Charlie spread the contents on the table, separating Jonathan's and his mother's homework while Jonathan munched and pointed, directing which went on what pile.

"What's our 'genda today?"

"Mom left a note. Can you read it?"

Jonathan scowled in concentration at Jade's printing, proud that a big first grader could read. "Looks like—'Put my work on my special place.' She means on her desk. 'Do your homework. Feed Roxie. Take Roxie outside. Wipe her feet if they are muddy. I will be home by five. Love, Mommy.' What did Miss Barbara say about me?"

"That paper is addressed to your mom, so I didn't read it. It may be personal—or something she'll share with you. The other one looks like a permission slip."

"The zoo! We're going to the zoo to study animal behavior if it's okay with our parents."

"Then you better make sure your mom's homework is on her special spot." With that, Jonathan jumped from his chair and, with Roxie at his heels, bolted for the stairway door that connected the two adults' worlds. Charlie's heart swelled with joy. How lucky he was!

c◡◠c◡◠

Charlie heard Ben's rattletrap before he saw it and recognized it from being parked nearby on their street. The skinny high school student unwound his tall frame through the open driver-side window. As he strode toward the front door, Charlie's first impression was *poor*. While clean and neatly pressed, his clothing was just shy of ragged, and not in a fashionable way. The kid rang the bell.

"Mr. Alderfer? I'm Ben Olinger. Mr. Greer thought you might need some help."

"Yes, of course. He told me all about you, and how pleased he is with your work. Please come in." Even though Charlie was six feet tall, he found himself looking up at the boy's pale gray eyes. His face was placid and calm with a smile that included his eyes. He extended his hand and shook Charlie's with a man's measured grip. He nodded in the direction of Mr. Greer's place.

"No one should be forced out of his home because he doesn't have family or friends to give him a hand. I volunteer whenever I can. Like when this old lady's toilet wouldn't stop running, and she couldn't afford a plumber or the water bill. It was a simple repair—a new flapper fixed it right up. She gave me some homemade cookies. When I shoveled her driveway, she gave me a loaf of bread, hot from the oven. I was so hungry and grateful!"

"You any good with cars? I have an old one that needs to be tuned. I've been, ah, away for four months and it doesn't want to start."

Ben jerked his thumb over his shoulder. "I love working on old cars. That compact out in the street? Had been just a shell that I got for six hundred bucks. All its parts I salvaged from the junkyard. You would not believe the perfectly good stuff that people discard."

"If you'd like to take a look at my project, it's in the

spare garage out back, which is more like an overgrown shed." The clinking of doggie toenails preceded Jonathan upstairs. "Jonathan, meet Ben. He might be available to help us a bit."

"Like Mr. Greer?" The three exchanged smiles as Roxie pawed at the door.

"Homework?" Jonathan's face fell. "Okay, a brief reprieve, but you'd better be finished before your Mom gets home."

The three walked downhill to the old frame two-car garage that anchored the right rear corner of Charlie's one-acre property. He reached for the handle, but Ben beat him to it, lifting the door as if it were weightless. In addition to all manner of garden implements—a rototiller, two lawnmowers, a chainsaw, snow and leaf blowers, long-handled implements, and shelves filled with hand tools, bags of potting soil, and fertilizers—was the tarped auto in question.

Charlie eased the cover off a vintage Corvette for Ben's inspection with the same care that one would unroll a Persian rug. Ben appeared stunned. "Oh, man! It's a Vet. That is one fine machine. It is—magnificent." He stroked the fender with the same care one would touch a newborn.

"Do you think you could tune it?"

Ben said nothing for a few moments, absorbing its aura. Finally, he took a deep breath and confessed. "Mr. Alderfer? Sir? I wouldn't let anyone touch this machine who isn't an expert. I don't have the experience or knowledge to work on it. Oh, I could take a stab at tuning it and take your money. But I'd leave you with a bigger problem that would take megabucks for an expert to fix. I'm sorry, but no."

Charlie thought, *I like this boy*. "Well then—how about tuning my lawnmower? The blades are shredding the grass, and it takes extreme cussing to start it. And it stalls at the most inopportune times. And then there's the roto-tiller—same thing. And the snow blower."

Ben brightened visibly. "That's more up my alley. And I can do minor plumbing as well."

Jonathan, who had been scrutinizing the contents of the perimeter shelves, turned his attention to their visitor. "Mr. Ben, could you teach me how to fix a lawnmower?"

"Perhaps when you're a lot older. The blades are sharp and could hurt you. You need to be bigger and stronger. And eat all that stuff your mom says is good for you."

"Okay." Apparently satisfied, and with Roxie at his heels, Jonathan sprinted toward the house to finish his homework.

"Do you think your little boy could raise the door high enough to squeeze under? He was awfully interested in those bags on the shelf, and the ladder is leaning against it."

"The old lock doesn't work. We've never had trouble with folks breaking in, but a new lock could be added to your list. What do you charge by the hour?"

"Like I said, for people with limited means, I do volunteer work. Or enough to cover gas and the parts they need. And a few extra bucks if they insist."

"I think we can do better than 'a few extra.' Why don't you check out the going wage for each type of work we're discussing, and we'll figure out what's fair. Deal?"

"It's a deal.

ﻌﻌﻌ

Charlie couldn't believe his eyes or his ears. From the kitchen window he spotted Ben covering the width of the back lawn that lay behind the flowerbed. The mower, which had lost its cough, splutter, and backfire, seemed to be gliding, gobbling grass and leaves in its wake. Ben had even managed to attach its persnickety bag, leaving a crisp, verdant path.

Charlie's eye next caught a blaze of light—or was it a reflection—on the closed garage door. A lock! Ben had already dealt with that issue. Stepping back from the sink, Charlie eyeballed the clock over the window, its hours painted with various birds. Hearing the bluebird's song, he knew it was fifteen past something, but could it really be seven? On a Saturday morning? What time had Ben arrived?

In the next forty-five minutes, Ben covered the entire lawn, located the refuse spot behind the garage, and was freeing the mower of clinging grass snippets with Charlie's garden hose. He wheeled it to a sunny spot to dry before striding toward his car, an old toolbox swinging from his hand.

"Ben. Wait up!" Charlie called after him as Ben was stowing his tools in his trunk. He loped back to the door. "Didn't expect you to mow as well—not first thing on a Saturday morning."

"That's one fine mower. Just got carried away, it was running so well. No charge for a test drive. Oh! Here's a pair of keys for the lock. No charge for that either. Picked it up at a flea market, keys and all. At the end of the day, they were throwing it away because it's an odd style that nobody wants. I just knew it would come in handy one day."

"Won't you come in and join us for breakfast?"

"Can't. Just got time to get to the gym and shower before swim team practice."

"Then take something with you," Charlie said, pointing to the fruit basket. Ben snagged an apple and a banana.

"Thanks. If I can stop by after practice and before I go to work, we can talk about what's next on your list."

"I'll be here all day."

Hired help. If anyone had mentioned that one year ago, Charlie would have laughed. The retirement he had planned meant serious living. Sprung! Maybe his church's bowling league about which the *old guys* had been pestering. Or hiking or cooking lessons. Caving with the Boy Scouts. But when? His lists had lists that covered two pages—paint the interior and all that wood trim, enlarge the gardens, travel more to see the kids. Maybe a river cruise with his buddies.

One day he was steeped in possibilities, the next waking from a coma in the hospice ward, reduced to being a grownup in diapers. Decades of goals replaced with hopes of walking to the bathroom unassisted to use the toilet. The VA's staff had been encouraging, upbeat, and highly professional, keeping him clean and comfortable, but he was humiliated nevertheless. Maybe the girls were right. Accepting a little help with the heavier tasks could be prudent insurance against a recurrence, however unlikely.

Chapter 2

*B**ing Bong!* Charlie opened the stairway door and called, "Come on up. I'm presentable." Jonathan thundered upstairs, Roxie practically Velcroed to his side. "Did your mom say you could have breakfast with me this morning? Let her catch up on her sleep?" The child bobbed his body *yes*, then scampered into the kitchen where Charlie had laid out the ingredients for waffles.

For the umpteenth time, Charlie blessed their foresight when he and Emma designed their house to accommodate visiting elders for the long term. Their contractor had installed two-way doorbells and locks on both stairway doors. Not only did that ensure each family's privacy, but eliminated the need to circumvent the house to knock on each other's front doors.

The red brick rancher, built on a slope, enjoyed a street-level front elevation, while the lower level, built into the hill, had a full view of the garden through expansive picture windows. They anticipated their retired parents would enjoy lots of time with the grandchildren, but it wasn't to be. Their elders opted for lives on their own.

The apartment was a blessing when their daughters invited hordes for sleepovers, then term breaks from college. Party central morphed into young married visitors, but they eventually moved out of state to follow their careers. When his eldest gifted him with two lovely grand-angels, he thought they would come often, the great room being the perfect play space. But careers, school, and sick days gobbled the parents' vacation time. Charlie's grandbabies called him Airplane Grandpa, and those rooms lay fallow for years until Jade and Jonathan swept into his life. The suite was complete with two bedrooms, two baths, a cozy kitchen, and lots of room for an energetic boy and his dog.

"Did you bring me your mom's *Ben list*?"

Jonathan pulled the strap of Jade's repurposed passport wallet over his head. He loosened the Velcro flap, carefully extracting a folded piece of paper. He handed it to Charlie. "Looks like that faucet is dripping again. Are you sure everyone's turning it off completely?"

Jonathan rolled his eyes. "So hard the handle bends all the way back. Mommy says the drip keeps her awake."

"And what's this about a trap?"

"I, ah—it wasn't on purpose, I promise! I dropped Mommy's pinky ring down the drain. I just wanted to see if it would fit on my thumb—all my other fingers are too skinny. It kinda got stuck, so I pulled real hard and it flew off my hand and rolled down the drain. Mommy said I shouldn't turn on the water—to use her sink until someone can trap it."

"A wise decision. Her ring might be caught in that U-shaped bend in the pipe under the sink. It's called a trap. Ben can unscrew the seal and see what falls out. He'll need a bucket to catch the water caught in the trap."

Jonathan scrunched his face in his perplexed expression. "Why don't they just make the pipe straight so the water falls down?" He reconsidered. "Oh. So you can get stuff back?"

"The water in the trap also prevents sewer gas from coming back up into the house. That would be really stinky." Jonathan giggled and scrunched his nose.

Roxie jerked her head to attention, then skittered to the front door before either human detected Ben's car. All three greeted him at the door. Ben stooped to greet Jonathan, deftly patting Roxie's head to keep her tongue at bay. "Papa's making waffles. And he makes lots and lots and lots."

"I really should get to work."

"Nonsense," Charlie said. "Join us. While we eat, we can go over our Ben list, as we've come to name it over the last few weeks. And we can fill you in on Jade's new schedule so you can access their rooms."

After they finished, Charlie took Ben into his office, which abutted the living room's front center wall. He'd once shared the space with Emma, and to that day could not bring himself to dismantle her collection of gardening books nor dispose of her last pair of gloves. Maybe someday, but he doubted it, and why should he if that made him happy?

Ben's eyes swept the room, taking a moment to look outside from which he spotted Old Mr. Greer. "This room is awesome. Some day I'd like a space just like it."

"Do you have post-graduation plans?"

"Not yet. Been too busy working. In a few weeks I turn eighteen, so I'll be expected to handle all my expenses. My parents—they're really good people—say the family income must support the foster kids too. I get that. They have nothing. Besides, I love working. In fact, I've picked up a second job, delivering pizzas at night. Seeing the fosters? I'm lucky to have a roof over my head. I clean house for them when everyone's asleep and it's quiet. And they feed me. The fosters never had that kind of a deal."

Charlie tried not to look as stunned as he felt about this teenager, who hadn't been a child for a very long time. "Let's go over what I owe you. If you prefer cash, that's fine with me, or a check if cashing it is convenient." He caught himself before saying he assumed Ben wouldn't have a bank account. "Our lists of jobs are growing exponentially. I had no idea how badly we needed a handy person."

"Mr. Alderfer. Sir. Please understand. I'm not looking for you to make things up to keep me in work."

"I'm not. I'm…

Ben held up his hand. "Just thought that needed saying. Because I'd know the difference if you were breaking things for me to fix. And you needn't feed me while I'm here. I get all the fast food and pizza I can eat, and there's food at school and at my parents' house."

Charlie laughed, which brought a relaxed smile to Ben's face. "Let's take a little tour of my tools and supplies—buckets, mops, cleaners, whatever—so you can see what's on hand. I'll let Jonathan explain about the trap."

❧❧

Ben's invitation to his high school's athletic banquet and award ceremony delighted Charlie while catching him totally off guard. Ben had said nothing about the event, which the invitation indicated was for two family members. Printed on cream-colored velum, it bore the school's seal and the particulars—a Friday evening in early December to be held in the school's cafeteria. An RSVP should be emailed.

"I was hoping you and Mr. Greer could come, although he'll need a ride and some coaxing. He says he doesn't go out in the evening anymore."

"What about your family? Don't you need these tickets for them?"

"Nah. They're already coming for a foster brother—he's a tenth grader on the football team that went to States."

"Other brothers or sisters? Grandparents? I'd hate for you to neglect your family on my account."

"The kids don't want to go, and I don't have grandparents. I'd really like you come." He handed Charlie a folded paper. "You can sit with my buddy's folks. They're really nice. You'll like them. Mrs. Quillen says to call her so you can meet on the phone."

"What about you? Where will you sit?"

"With the team. It's a very special night for us, accepting awards and the letters we've earned. For some seniors, it will be our last time together."

"Thank you, Ben, for thinking of me. I'd be honored to come. And I'll check with Jade to make sure I'm not needed, but she's always home Friday evenings—that's their movie and popcorn night.

♋♋

The first Friday in December, Charlie picked up his nametag and table number outside the cafeteria. He navigated the sea of festively skirted tables, which bore perky floral arrangements of mums, ribbons, and miniature flags denoting a plethora of athletic activities. Table twelve, to which Charlie was directed, was already occupied by five adults, the three remaining seats for himself and the Quillens, who had not yet arrived. Mr. Greer had sent his regrets.

Charlie introduced himself, smiling a greeting over the racket to the couple on his left, but translated her scowl as not wanting to chat with a stranger. Her companion, a skinny man with a vacant expression, nodded, then resumed staring straight ahead. The three across the round table seemed to know each other quite well. After returning Charlie's smile with large grins and finger waves, they resumed their conversation over the din. That was all right—Charlie was here for Ben and his teammates, and the noise level made cross table chitchat impossible.

As the principal stepped to the mike and the hundreds assembled quieted, the Quillens scurried toward their table and took the seats to Charlie's right. "Sorry. So sorry to be late. Parking's a zoo," Mrs. Quillen whispered as the principal continued his opening remarks. After brief speeches by the athletic director and various coaches, dinner was served, generous compliments being offered for the cafeteria staff's attempt at gourmet cuisine. Mrs. Quillen chattered nonstop about her youngest's scholarship offers and their eldest's Olympic potential.

Turning to his left Charlie asked, "Which of the athletes is yours?"

She turned snake eyes in his direction. "Benjamin Olinger."

"You're Ben's mother? Oh my goodness! I was hoping I'd meet you. He's a wonderful boy—does odd jobs for me and is so kind to help an elderly neighbor. So bright and resourceful. You must be so proud of him."

No reaction. Her still, vacant face seemed to register no comprehension of what Charlie had said. In fact, she looked annoyed by Charlie's compliment. He studied her surreptitiously. She was what his Emma would have called *dumpy*, her generous body enveloped in tent-like fabric, her wispy gray hair a wind-blown cloud. Chiding himself for unkind thoughts, Charlie remembered two things—the expense of providing for foster children and Ben's own shabby clothes. How dare he judge this generous woman!

Maybe she hadn't heard him? Perhaps she was hard of hearing. As he was relating an example of Ben's exceptional character in a much louder voice, the woman recoiled. "I'm not deaf!" With that, she pivoted away from him, staring in the opposite direction.

Stunned, Charlie turned questioning eyes to Mrs. Quillen who shrugged. Evidently, this woman wasn't a stranger to the swim team mother. When Mrs. Olinger glanced Charlie's way, he tried another tack. "Ben tells me you're foster parents. That's a noble undertaking. How many kids do you have? Two daughters kept my wife and me hopping."

"Everybody works. Benjamin especially, since he's the oldest. He understands that the household income must support the foster kids too. They have nothing."

The athletic director, tapping the mike, launching the awards' segment of the evening. Charlie swelled with pride as Ben accepted the plaque on behalf of the swimmers' spectacular season. His teammates cheered, hooted, and whistled, "Ben-jee! Ben-jee! Ben-jee!" as he was called forward again to accept the school's plaque bearing his name for a weight-lifting record.

Charlie stole a look at Mrs. Olinger, whose stony face reflected none of the other parents' jubilation, some mothers dabbing their eyes as their kids' names were called. She brightened a bit when the football team filed past the dais to claim their letters and certificates. "Which one of them is your boy?" Mrs. Olinger pointed to a bulky kid who was shambling along, looking out of place in grungy clothes. "He's a big kid. Does he hope to play college ball? Maybe go to the pros?"

Mrs. Olinger shrugged. "Too dumb for college. When he finishes vo-tech, he'll get a job in construction."

As the ceremony concluded, Charlie lost track of Ben in the milling mob of jubilant parents, excited siblings, and victorious athletes, the excitement deafening in the low-ceilinged enclosure that wasn't designed for that decibel level.

With quick goodbyes and promises to stay in touch, the Quillens swam upstream to join their son and his friends. Charlie noted the Olingers exiting the cafeteria alone.

☙❧

Charlie followed the meandering mob from the cafeteria, hoping they would lead him through the vast complex's maze to the parking lot. Ben, he knew, would be joining his friends for a post-awards celebration at another kid's home. *Good for him! About time you had some fun.*

"Mr. Alderfer! Wait up." Charlie recognized the swim team coach jogging toward him, nearly out of breath. "I was hoping I'd get a chance to meet you and to thank you for being there for Ben. He's a wonderful kid with a meager support system. And, I wanted to thank you for defending our country and our freedom. You're a bit of a folk legend, stopping a serial medical murderer at the VA."

Embarrassed, Charlie hung his head. "My service was nothing compared to what millions of soldiers have endured throughout history. They fought and died, some returning with life-limiting wounds to an indifferent country or worse. And now, so much PTSD is coming to light. Freedom isn't free.

"I couldn't do what you do, teaching, coaching, and mentoring. I remember Sally Ride, the astronaut-teacher who died in the Challenger explosion. Her motto was, 'I touch the future. I teach.'"

"I was hoping, since Ben obviously has your respect and admiration, that you could help talk him out of dropping the swim team. He's as amazing in the water as on the board. I couldn't believe my eyes the first time I saw that skinny six-footer do a perfect jackknife. And his sprints in the water? Even if he wasn't a perfectionist, he has the reach of an orangutan. He's college scholarship material for sure."

Charlie was stunned. "He didn't mention quitting to me. But then he doesn't talk much about his personal life or his goals. Come to think of it, he's all about us."

"He mentions Jonathan, and that makes sense. His friends, who have breached the Olinger's fortress, tell me its overrun with little kids who adore Ben. They nag him to read to them, talk to them, and give them the attention they simply aren't getting. The mother's idea of child care is parking them in front of the TV and feeding them junk food."

"Coach, I sat next to his mother at the banquet, and frankly was surprised by her attitude. Say something nice to a mother about her kid and you can't shut her up. You won't get a word in edgewise for the next fifteen minutes, and you'll see all her pictures, shared with excruciating details. But she didn't have one kind word to say about Ben. I shouldn't be judgmental—she's probably had different life experiences. But loving your child—isn't that universal among mothers? Especially with a kid like him? What parent wouldn't be proud?"

"In a rare unguarded moment en route to an out-of-town meet, Ben shared a bit of his background. It started with my sharing ideas to improve his breathing technique in the water. He said he's plagued with sinus headaches that interfere with normal breathing. As a small child, he was taken from his teenage parents—drugs, alcohol, you know—by Child Protective Services and placed in foster care. There was an altercation—he doesn't remember the particulars—but he woke up in the hospital with smashed facial bones."

"Ah. That explains the prizefighter's dip in his nose. I assumed it was genetic or the result of an accident. Go on."

"Somehow he ended up with the Olingers, whom someone prevailed upon to take him. The adoption was private. They adopted a younger girl at the same time. Then they had two of their own, followed by a string of fosters. Ben says he realized, by the time he was older, that they regretted adopting him—that adopted kids are as expensive as their own. They viewed him as a mistake; excess baggage."

"What puzzles me, then, is his optimistic attitude—his joy in helping. His cheerful demeanor. His work ethic. Where does that come from?"

"Nurture vs. nature, I guess. Who knows what his birth parents' potential and personality might have been, had they not become addicts?"

Charlie scoured his brain for the details of Ben's work history, about which the coach was well aware. "Still, they have instilled in him the necessity to provide for those who have nothing—like foster kids and the old folks he helps. I've got to admire the Olingers—stretching their income to support homeless kids."

The coach stopped so abruptly that exiting parents bumped into him, causing a domino effect. "Who told you that?"

"Ben did. In fact, he said he has turned over his earnings for the family's support since he was fourteen. They give him a small allowance."

"Huh!" the coach exploded. "That's a lie! Foster parents get five hundred dollars a month tax free per child to house and feed them. Period. The foster kids also have medical and dental cards, insurance, and a clothing allowance—even a small amount for gifts. You might say, 'they need to provide a big enough house which the kids will tear up,' but a house is an investment that appreciates in value. And I understand Ben does the cleaning."

Charlie was stunned, doing quick mental math. "That's still only thirty thousand dollars a year for four fosters."

"Until you add the father's income—he works for the county—and the mother does hair."

"Does Ben know about this?"

"I doubt that he'd care. He's grateful to have a home and loves helping with the kids."

"Are you sure about what the parents are paid?"

"We had a teenage foster girl ourselves. It didn't work out. She needed serious intervention for which we were unqualified to provide. Then she got in trouble with the law and was aging out of the system anyway. No, I'll contribute to the community by coaching neighborhood midget swim teams and at the Y."

Charlie took the coach's offered hand and they shook, both clapping the other's shoulder. "I wouldn't share our discussion about Ben," the coach said in parting. "I could be fired, and I wouldn't embarrass him for the world."

"I wouldn't dream of it." As Charlie scanned the emptying lot for his Buick, he reran his conversations with Ben. Best leave it alone, he thought, sensing the teenager had no idea about his parents' deception.

Chapter 3

It was unusual for Old Mr. Greer to ask Charlie to take him anywhere. Ever since Charlie was discharged from the VA, he asked his dear neighbor to accompany him on his own weekly grocery run. Mr. Greer was an excellent cook and made it his mission to tutor Charlie on the finer points of gourmet cooking. Charlie would ask if he'd also like to go to the bank, the pharmacy, run errands, or have lunch. Mr. Greer never asked anyone for rides, but Charlie was keenly aware that his various friends *happened to be going places* or *needed companionship* for professional appointments.

On this occasion, however, his neighbor did ask. "Ben keeps telling me about his swim meets and his diving competitions. I've run out of excuses, especially since his friends keep offering to take me. There's a meet on December nineteenth, and he tells me scouts will be there from several universities. His friends plan on doing some cheering. You know—ramp up the scouts' interest. I was wondering if…"

"We'll go! Just tell me where and what time, and I'll pick you up."

"Um, well, it is an away meet in another county."

"Not a problem. We'll get an early start. Go on the eighteenth if it's in Pittsburgh. We can stay overnight."

"Naw, just twenty-five miles or so. I'll give you the address."

Charlie felt ashamed. How many times had he heard Ben mention his practices and meets, and Charlie hadn't considered attending? Besides, this would be an opportunity to spend more time with his old friend.

December nineteenth fell on a Thursday, the meet being held from two to six thirty p.m. If they left immediately after the meet, Charlie could get his friend home before Mr. Greer was exhausted and in time for his evening meds. Unlike many seniors, he never complained about his aches and pains or his declining strength. He'd quip, "Being old sure beats the alternative, and I intend to top the upper end of the statistics."

That Thursday, as Charlie approached the Quad-A high school's sprawling campus, he grasped its reputation as a bastion for affluent professionals' kids, not only by the beautiful facility but by the high-end vehicles in the student parking lot. He circled a driveway that fronted the expansive glass doors, above which bore the brass letters, NATATORIUM. "I'll park the car and meet you inside," he told Mr. Greer.

Before the old gentleman could grasp his door's handle, two strapping young men in school letter jackets materialized, opening it for him. One extended a hand while the other shot Charlie a smile that revealed perfect orthodontia. When Charlie pointed to the doors, the kid nodded. They ushered Mr. Greer toward the entry, holding the door for him. As Charlie inched from the curb, he could see the young men chatting with his friend. Someone was raising these kids right.

When he rejoined Mr. Greer and approached the ticket counter, a volunteer asked if he was a veteran. "We are," he said.

"Please be our guest. And thank you for your service." She beckoned to someone behind Charlie, and another student materialized. She escorted them poolside to a reserved section for people who might not appreciate climbing the bleachers. Charlie greatly appreciated not having to ask for accommodation. To his right, circling the end of the pool, another section served patrons in wheelchairs. He was surprised that its occupants included students with serious disabilities. As they waited for the meet to begin, numerous students swept past their less fortunate classmates to chat, share a giggle, or the latest gossip. Nice kids!

The natatorium, which he had researched while Googling for directions, was newly refurbished, largely by the generosity of a wealthy benefactor and former student who had gone on to Olympic glory and a hugely successful professional life. The Olympic-size pool sparkled, throwing reflected light onto pristine tile walls. The effect was stunning. As the men shrugged off their jackets, scarves, and sweaters, a half dozen cheerleaders in their home-team's colors, pranced into position in front of their students. They clapped and stomped and joined into whatever the cheerleaders initiated.

A microphone's squeak silenced the crowd as the principal began opening ceremonies that would befit a national event. They pledged allegiance, sang the national anthem accompanied by a small band, and belted out their alma mater. The principal then introduced the visiting principal, coaches, and dignitaries, after which the coaches introduced their team members.

Old Mr. Greer pointed to Ben, who was a head taller than any other swimmer. Charlie swore he could count his ribs. When his name was called, his student section chanted "Ben-jee! Ben-jee! Ben-jee!" Charlie took a moment to scan the crowd for Ben's parents. If they were present, he couldn't find them.

As the races progressed, both student sections cheered in thunderous volleys, as if this were the playoff for the state title. At long last, the diving competition began. The athletes, lined up with their teams, all took dips in the pool then shook off the drips and dabbed their faces with towels. As Ben mounted the steps to the high dive, his classmates cheered, "Ben-jee!" repeatedly.

When he stepped onto the board, a hush fell over the natatorium. He covered the board in several long strides, paused, and pivoted, balancing his size-thirteen feet by his toes at the edge of the board. Silence. Like a soldier at attention, he paused. A statue. Then in a snap, his knees dipped hard, depressing the board, arms shooting upward, the board's spring propelling him skyward. Touching his toes, then arching backward, ankles together, toes pointed, he knifed headfirst into the water with barely a ripple.

The students jumped to their collective feet shouting, "Ben-jee! Ben-jee! Ben-jee!" as he emerged, hoisting himself onto the concrete. A teammate tossed him a towel as the cheering continued. He mopped his sheepish expression and gave a little wave to his friends.

Charlie clapped until his hands hurt, knowing he had just witnessed magic. Mr. Greer was wiping tears from his face. They agreed that they'd never witnessed anything like it. As soon as the diving competition ended, Charlie hustled his friend from the building. Having brought Mr. Greer's handicap hanger, he had snagged a prime parking spot to which Mr. Greer insisted on walking.

⌘

A December twentieth snowstorm delighted the children who frolicked in its wind-swept drifts, thrilled that Christmas vacation had started a day early. Ben had followed the snowplow to Charlie's street, pleased that Charlie's oversized snow blower could clear the driveway and flagstones to the lower level. He made quick work of Mr.

Greer's driveway, even though the old gentleman never drove unless conditions were perfect, and then only a few blocks to the nearby strip mall. Still, emergency vehicles might be impeded should the need arise.

Jonathan made snow angels and aimed clumsy snowballs at Ben, whose raised arm deflected most while letting a few hit home. Charlie, watching with Jade from the living room window, beckoned the pair inside to warm up. Over hot chocolate and cinnamon rolls, Ben proposed an adventure for Jonathan.

"There's this humungous hill on the schools' grounds near my folks home. It's perfect for sledding. We have a bunch of sleds and saucers for the kids. Want to go sledding? You too, Mr. A."

Charlie grinned at the thought, not having been sledding since his girls were little. He missed it when they became too sophisticated to be caught dead sledding with a parent. Besides, there were boys to impress. He thought of Jonathan and frowned.

"I know what you're thinking," Ben said. "The roads have been plowed and salted. If you'd be more comfortable driving, I'll meet you there. If you don't want to sled, you can take pictures."

Jonathan leapt from his chair, arms flapping in excitement. "Can we? Can we?"

"I'll toss his ski pants and jacket in the dryer," Jade said, gathering the discarded garments from the laundry room floor. "Would around one o'clock be okay?"

"That works for me, since school declared a snow day, and I don't have to report to work until six."

⁂

Dozens of children's fluorescent clothing dotted the vast sloping hill that bordered the high school's athletic field. Squeals of delight pierced the crystalline air under a weak winter sun that struggled to break through retreating gray clouds. Adults huddled in groups on the shoveled sidewalk, chatting in between breaks to warm their faces with woolen mittens.

Spotting Ben with the others, Charlie parked at the curb. By the time he reached the rear door to liberate Jonathan, the child had disengaged his seatbelt and was jumping up and down in the limited space. His breath fogged the window, punctuated by nose prints as he poised to bolt from the car. He erupted the minute Charlie opened the door.

"Hey, buddy! You ready? Then let's go." Ben shouted their itinerary to Charlie. "The best place to snap pictures is where the hill levels off. That halts everyone's progress. Trust me—you won't be run over. Would you hang onto these?" he asked, handing Charlie the tow ropes to a second plastic sled and a saucer. "I'll ride with him for the first few runs until he wants to do the bunny hill alone. Don't look so worried. I do it all the time with the kids, and they're pretty little. Haven't lost a single one yet."

By the time the pair did the long hill twice, Jonathan was begging to fly solo, choosing the saucer on which he'd seen a kid he recognized making his spin. Edging to the hill's bottom, Charlie snapped pictures. "Watch us! Watch!" Jonathan screamed as the pint-sized pair struggled back up the hill, jumped into their saucers and, whooping with delight, hurtled downhill while Charlie captured the action with his phone. "This is Alan. He's my best friend," Jonathan gasped. "He's in my class."

The little boy grinned, then turning, waved to a woman who was bobbing on her toes, arms clutching her body. "That's my mommy! Over there with the ladies." She waved with the same energy that a shipwrecked sailor would flag a passing ship. As the boys took off again, the mother beckoned to him. Introductions dispensed, Charlie texted her and Jade the movie he had just shot.

By mid-afternoon, the temperature had plummeted. Chilled parents collected their charges, some barely able to walk while others begged for just one more ride. Jonathan was visibly saddened by his friend's departure until Ben proposed an additional adventure. "Do you like trains?"

"Yea. I have a Tommy the Train in my bedroom."

"We have special trains at my house too. We put them up every year around Christmas instead of a tree. Would you like to see them?"

"We wouldn't want to intrude on your mother and her routine with the foster kids," Charlie interjected, fearing the hostility Mrs. Olinger had exhibited at the athletic banquet.

"It's OK. Dad's at work. It's just my sister. She's a sophomore who's babysitting two little ones who will be napping. Mom took my eight-year-old brother and ten-year-old sister Christmas shopping, and Matt, the football player, is at a friend's."

Charlie did the math, accounting for all ten. "Well, if you're sure it's okay. Perhaps for just a few minutes…"

Ben drove a few blocks to a quiet, tree-lined street of red brick split level homes. The spacious yard, while fenced and outfitted with playground toys, tested his ability to envision the house accommodating ten people. Perhaps one large bedroom was used as a dormitory. They parked, Ben leading the way through a screen and storm door combination. It screeched as he swung it wide to admit them. "Watch your step!"

Without being asked, Jonathan toed off his boots, dumping them in the entryway's corner, and topping them with his snow-caked mittens. Charlie followed the child's lead, shoving his gloves into his pockets. Ben led the threesome down a narrow center hall. Jonathan saw the scene before Charlie. "Oh wow! It's a huge train!" Tracks looped multiple routes on a low platform that consumed half of the large living room floor.

Jonathan gaped at the display, dropping to his knees and crouching to examine the locomotive. Without touching, he absorbed every detail of the magnificent engine. He scooted on hands and knees to each car, peppering Ben with questions about each one's purpose before moving on to the next. He giggled in delight at the red caboose.

"Come on—there's more." When they could coax Jonathan away from that train, they cut through a kitchen that Charlie thought smelled of cabbage and something unpleasant. The sink and counters were neatly stacked with dishes that looked rinsed, but dirty. Beyond the kitchen they descended a half-flight of stairs into a spacious family room. At one end another train looped in lazy circles. Ben flipped a switch; two locomotives began moving, each pulling several cars and a caboose.

"Listen!" Ben directed Jonathan toward the sounds coming from living room. The boy sprinted up the stairs. "What do you see?" Ben called after him, obviously having as much fun as the child.

"They're all running!"

"Be careful!" Charlie hurried after the child. In spite of Ben's easy-going nature, Charlie was terrified that Jonathan, unfamiliar with the layout, might cause some real damage. To his relief, the child had resumed his crouched position to follow each train's journey.

"This is the very, very, very best thing I've ever seen! When I'm all grown up, I'm going to have a house just like this."

"Well, the trains are packed away after Christmas."

"But why? Why wouldn't you want to keep them up all the time?"

"Then they wouldn't be special. They'd be so ordinary we wouldn't even notice them any more. And they'd be hazardous if new foster kids were babies or toddlers."

"Jonathan, we'd better be going. Ben must get ready for work. Let's thank him for a fun afternoon."

Jonathan threw himself into Ben's outstretched arms. "This was the best!"

"You're welcome."

Chapter 4

Charlie admitted to being an odd duck, finding January a joyful time. The holidays, while happy, were accomplished. The lawn was dormant, the mosquitoes and their biting ilk were gone, and the garden grew exquisitely in his imagination where no diseases, blights, or mildews attacked Emma's perennials. And the daylight hours lengthened a few minutes per day.

Thanks to a heated birdbath and a mealworm feeder, his bluebirds stayed throughout the winter. Cardinals, juncos, woodpeckers, chickadees, wrens, and finches entertained him by the hour. He made a note to order more mealworms and seed online. Over the Christmas holidays, he'd flown the triangle from Harrisburg to Atlanta to San Diego and back, spending precious days with his older daughter's family. The little believers thrilled at every holiday surprise. During Christmas Eve service, after the choir's splendid anthem, the three-year old jumped on the pew and shouted, "Do again!"

He'd next spent a week with his youngest, saddened by her wistful confession that the stork had missed them again. And again. He listened, his heart filled with compassion, as she detailed a planned visit to a fertility clinic at a prestigious hospital. If only they lived closer—he'd take her—where?

With a heartfelt apology to his Emma's memory, he enjoyed a decision made without negotiations. Emma disliked and distrusted fireplaces. Central heat was a gift, as witnessed by homes built in the early 1900s without chimneys, bragging rights for homeowners who could afford furnaces. As autumn leaves fell, Charlie yearned for a fire and hired a mason to install an outside source of air. A fireplace shop fitted both hearths with snug glass doors to block cold air when there wasn't a fire.

He bought storm-felled logs from a farmer and paid Ben to cut, split, and stack them. They'd only smoked up the house—twice—by forgetting to open the damper. Jonathan loved to toast marshmallows and make smores. Charlie smiled with contentment, grateful their two-home arrangement worked, ebbing and flowing to share togetherness and privacy.

Charlie's joy was cut short one twenty-degree Saturday morning in February. He was sipping his coffee and enjoying the comics, which he always read first. Jonathan was at his best friend's house for his first sleepover, a milestone for a boy with no other relatives. The stairwell doorbell rang multiple times, accompanied by fist banging and Jade's imperatives to admit her immediately.

Jonathan! An emergency! Something must have happened to him. His coffee cup missed the saucer, clattering sideways, spilling its contents onto Dick Tracy. Disentangling himself from the stool's legs, he bolted to the stairway door and unlocked it. Jade's face betrayed sheer roiling emotions as she flung the local section of the morning's paper at Charlie. "Read this!"

Riveted, Charlie scanned the Court Log where Jade's finger was stabbing.

> *Local Man Pleads Guilty To Sex Offence.*
> *The Assistant District Attorney has charged*
> *Benjamin Duane Olinger of Lancaster*
> *County, local address unavailable, with*

indecent assault, corruption of a minor and harassment. At his arraignment, Olinger's public defender entered a guilty plea for Olinger who was released on his own recognizance. A sentencing date is pending.

"What the hell!" Charlie boomed. "This has got to be a mistake. It can't possibly be our Ben. It must be a typo. Two guys with the same name."

Jade shook her head. "His name isn't common."

Charlie lunged for the landline and stabbed Ben's cell phone number into the handset. *The number you are trying to reach is not in service. Check your...* He banged down the receiver, rummaging through the kitchen drawer for his address book. He dialed the Olingers' landline, which he never used. A gruff voice answered on the fifth ring, "Yea?"

"Is Ben at home, please?"

"Doesn't live here no more. Don't call again." *Click.*

Charlie then remembered the Quillens with whom he'd sat at the athletic banquet. He dialed. When a familiar woman's voice picked up, Charlie identified himself. "Mrs. Quillen? I'm trying to reach Ben. His cell phone isn't working, and I'm told he's left home. Do you know how I can reach him?"

Mrs. Quillen choked and began sobbing as if her heart would break. "Those terrible people. This is just awful. How could they do this to him?"

"I gather you read the paper."

"They dumped him near our home last evening with a box of broken trophies and the clothes on his back. Not even a jacket, and it's freezing outside."

"Is he there now? Can I talk to him?"

"My husband's driving him around, trying to find where they towed his car."

"Please tell him, 'Come see me! Now!'"

જ્જ

Just before noon, a bleary-eyed but joyful Jonathan by-passed Charlie's door en route to his own lower-level front door. Jade, who had kept the vigil with Charlie, excused herself to let him in, thundering downstairs to their apart-ment. As he heard the door latch, Charlie breathed a sigh of relief. At least the little guy wouldn't see him upset or witness his meeting with Ben. If the eighteen-year-old got the message and was willing to face him. The moment he dreaded arrived two hours later with Ben's tentative knock.

Without any preamble, Charlie motioned him into the living room and pointed to the couch. "Sit!" He did. Char-lie sat beside him, pivoting to speak. "Tell me what this is about. Everything. Start at the beginning and don't leave anything out."

"I didn't do what they're talking about. It's all a terrible mistake."

"Guilty pleas don't just happen. Talk to me, Ben."

Ben stared at his hands.

Charlie waited until he couldn't stand it any longer. "Ben?"

"It's a long story."

"Just tell me what happened. The whole story."

"It started last May with this foster girl, Izzi. She waited until we were alone in the house, supposedly babysitting the younger foster kids. My folks were out shopping, and the little kids were in bed. She comes on to me, all sexy and seductive. 'You show me yours and I'll show you mine.' I told her no—that it's inappropriate. She goes all pouty. Says, 'You don't know what you're missing.' Tries to rub up against me. I yell 'no! Back off, bitch.' She shrugs and walks away.

"The next day I come home and the cops are waiting for me. She told the guidance counselor that I'd tried to rape her. That she'd fought me off. Even showed scratches on her arms. They questioned me at length, seemed satisfied with my answers. But my folks ordered me out of the house because of the foster kids. They were afraid Child Protective Services would take them away. So I stayed with friends for a few days."

Charlie's mind clicked. Of course! Those two ladies in the grocery story! Talking about the girl in the cafeteria, bragging about what she had done. That junior had been Ben! The timeframe worked. It would have been just before school ended and Charlie's aneurysm had ruptured. If only he'd asked for the names of the shoppers. "How old were you then?"

"Seventeen. End of my junior year. My parents got in touch through the school, told me it was all over, and that I should come home. So I did. My friends at school said she'd bragged about doing it before."

"Surely they're not charging you for that now."

He shook his head. "Right after New Year's, I was walking home from a friend's and spotted another cop car. 'Oh no!' I thought. 'Not again!' I was so angry after that awful lying bitch accused me of attempted rape. Worse— my parents didn't even ask me first if it were true. They just called the cops. How could they have taken her word over mine? They raised me since I was four, and I've never been in any kind of trouble.

"Thank god that girl had a record—a pattern of accusing her foster families of anything and everything, just for the thrill. I calmed down, remembering that and thinking, *What will she do for kicks after she ages out of the system? She must be eighteen by now.* I stomped into the house, tried not to look angry or act rude. Two cops were sitting on the chairs facing my mom on the couch.

"'In here,' she called without a trace of emotion. She just got up and left. No introduction. No explanation. The cops didn't stand up to greet me. I didn't sit. Their faces were menacing when they should have apologized for raking me over the coals for Izzi's lies. The younger one said, 'You dodged a bullet on your previous offense—at least the one your parents brought to our attention. Got away with it because of that girl's prior bad acts. But this…'"

Ben was quiet for a minute until Charlie said, "What? What happened next?"

"The old one said, 'Your ten-year-old sister told her mother that you *committed criminal acts against her person.* Of course she didn't word it that way, but to the social worker it was pretty clear what she meant. Your parents have filed a complaint.'

"I said, 'Tori? That's impossible! I've never touched her inappropriately. Even when she was a baby, I didn't bathe her, change her, or help her in the bathroom. Why would she say something like that?'

"The officers looked like they meant business. 'If you'll come with us to the station, we'll get this cleared up.'

"I said something like, 'Well I should hope so!'

"'Are you willing to take a polygraph test?' the older cop asked. I said, 'of course.' First, they questioned me at the township police station. They started with easy questions—name, address, age, occupation, family members, etc. Then they zeroed in on my relationship with my sister. It got ugly. They were relentless. Asking the same questions over and over. In all different ways. Yelling in my face. Like a Marine sergeant at boot camp. Starting way back when I was little.

"They kept saying, 'If you *confess to something,* we'll make it go away. But if you don't, you'll go to a supermax prison where you'll be raped and sodomized every day. A skinny guy like you wouldn't stand a chance, maybe be killed. But if you take a plea, we'll make it go away, you'll get some counseling. Maybe a little community service. With no felony conviction to follow you around.

"I asked for the polygraph test again. 'Bring it on. Let's get this settled, once and for all. I'm innocent.' The test, they said, would be given at the state police barracks. I drove myself because I had to be at work at six, and it was already three-thirty."

"So you weren't under arrest?"

"Not at that time. The barracks wasn't a bad place—I signed in at the main door, showed them my driver's license, then the woman behind the glass window phoned someone. A trooper opened a door that led into an open area where a bunch of people were doing deskwork on computers and phones. I wasn't scared or anything. I knew I hadn't done anything wrong.

"The trooper led me to a small room at the back. I thought a technician would roll out a machine and they'd ask me questions. You know, with the needle tracing squiggles when you're lying or telling the truth? But it wasn't like that."

"How many of them were there?"

"Three. The detective, a corporal who'd come to my house, and a state trooper I'd just met. I don't remember their names. I was getting nervous about the time because they started hammering me about Tori's lies. I needed my job, and if I were late, I'd be fired. I'm homeless. I need that paycheck. Finally I asked, again, about the polygraph test. They read me my rights."

"Was anyone there with you? A parent? An attorney?"

"My parents were bringing the charges, and I'm eighteen, so the cops didn't need them. I said 'yes,' when they asked if I wanted an attorney."

"So—did they stop the proceedings immediately?"

"No. They just kept hammering at me. All three of them. I thought they were waiting for my attorney. But he never showed up."

"Do you know one? Call someone? Did they?"

"No. They said I had to sign a paper to get an attorney."

"Did you? Sign something? What did it say?"

"I don't know. It was just a bunch of fine print."

"Ben, you should never sign a legal document without reading it. Don't you watch *Law and Order*?"

"I don't have time to watch TV."

"So what happened next?"

"They said, 'Okay.' They'd give me the test. But if I said anything wrong, any tiny little thing, or if I misspoke, it would prove I was guilty. And I'd be going directly to jail. Taking a polygraph was a terrible idea. I had two choices—to confess to something or go to prison. If I confessed to something, they could drop the charges and let me go. It would be over. So I made something up. About us kids wrestling when we were little. When I was eleven or so."

Charlie sighed. "How did that get you arrested?"

"They read parts of the complaint, asking me if I'd heard it before. I said 'yes,' since they'd gone over and over and over it at the police station. They asked if I understood what she meant. And I said 'yes, but she's lying.' They said they'd type up what I'd just told them. I assumed they meant what I'd said about when we were little and messing around, wrestling and tickling each other. I was to sign it."

"And they did?"

"Yes. They typed up a form."

"And you signed it?"

"Yea."

"Before you read it?" He hung his head.

"What I don't understand is why the attorney never showed up. I signed the paper and everything. Maybe he got stuck in traffic."

"What happened next?"

"They let me go. I went to work then slept at my buddy's house. He lets me keep a sleeping bag behind his couch. The next day the cops showed up—same two—and arrested me. They handcuffed me, put me in their car, and took me to some justice who said a bunch of stuff. He asked if I had an attorney, and I told him he hadn't shown up. A long time later, this dude showed up to waive what he called a preliminary hearing, and he entered a guilty plea for me. And I was allowed to go home. I thought it was over."

"What happened next?"

"That guy who came is a public defender. He works for free for people like me. I have to go see him to learn what comes next."

"You shouldn't go alone. I want to come with you. Is that all right?"

Ben nodded.

"Ben. Tell me the truth. Just between us. You can trust me. Did you ever do anything inappropriate with your younger sister? Don't take this wrong, but if you did, I still want to help you—get you counseling, housing, medical care. Whatever you need. But you must be honest with me."

"Mr. Alderfer. As God is my witness, I never touched my little sister beyond giving her a hug and a swat on the butt when we were little."

"I believe you." Charlie glanced at the paper Ben handed him with the particulars of his first real appointment with the public defender. That meeting would be held Monday morning at ten-thirty a.m. "I'll pick you up and we'll go together. Ben, I promise, you will not face this alone."

Chapter 5

C harlie found Ben's friend's apartment in a run-down section of a once-thriving steel town. Ben was waiting on the curb, wearing yesterday's clothes. He was coatless. Motoring down the window, Charlie called to him, "Go back and get a jacket. It's freezing this morning."

"I'm good," he responded, jumping into Charlie's passenger seat. "Let's go." His face showed nary a care in the world, his gentle smile looking downright normal as if they were going to breakfast or to run a few errands. Only his hands betrayed his nerves, as he rotated a worn manila envelope in his lap.

He'd better get serious, Charlie thought. Having confessed to god-knows-what, he'd better be prepared to explain how it happened and defend himself. Charile knew what corrupting minors involved—having sex or giving alcohol to an underage person—but the rest of it? Just what was indecent assault? He'd seen plenty of crime shows on TV, but didn't assault mean beating someone up? Guess they'd find out soon enough.

If Charlie had expected an opulent law office, he would have been sadly mistaken. Finding curbside parking near a dilapidated building that matched the address Ben had been given, he led the young man into a large open area where sloppily-dressed women and tieless men in short-sleeved dress shirts worked at old metal desks. He stayed back, letting Ben approach the receptionist's counter. Scanning his paperwork and his driver's license, the woman pointed Ben toward a stairway.

Steeply pitched steps, edged in metal, were covered in dirty black and white linoleum that was losing touch with the edges. Charlie made good use of the handrail, even though it wobbled under his grip. On the landing, a hallway emptied into a reception area and led to several closed doors toward the rear of the building. Ben again showed his documents to a bored looking woman behind yet another counter. "Down the hall. Second door on the left." They turned toward the hall. "Not you, unless he's under age, you're his legal guardian, or a co-defendant. Didn't see another name…"

"I'm his friend. Additional eyes and ears."

"Don't work that way. This ain't a doctor's office. Have a seat."

"You mean I can't be with him?"

"Nope. Have a seat or come back in thirty minutes."

"It's all right," Ben said in his calm, easy way that worried Charlie. Heat inflamed Charlie's face, his heart rate ratcheting, as he spun to follow the boy.

With his peripheral vision Charlie absorbed the woman slowly rising, a security guard closing at her side. "One more step and we're calling the cops. Now, sit! Or you're outa here."

"Sorry. So sorry." He made a calming motion toward the guard. "This is all new to us."

"From the looks of those papers, he's pled guilty, so you better learn fast."

Charlie sank into an old metal chair, its cracked vinyl seat curled so badly that he could feel it beneath his wool slacks. An industrial clock's red second hand jerked unmercifully on the wall behind where the woman had resumed ignoring him. Tick. Tick. Tick.

At exactly eleven, the second door down the hall opened and Ben emerged. Nobody followed him. No goodbye, clap on the back, words of encouragement following him. All color had drained from Ben's face. "How did it go?" Charlie asked.

Ben sighed. "He said it didn't matter if he believed that I was guilty or not. That wasn't his job. Because I'd confessed and a guilty plea had been entered, there's no do-over. I should have said nothing. Insisted on an attorney. Shut the hell up. I told him the cops said they'd make it go away if I just told them something—so I made something up. And I don't even remember what I said. He said, 'They lied, which is a legal investigative technique. They have to clear ninety percent of the cases without a trial.'"

"So—now that you have an attorney, what's he going to do for you?"

"He'll see me once a month before *calendar call* at the courthouse to touch base on my case. I have the dates. I have to show up to prove to the judge that I haven't skipped. If I don't, the judge will issue a bench warrant for my arrest and retract my ROR—being free on my own recognizance—and throw me in jail. He'll represent me for sentencing in March."

"He can't let you take it back?"

"No. He'll try for a light sentence since I have a clean record."

"Ben! Nobody should go to jail for something he didn't do."

"He said they'd go much harder on me if I insist on a trial. It would be my word against a 'sweet little girl.'"

"Can't somebody talk to her? Can't you?"

Ben shook his head. "There's a restraining order that I can't come anywhere near her or her house or her school or anywhere she *frequents*. That they'll throw me in jail if I do. I just don't understand…"

"Come on. Let's get out of here and go get some lunch."

"If I try to eat anything, I'll throw up."

❧❦❧

Charlie dropped Ben off at the high school, knowing that his showing up with an excused absence would count as a full day. He was missing way too much school because of this ordeal. His graduation must not be threatened. As he drove away, an idea percolated. He made a U-turn and parked in a visitor's slot. Inside the administration building, he located the principal's office to beg for a few minutes of his time. Luckily, the secretary recognized Charlie, having been on the job since his girls were in high school. She ushered him into the principal's office who recognized him immediately.

"Well if it isn't our crime-fighting veteran." The principal jumped from his chair, circling the desk, arm extended to shake hands. "To what do I owe the pleasure of a visit? Not that you ever need an excuse. Please. Have a seat. Tell me how our wonderful girls are doing."

The principal settled into the second visitor's chair and gave Charlie his undivided attention. "I'm here on behalf of Benjamin Olinger." The principal's smile vanished. Charlie rattled off his best executive summary of Ben's predicament, embellished with his take on the unfolding miscarriage of justice. When he finally paused, the principal's face was an ashen study in grief.

"If what you say is true, there's no up side to this. Neither child will be unscathed. Best thing he can do now is to get an excellent lawyer. I'll call him in for a talk, see what I can do within my constraints. But, Mr. Alderfer, I must tell you that his mother calls every day, demanding an accounting of his attendance and activities. I'll remind Ben, that since he's eighteen, he can choose who may and may not have access to his personal information. At this time, his parents are listed as his contacts in case of an emergency. He can not only bar them from accessing information but appoint someone else."

"Would it be ethical for you to suggest me? Of course I'd be willing."

"I'll recommend he choose a responsible adult with no conflict of interest—a relative, family friend, a minister or spiritual advisor, and so on. If you'll jot down your contact information and he chooses you, we can shut down the pipeline immediately."

"You sound as if you've made up your mind."

"If you can prove his side of the story, do it. I've dealt with those parents before."

♥♥♥

Charlie entered the VA's outpatient building and approached the sign-in kiosk, knowing what to expect. Once he was spotted, word quickly spread, a ripple of employees, volunteers, and escorts, their well-wishes swelling a chorus throughout the lobby. Old friends, visiting veterans, and even strangers pressed to greet their local hero who had rid the hospital of a serial killer. After pressing many hands, Charlie escaped to the elevator that took him to his primary-care physician.

After the obligatory weigh-in, temperature, blood pressure, and oxygen-level checks, his doctor ticked through the examination. "I wish all my patients were as healthy. Who would guess how close we came to losing you? What a waste that would have been. I'm obliged to ask you and all my patients if you are ever depressed. Have any suicidal thoughts about harming yourself?"

Charlie belly laughed. "I was born happy and have no reason to change. And since my near-death experience with that aneurism, I greet every new day as a gift to do something important. I do, however, have a little problem, for which I need a referral." Succinctly, Charlie relayed Ben's situation and his determination to help him. "If he were a vet, he'd be seeing a lawyer, a family therapist, an ophthalmologist, and an ENT for his sinus infections. I don't know where to begin researching civilian doctors."

"Might I suggest the chaplain? I can see if he's available. He knows a plethora of specialists beyond our walls, many of whom do pro bono work. First, though, let's concentrate on you. I'm sending you to physical therapy for relaxation techniques. Sounds like you're going to need them."

Appointments and a quick canteen lunch later, Charlie hiked the connecting corridors to the chapel where the chaplain was waiting. Given his choice, they met in the sanctuary where Charlie felt he wouldn't be tempted to exaggerate or cuss. The chaplain listened intently to Charlie's summary, which was becoming more streamlined and less emotional. More facts; less drama.

"Of course I will pray for you and your young man. And, for the practical aspects, I have resources to recommend." From a pocket he extracted a pack of business cards and riffled as if searching for the ace in a deck. "Ah. Here. This fellow, Brownie, is a private detective. Lost both legs to an improvised explosive device in Iraq, but hasn't let that stop him. Police and lawyers in the tri-county area swear by his expertise in getting to the truth.

"This ophthalmologist donates ten percent of his time to un- and underinsured youth." He thumbed further into his deck and produced a third card. "This criminal attorney is the best. His father's a judge. He's religious and honest. Fair warning, however. He will not let a client lie under oath."

"Thank you so very much. I'm determined to see justice done."

"Charlie, I've known you throughout your ordeal—nearly dying and months in recovering. You've got a huge, compassionate heart. Don't let anyone abuse that."

"Don't worry, Father. I'm nobody's fool."

✿✿✿

The minute Charlie got home, he logged onto the county law library to research the polygraph law. Every topic he entered yielded no references, suggesting he refine his topic. And the website was huge—he'd need a law degree just to navigate the topics. A librarian—he'd go in person. The main number offered general information about the facility's capabilities and contents, hours and directions—round and around. Grabbing his jacket and car keys, Charlie launched his mission.

He parked and entered the vast courthouse complex, passing through security. Two guards, who barely took note of him while x-raying his satchel, continued chatting. Maybe a life of crime would be fun, he speculated, as everyone looked through senior citizens as if they were transparent. He elevated skyward toward the bastion where fine legal minds researched arcane topics. Having dressed to impress Ben's public defender, Charlie blessed his wardrobe decision—dress slacks and tassel loafers, oxford cloth shirt, and cashmere vest—a gift he swore he'd never wear but now felt nattily attired to pass for a peer.

The library was vast, cocooned in silence, its highly polished tables and pendant lights as elegant as an Ivy League university's faculty lounge. He'd expected banks of computers lining every wall—they were probably somewhere—but not among the sea of lofty open stacks that held weighty leather-bound volumes. Their dates spanned decades and dealt with case law, statutes, rules of court and so on. At a librarian's suggestion, he chose two green volumes and lugged them to a table. He struggled to understand the legalese, which meant nothing to him.

"Charlie? Is that you? Oh my God. It *is* you!" Charlie rose to shake hands with the VA volunteer named Paul who had spent many evenings playing Bingo with hospitalized patients. "When you no longer came, I'd assumed you had passed. This is—amazing! What brings you here?"

The elegant man in a well-cut suit, starched white shirt, and silk tie obviously must be a lawyer in real life on a break between courtroom appearances. "I'm hoping to find a ruling that enables a polygraph test to be introduced at trial. Also a ruling against police lying to a suspect." He spread his arms wide, palms raised in supplication. "I don't know where to start."

"How about at the beginning? I'm a civil attorney, but I have time to listen." Charlie unloaded the facts as he knew them, interspersed with a generous helping of his own fears and indignation.

"This much I do know. The Supreme Court has ruled that lying to a suspect is legal, the exact wording of that decision escapes me, but you can Google it."

Charlie felt his spirits tank.

"My partner, Ezekiel Geoffrey—Zeke —is a criminal lawyer. We've had success with a polygraph expert who practices in an adjacent county. He has twenty years of experience and is respected by law enforcement in multiple jurisdictions." He pulled out his phone, directing Charlie to the expert's particulars, which Charlie added to his notes. "Here's my card. The case is beyond my expertise, but my partner gives potential clients a free hour to explain their situation."

"I'll pursue both. And thank you so much."

Chapter 6

Charlie leapt for the kitchen phone, which he could hear ringing even before he got the door open. He grabbed it. "Mr. Alderfer? It's Ellen Quillen. I'm so glad I caught you. I've got some bad news for Ben." Her shaky voice betrayed that she had been crying. "Ben's awful mother phoned every swim team family, warning them about *guilt by association*. I've known these women for years. They're level headed and strong, not the kind to be bullied. I hope they stood up to her.

"Then I had a visit from a social worker from Child Protective Services, suggesting it was unwise to house a confessed child molester, given that we have a little girl. She caught me completely off guard, hinting that our daughter's situation might need to be questioned. I could not believe it!"

"What did you do?"

"After I pried out of her that she'd had an anonymous tip, I gave her a piece of my mind about Mrs. Olinger. Knowing that I knew the source, the details, and the implications, she backed down. I ordered her out of my home."

Charlie was too stunned to speak. The woman continued. "So then I phoned every one of the moms who had only high school boys still at home. They had lots of supportive things to say about Ben, his character, the deplorable accusations—but all of them had reasons why they couldn't accommodate a long-term guest."

"Don't worry about it—you've done all you can. I'll leave a message with the school for him to come straight here. And if you see him first, please tell him."

"Thank you! And God bless you, Charlie. We'll do everything we can to help—food, clothing, some money—whatever he needs."

He set the phone quietly in its cradle and eased into a chair to think. He took deep breaths, exhaling slowly through his nose to expel his negative feelings. A plan of action trickled into the void. He hurried into his office, grabbing a notepad and pen en route. He dialed. The polygraph professional picked up on the first ring with a cheerful, "Snyder Bureau of Investigations. How may I help you?"

Charlie cut straight to the chase, starting with their mutual friend's recommendation, the eighteen-year-old boy's case, and what Mr. Snyder would need to know if he took the case.

The conditions sounded pretty straightforward. "Benjamin, not you Mr. Alderfer, would be the client, and confidentially would apply, as I hold a law degree. He can share whatever he wishes with you, but I cannot give you the results myself without his consent.

"I'll need some information for baseline questions, such as his age, date of birth, eye color, car that he drives, etc. Personal details only he might know. I'll prompt him to either tell the truth or to lie for a baseline to test his reactions. I'll need a copy of the charges—you can fax them to me—and five hundred dollars cash at the time of the interview, for which he'll get a receipt." To the latter he added an apology. "Cash isn't to let us cheat the IRS. Clients' checks sometimes bounce."

Charlie made the appointment with Snyder for the following week, then called his VA friend Paul's lawyer to make that appointment. He could cancel if Ben balked or simply could not face just how desperate the situation was. But he'd convince him. The new attorney, who would be in court the following morning, would see them at one o'clock the same afternoon.

❧

What to tell Jonathan, Charlie mused, as the clock ticked toward three-thirty. Was this all the same day? A black and white streak caught his attention as Roxie careened across the snowy front yard, skidding to a stop at the end of the driveway. Boy and dog frolicked in the snow briefly, then pelted toward Charlie's garage door. Yanking off his snowy mitten with his teeth, Jonathan punched in the code. The door lifted. As instructed, he waited until it was fully raised, then entered and pushed the corresponding button by the laundry room door, obviously tickled with his big boy accomplishment.

That Charlie was hurrying through their after-school routine wasn't lost on the child. "Is something special happening today?"

"Ben's coming over. In fact, he's going to sleep here for a few days while he sorts out some stuff."

"Is he sick?"

"Not really. I'd say, over-extended. Exhausted. Needs to be by himself for a while when he's not in school or at work. We'll need to leave him alone; give him his privacy."

Satisfied, Jonathan turned his attention to his backpack, which he dumped on the kitchen table. Charlie grinned at the child's nonchalance, his cue to remark about Jonathan's competence in completing a multi-part task, as the teacher's notes indicated the first graders were learning. His homework, mommy's homework, mommy's notes from the teacher. He grinned. "May I have one more cookie? They were kind of little, and I'm still hungry."

"How about a banana? Or a tangerine?" Jonathan pounced on the fruit bowl, retrieving an orange. "Hang up your coat to drip, and gather up your work. And take some fruit you think your mom would enjoy." He snagged a red delicious apple and bundled his papers. Charlie sighed with relief. He could greet Ben without an audience.

☙❧☙

Charlie paced from the living room bay window to the kitchen, to the front door's sidelights, to the dining room's sliders that overlooked Emma's frozen garden and back to the kitchen. The minutes dragged, making the Audubon clock birds seem to forget to sing. As he circled through his study, glancing toward Old Mr. Greer's home, he isolated the conflicts he hadn't been able to resolve.

Ben, officially homeless, desperately wanted his family to believe him and love him again. Conversely, Ben needed to rage at his so-called family, which meant divorcing his yearning for family. His knotted emotions were bundled with layers of denial. Charlie incubated the challenge du jour: how to make humble, polite, sensitive Ben feel at home and not like a nuisance or a burden while energizing his need to fight. Roxie's toenails on the steps announced Ben's rattletrap. *First, just get him settled.*

Bing bong! Charlie flashed to Mrs. Olinger's calling all the swim team parents. Privacy—she must not know where Ben was staying. He should give Ben the combination to the garage's keypad to access Emma's empty space. If oil leaks worried the boy, heavy cardboard could protect the floor. He smiled. With the door down, Ben's privacy could be safeguarded. Charlie's lower level was zoned as a separate apartment, meaning nosey do-gooders could not question Ben's proximity to Jonathan; i.e., no harassment from Children's Protective Services and their ilk.

He opened the door to the teenager, whose demeanor betrayed rejection and resignation. "Welcome! Come in! Come in!" Charlie was so relieved by Ben's accepting his invitation that he couldn't stop himself from chattering. "You'll need your own hook for your coat. And a place for assorted outdoor shoes and boots. Let's do that first. Then a snack. I baked cookies, which Jonathan says are delicious. And there's fruit. What would you like to drink with your snack?"

Ben dropped a battered suitcase that predated wheeled luggage onto the slate entryway. "If you have any coffee— leftover or instant would be great. Or water is good."

"I was just thinking that coffee would hit the spot. I'll put on the pot. Regular or decaf?"

"Whatever you have."

Charlie ground fresh-roasted beans, the aroma filling the house. While it dripped, he piled cookies onto a plate and urged Ben toward the kitchen table. They sat, sipped, and munched, giving Charlie time to pitch his proposal. "It's time to take the proverbial bull by the horns. I've taken the liberty of making an appointment for you with a criminal lawyer who's highly recommended. Your principal is on board to expedite excused absences. The secretary will hand you his sealed note. I'll pick you up in front of the admin building tomorrow morning at ten."

"I don't have nice clothes to visit a law office."

"From day one, I want you to just be yourself. Whatever you own will be fine. And, if you wish, you're welcome to use the washer and dryer any time." Next, Charlie explained about the polygraph expert for whom he'd already made an appointment for the following week.

Ben startled, mid-chew, at the price. "Five hundred dollars? I don't have that kind of money."

"I'll get the cash and give it to you. But you must fill out the forms to hire Mr. Snyder yourself upon our arrival. The test will be completed that day, you'll get his verbal findings, and he'll mail you his report. He can fax it to me, here, with your written approval."

Ben hung his head. "I'll never be able to thank you enough. I'll pay you back after graduation as soon as I can work longer hours."

"That's all right. It's a gift. Someday someone in your future life—a deserving person—will need your help. Just pass it on. Now—let me show you your suite." A hall, which separated the living room from the kitchen, bisected the rancher and led to his daughters' former rooms. One faced the front yard, one the garden, with a Jack and Jill bathroom connecting the two. Charlie directed Ben toward the rear, in which were installed blackout blinds behind the curtains.

He opened that room's bathroom door, which had a second door connecting to the front bedroom. Each had a lock. "Make yourself at home. Pardon the sweet-smelling girly stuff. There's guy products too—help yourself to whatever's in the vanity. The TV's on cable. Lots of room in the drawers and closet for your things." He repeated, "Please consider this home indefinitely. By the way, I've never adjusted to eating alone, so you're welcome to join me any time."

"They give me breakfast and lunch at school—the principal said that I qualify. And I eat at my jobs. But thank you."

Another call to the principal was needed to see if the Olingers had cut Ben from their medical insurance. If so, Ben would need to apply for public assistance. Hell, wasn't that what he paid taxes for? Nobody should go hungry or without medical care in this land of plenty.

Chapter 7

If Charlie had been expecting Perry Mason or a Marine sergeant-type, those stereotypes vanished. The attorney's office reminded Charlie of the brick row houses in Philadelphia's Society Hill, this building undoubtedly dating to the mid-1800s when professionals chose to live near the courthouse. Beside the shiny black exterior door with a stained-glass transom hung a tasteful plaque bearing the law firm's name. Climbing several brick steps, Charlie led Ben into a large reception area, tastefully decorated in Williamsburg style. It was charming without looking pricy.

A secretary of indeterminate age rose and greeted them as warmly as she would any valued clients. She circled her desk to shake hands. Charlie did not miss that she approached Ben first. She was neatly dressed in a pantsuit, a crisp white blouse with a high collar, and black flats. Her anchor-bob hair was tastefully colored, and her gold-stud earrings and oversized watch completed a professional image.

"Mr. Geoffrey is expecting you," she said, rapping twice and then leading them into his office, its width encompassing the building's footprint. To Charlie's glance at a door to the rear, she said, "That's where we keep our worker-bees and office equipment." Ezekiel Geoffrey, Esquire was as mild mannered as a certified public accountant. Charlie judged him to be early fifties—old enough to be experienced but young enough to wrestle with demons. He was slender, no taller than five-nine, and dressed in a conservative off-the-rack suit that looked custom tailored. His blue oxford shirt's cuffs bore no monogram. A Seiko watch looked utilitarian.

As the secretary departed, Zeke Geoffrey's partner, whom Charlie knew from the VA, entered. Introductions completed, Zeke said, "I've asked Paul to stay, if that's all right. He tells me, Mr. Olinger, that he's familiar with your situation, but, with your permission, I'd like him to listen.

"Sure. And it's Ben." Without further chatting, the boy launched his story while the attorneys listened attentively. Zeke jotted notes on a white legal pad.

Charlie jumped in. "Can you help him? Nobody should go jail for something he didn't do."

Zeke addressed Ben. "You must understand that I am an officer of the court. I cannot plead you innocent if you are guilty. That would be suborning perjury, which could not only get me disbarred but brought up on criminal charges. One does not lie to the court. For me to help you, you must be honest with me. If I find you're lying to me, you will be fired. Do you understand?" Ben nodded. "I'm not saying you can't conceal anything, but if there's something you don't want revealed, do not tell me."

For the first time in days, Ben grinned. "That is so easy because I am completely innocent. And I have nothing to hide."

"There is a very remote possibility that something you did in the past is illegal. If so, you can't conceal it after the fact."

"I understand."

"All right. You need to know what my firm charges. Criminal law isn't like what you see on TV about civil suits, where the lawyer says, 'I don't get paid until I get you money.' I charge by the hour. All hours don't cost the same, as staff handles what they can at their lesser rate. If you call and we chat for five minutes, that isn't an hour—it's five minutes. Most of my time will be spent working your case. If you choose to hire me, my secretary will draw up papers for you to sign. We'll need you to set up an escrow account from which the firm's fees will be drawn."

"But I don't have any money…"

Charlie held up his hand. "I'll lend you the money. We'll figure out a repayment plan after they make the charges go away. How much do you need to get started?" Charlie asked the attorney.

"The final figure depends upon how far this goes. Once I start the process, the witness may recant, the charges being dropped. If the case goes to trial, and the verdict necessitates appeals…"

"But if the charges are dropped, could they be re-filed against me at a later date?"

"Let's not get ahead of ourselves, Ben. Do you want to retain my firm?"

"Yes!" Ben and Charlie responded in unison.

"Good. First order of business—I'll file the documents to retract your guilty plea and enter 'not guilty.' And I'll file for discovery, which will require the prosecutor to divulge all evidence they're holding against you. Then we'll plan the best course of action."

"Will my parents know what I'm doing?"

"All concerned will be notified."

Charlie addressed both lawyers. "I'm taking him to the Snyder Bureau of Investigation next week. Thank you for the referral, Paul."

"You do understand," Zeke said, "that even the most positive results won't be admissible in court."

"I know, but I don't understand why," Ben said.

"There's no uniform certification for practitioners or their equipment. Still, a good result might convince some people to accept your innocence."

"Can't we leak it to the press? They jumped on his confession quickly enough," Charlie asked.

"No! That can only hurt him."

"But why?"

"The police could insist that he take their test to dispute Snyder's findings."

"They'd find me innocent and owe me an apology, although I'd be fine if they didn't."

Zeke raised his hand in the stop position. "They could lie about their findings."

Charlie exploded. "They couldn't do that!"

"They can and they have. Let's not put temptation in their way, no matter how fine your local law enforcement department appears to be. If Ben wins, there will be enough egg on their faces."

ᴄᴈᴇᴈ

Ben's appointment for his polygraph arrived on an uneventful weekday morning. Jade had departed at six while Charlie stayed with Jonathan until he'd completed the morning's ablutions. Together they locked Jade's exterior door and trotted upstairs for breakfast. "Bacon! My favorite! May I have my egg scrambled, please?" Charlie was way ahead of him, having lined everything up in the fridge the previous evening. They sipped coffee and cocoa respectively before the usual briefing began.

Jonathan spread the contents of his backpack on the table. "My homework. Mommy's. Her note for the bus driver to drop me at Alan's stop after school. I'm to give it to Miss Smith in the office."

"I might be home before you are. I can pick you up at Alan's?"

Jonathan shook his head. "Mommy said to tell you she'll pick me up at four. It's okay with Alan's mom. Besides, Alan's mom and my mom have tea together and talk about stuff. I think Mommy needs friends. Do you think she needs friends?" He paused, catching his error. "I mean, besides you. My friends' mommies have husbands or boyfriends or girlfriends. Do you think I should tell Mommy she needs a boyfriend? I don't want her to be lonely."

"If you suggest that, she might think *you're* lonely. So I think you should tell her what's on your mind and why. You know, Jonathan, your mom's awfully busy. Making and being a friend takes real time. As for a boyfriend, she'd be extra picky, not wanting to choose someone who's not family-friendly. She's a wise lady. You can trust her to know what's best for you both. So—what's new at school?"

"There's this kid—he's really big. Humongous! He's older. Been six for a long time. His father played football. Says he will, too. That his dad wants him to be a … a … greg … "

"Aggressive?"

"Yea. That's what he says. He bosses the other kids around on the playground. Has to go first. Pushes the guys out of the way. Yesterday Suzy—she's really little—she pushed him back and he decked her. She fell and hit her head. The other girls were all over him. Then the teachers came running. We were sent back inside. A teacher took Suzy to the nurse."

"What happened to the bully?"

Jonathan shrugged. "I don't know. Papa, should I have tried to stop him?"

"No. That's the teachers' job. Next time, get whoever's on duty to intervene. I used to tell my girls, 'if there's trouble over here' and I'd point to my right, 'I want you to be over there.' And I'd point left. Avoid being part of a mob."

"Can I tell you a secret?"

"What kind of a secret? Did you promise not to tell about somebody's surprise, like what they're getting for their birthday? Those secrets you must keep, unless it involves something dangerous or illegal. Like someone planning to steal something from a store. Then you tell them, right then, that you cannot keep that kind of secret."

"This lady told me something and said, 'don't tell your mommy. It's our little secret.'"

Charlie jerked to attention. "What woman? A teacher? A friend's mom?" Jonathan shook his head *no*. "Where did you see this woman? Is she someone you know? Start from the beginning."

"I was outside, waiting for my going-home bus. There were lots of kids and moms and dads, walking around cause the bus was a little late. This woman came up to me and said, 'Are you Jonathan Kepley?' I thought it was okay—that she was someone's grandma or a friend of my mom's. Then she said, 'Can you keep a secret?' I said 'yes,' cuz I can. Then she said, 'I'm your long-lost grandmother. Your grandfather and I would like to get to know you. But don't tell you mom. It's a surprise.'"

"Then what happened?"

"I remembered *Stranger Danger* that we talked about in kindergarten last year." He scrunched his face in contemplation. "But she didn't look strange."

"How so? What did she look like?"

"She had on her Sunday school clothes and fancy shoes. She had pretty hair, and she smelled nice. And she looked like that picture of Daddy that Mommy keeps in her room. Mommy made one for me too. Only this lady was old."

"Did you promise?"

"Nooooo! I felt scared. So I ran to the bus."

"You did the right thing. Bad people sometimes look harmless—even helpful. They aren't your friends. If it's all right with you, I'll relay your story to your mom. She'll know what to do." The scarlet tanager chirped the hour on the Audubon clock. "Do you have everything?" Jonathan rolled his eyes and loping toward his hook, got his jacket."

"Don't forget your backpack."

He groaned, then shot Charlie a conspiratorial smile. "I won't forget. But I like it when you ask me. I love you, Papa."

"I love you too, precious boy."

As the bus stopped at Charlie's driveway, red lights flashing and side bars extended, Jonathan ran, backpack flapping. Without losing his forward momentum, he turned to wave to Charlie, who waved back from the living room picture window. *Damn*, Charlie thought. *The evil ex-mother-in-law surfaces again. Jade will explode.* He knew she'd call the school and praise Jonathan for doing the right thing. And reinforce that whenever anyone says, *don't tell your mother,* that's the very thing he should tell her.

⌒⌒⌒

Charlie's plan of action went as smoothly as a military stealth operation. He pulled up in front of the school's admin building at the exact moment that Ben strode into the sunlight. He looked frail and so much thinner than when Charlie had first seen him at Old Mr. Greer's.

He'd have to check in with his neighbor—bring him up to date on Ben's legal defense. But first, he'd better okay it with Ben.

The young man fit his lanky frame into the Buick's passenger seat and shot Charlie a smile. "Took early lunch, so

I'm stoked and ready to kill my test." Charlie wondered if too much enthusiasm and bravado, however feigned, could influence his answers, but Snider had emphasized that even if his vitals were elevated by his emotions, that would be his *normal* for that day. So, not to worry about being scared, nervous, ill, emotional, or whatever.

First stop—the bank. While Ben waited in the car, Charlie withdrew five hundred dollars from his checking account. He counted it, then tucked it back into the envelope. Back in the car, he handed it to Ben, who stared at the envelope without opening it, murmuring his thanks. They drove into a glorious morning that hinted of spring and exquisite possibilities—if only. As they drove southeast, Charlie tried to concentrate on signs of spring, letting that whisk negativity from his mind. What if—was there even a remote possibility—he was wrong?

Could Ben be one of those rare individuals who appeared genuine and compassionate, but wasn't? Or didn't grasp the difference between right and wrong? How deep were the scars from his life's experiences? Nature versus nurture. But, of the latter, he'd had a village of positive influence. Had it worked? *Stop it!* He made a decision. If Ben wasn't innocent, he'd move heaven and earth to secure appropriate treatment and a fair disposition.

Having crossed into a third county, Charlie located the Snyder Bureau of Investigation, located in a pleasant section of small-town businesses. Unlike Zeke's office, this site spoke of postwar structures built by blue-collar enterprises that had passed through many turnovers. He parked in front of the building that sported no meters.

The expanse inside was cool and dark, the reception area resembling a doctor's office with mismatched chairs bordering three walls. It reminded Charlie of the public defender's office only cleaner and better smelling. The continuous, faux-wood walls were broken only by closed doors, stained the same milk chocolate brown. Vinyl of a bygone style carpeted the floor. Behind a sliding Plexiglas partition, a receptionist looked through myriad scratches and motioned for Ben to approach.

Charlie found two vacant side-by-side chairs, sat down on one, and placed his canvas briefcase on the other. In it, he'd brought Ben's copies of the Criminal Complaint affidavit and Probable Cause that he'd faxed to Snyder. Forcing himself not to stare, he took in the sad-looking men—and no women—who stared at the floor, their hands, their feet, or their eyelids. The place was quiet as a meditation chapel. What a sorry looking lot!

Charlie wondered why they were here, uncomfortable that he and Ben had the only white faces. Collectively, those who waited were shabbily dressed, some in work clothes that bore company logos, others in camel-colored overalls and dusty Wolverines. Not a suit in the mix. Charlie bet that no white-collar criminal would have pleaded guilty to something he didn't do. Or, if he did, he'd holler for his five-hundred-dollar-an-hour attorney, perhaps one he kept on retainer.

"Mr. Olinger?" Ben barely had time to settle beside Charlie before he was directed to proceed down the hall.

"Told ya we shoulda made an appointment," someone scolded one of those waiting. "We're gonna be here all day."

Chapter 8

Charlie followed Ben, expecting the receptionist to snag him, just like the woman in the PD's office. Instead, Snyder welcomed both into his office and motioned them into his visitors' chairs. Charlie skimmed the modest office, its walls hung with plaques of appreciation from numerous law-enforcement agencies. Evidently, he was well known in numerous cities and counties. After repeating to both everything Snyder had told Charlie on the phone, he said it was time to begin.

"Mr. Alderfer, if you wouldn't mind waiting in the reception area, I'll proceed with Ben's test. My equipment is in the private extension of my office," he said, motioning like a hitchhiker to a closed door behind his desk. "The rules state that nobody else can be present—just the examiner and the subject. It's a lengthy exam. The interview segment and the actual test take two or three hours combined. You may want to pick him up later or, since I know you've traveled a great distance, I can recommend a nice diner, our little community park, or the library. Just let my receptionist know where we can reach you, just in case."

In case of what? Charlie wondered. That Ben would freak out, change his mind, or have a stroke—no, he wasn't leaving without him. Finding his original chair taken, he took another that bordered an end table that held a surprising array of new magazines. He found a *National Geographic*, demanding himself to become so engrossed that time would pass quickly. As an institutional clock ticked precious moments from his life, Charlie tried hard not to picture Ben's life in a prison cell. Concentrating, he read the magazine from cover to cover, then rested his eyes—just for a minute…

જ∾જ

Charlie jerked to attention as his napping brain recognized his name. He looked at the clock. Two hours had passed. Snyder had opened his office door and was calling his name, beckoning for him to join him. Charlie leapt to his feet, stopping only to rescue the *National Geographic* that had slid to the floor and replace it on the end table. He hurried down the hall. Ben, his expression unreadable, was sitting in the far visitor's chair. Charlie took the seat next to him.

Snyder folded his hands and rested his forearms midway across his desk. He leaned forward, high drama emanating from eyes that stared straight into Charlie's. The oversized clock behind Charlie's head ticked—one, two, three times. *Get on with it or I'm going to die of a heart attack, right on this spot. Breathe in. Breathe out.*

Snyder's voice boomed, echoing in the confined space. His pronouncement was clipped. Starched. "He didn't do it. He's innocent."

Charlie felt his mouth drop open, his heart leap in jubilation. Ben's nonchalant face was calm—he already knew the results.

Even without notes, Snyder ticked through the salient points. "Did you pick her up? No. Did you carry her upstairs? No. Did you put her on her bed? No. Did you close her bedroom door? No. Did you then lock the bedroom door? No. Did you pull down her pants? No. Did you say, 'don't tell mom'? No. And so on and so on, through all the charges on the criminal complaint, to which I added a few questions of my own, just for good measure."

To Ben he concluded, "My recommendation is that, when this is all over, you bring criminal charges against your father. And someone should investigate the suitability of that family to be foster parents. All that will be in my written report, which my office will overnight to you. It's up to you, Ben, with whom you share it."

Charlie asked, "Of all the people you see, how many are innocent?"

"Most of them. A few think they can fool the polygraph, but that would take a sociopath who has practiced his technique. For the police who request my services, it's an investigative tool to rule in—or out—suspects. But no parent, however innocent, should ever take a polygraph test, because at some level they feel guilty for not realizing the danger, for not intervening, or for allowing the crime to happen to their child. Which is why I don't ask subjective questions, like 'are you innocent' or 'are you guilty.'"

"Thank you! So very much. You have no idea how helpful this is," Charlie said, as he and Ben shook the expert's hand.

"Good luck to you, Ben," he called after the innocent man. "Days like today make my work worthwhile."

Charlie glanced at the clock, memorizing the time, which he hoped, in time, would prove to be the innocent hour.

⌭⌭⌭

Charlie skidded to a stop in front of the public defender's office, leaving Ben asleep in the car. He bound up the stars, prepared to muscle his way past the rude gatekeeper woman. He was prepared to do battle, but the woman wasn't there. He glanced at the clock—four ten p.m. Quitting time came early for that public servant.

Glancing down the gloomy corridor, he could see that the PD's lights were still on. He listened as he crept down the hall, proceeding when he heard no voices, such as a client or phone call in progress. He peered around the corner at the man, jacket off, tie loosened, munching an apple, having just taken a huge bite. He looked up mid-chew in surprise.

"I brought Ben Olinger to your last meeting with him. Remember Ben? The poor sap who was duped by over-zealous police?" He tossed the polygraph expert's card on his desk. "If you don't know this guy, you should. This should have been your first course of action. If it wasn't in your budget, Ben could have raised the money himself. Call this guy," Charlie thumped the card with his index finger. "Check out his website. As his attorney, at least for the moment, you can ask him about Ben's polygraph test. FYI, he passed every point with flying colors."

The man swallowed, a smile spreading over his face. "That's great! Congratulate him for me. But you've got to understand there was nothing I could do for him after he muddied the waters. And you're right—I do not have the budget to pay for private services. Whatever you paid for that test is about half of what I have for all my cases for the entire year, and that includes private investigators for murder cases."

"So—you're in the plea-bargain business?"

"Not me personally. It's the reality of our criminal justice system. Ninety percent of cases must be cleared without going to trial. Otherwise they'd go free because of the *speedy trial* requirement. That's why you hear, what may sound to you, that criminals get a slap on the wrist in exchange for a plea. Since Ben pled guilty, I had nothing to bargain with. They had him.""But the circumstances. The police lied."

"The US Supreme Court has ruled that lying to a suspect is an acceptable investigative technique."

"But how would an innocent young man, who does nothing but go to school and work and has never been in any kind of trouble, know that?"

"I agree. If this young man is important to you, I suggest you retain private counsel. And let me know who, as soon as possible, so that we can change his attorney of record. Otherwise, we'll be proceeding to sentencing."

Feeling a little sheepish for storming his office, Charlie extended his hand and muttered his thanks. "I'll do that."

"Give Ben my best, and tell him good luck. And thank you for getting involved."

⌘

The next day started with Charlie retrieving Ben at the school for a ten o'clock meeting with his new attorney. "Do you have a bank account?" Charlie asked.

"A small checking account. I did have a savings account—it was an 'and' account—with my father's and my name, but the bank told me that he had drawn down the balance to zero and closed the account. He asked for a cashier's check and took it with him. Everything I'd saved since I was twelve—my very first job, gift money, awards—everything is gone. That was my start-up money—maybe for a dependable car. My first apartment." He shook his head, resignation already in place. "And now this. How can I—"

"Here's how we're going to pay Mr. Geofrey. I'll have his office draw up a promissory note for you to sign at two percent interest per year. The interest is to keep the IRS happy that it really is a loan. I'll write him a check, today, for his retainer—that will be 10,000 dollars—and I'll pay for additional hours when costs exceed the retainer. Is that all right with you?"

"*Why would you ever do that for me*! If I'm found guilty anyway and go to jail, I'll never be able to pay you back. It's a shit-load of money!"

"In the first place, I can afford it, so don't worry about that. The house is paid for, my girls are educated, I have health care for life through the VA, and my income exceeds my expenses. I have no desire to travel the world—I saw enough of that in the service—and no interest in riotous living. More important, however, is my absolute outrage about what has been done, and could be done, to any innocent eighteen-year-old homeless high school kid with no means of support."

Charlie refrained from adding the most salient point—that his parents were not trying to right a wrong or see justice done. They were trying to destroy him. But why? Arriving downtown, he maneuvered the Buick into the exact space he'd snagged the previous week. "Let's wrap up the financials first, then let your attorney see that polygraph report. He'll give us copies of the evidence the DA is holding against you."

The lovely secretary, who had been chatting with Charlie's VA friend Paul, greeted them warmly, offering coffee, tea, soft drinks, or water—sparkling or plain. "Charlie's a Bourbon man," Paul supplied, and everyone smiled, although Jim Beam wasn't added to the selections. The secretary handed Charlie the paperwork for the demand note, which Charlie had already requested by phone. To retain Zeke to represent Ben, Charlie gave the secretary his personal check.

"Just sign here," she said, directing Ben to the appropriate lines that were marked with removable stick-on red arrows. "And Mr. Alderfer, if you'll please sign at the green arrows, I'll notarize them and have them ready when you leave." That accomplished, she left the three with

Zeke.

"You owe me a drink," Charlie scolded as they shook hands.

"We'll all have a toast when this is over. Please sit."

"I've got to ask—am I paying for Paul too?"

"No, Charlie. I'm here as a friend with extra ears. I'd say it's a debt for your service to our country, but I'm dying for a peek at Snyder's report. From everyone's demeanor, I'm guessing that it went well."

Having read it multiple times, Charlie watched Zeke and Paul's faces intently, knowing experienced attorneys should reveal no reaction. But both did—at the top of page three, as their eyes swept three lines and stopped at line four. "What the hell..." his friend mumbled, frowning, then rereading the passage. Then both resumed reading.

"I want to throw the report in that detective's face and tell him to put it in his pipe and smoke it! Then go after the parents," Charlie said.

Zeke shook his head. "Charlie, the case is about Ben and the charges brought by the district attorney's office on behalf of a ten-year-old girl. That's where our focus must be. Even if your cop friends uttered a *mea culpa*, that won't make the DA's case go away, unless his sister recanted—admits under oath she lied and takes her medicine. That, I'm not expecting because this has gone way too far. The parents themselves are in hot water, as they're responsible for child support until you are eighteen or graduate, whichever comes last. But for now, let's take a look at these documents." Zeke passed the packets to them. All read in silence.

Charlie scrutinized them, which included a detailed affidavit, as witnessed by the three law enforcement types, and a Miranda warning. The latter was typed on a form that showed ink accumulation from dirty keys. A *Probable Cause* affidavit, which contained a statement supposedly attributed to Ben, was typed at the bottom. His shaky initials were written beside what Ben had told Charlie had happened.

Page two, *Rights Warning and Waiver*, was filled out by the trooper who signed it. The word *Waiver* was underscored in blue ink and starred by Ben's signature. Page three contained Q and As about all three pages being true: that it was given of his own free will, that it was given without any promises or threats, that he understood the statement, and asked if he wanted to make any corrections to the statement he had made. Yes, Yes, Yes, and No were typed. He had signed it at four p.m. with three witnesses' signatures.

Supplementary reports detailed Ben's first interview with the police that spelled out his adamant denial and his profound confusion as to why Tori would say such a thing. He agreed to take a polygraph test. The next pages contained copious reports: Ben's father's version of the incident, supposedly as told to him by his daughter. Children and Youth Services' statement about their interview with Tori. A criminal investigation report about the request for a polygraph, reporting that during a *pre-test interview* he made admissions, signed a statement, and waived his Miranda Rights, a copy of which was appended among the fourteen pages.

If Charlie or Ben were expecting a scolding for Ben's naiveté, they would have been disappointed. "First, we withdraw the guilty plea. Then I will conduct interviews with the DA's office, the police, and any witnesses permitted. I cannot, in any way, harass your sister."

"And I," Charlie promised, "will rally all the support I can muster."

"Just be careful. Do not do anything illegal. If uncertain, keep me in the loop, and I'll rein you in if you stray."

"Is there any way I can get my stuff out of my house?"

Ben asked.

"I'll arrange for a constable to escort you into your quarters. Your parents, who will receive legal notice, cannot interfere or prevent you from entering. If they have disposed of your possessions, you'll make a list of their approximate value, and they'll be compelled to compensate you for your loss."

"What's going to happen to my sister? She's always been a sweet little kid."

"Not your problem, Ben. She'll have to live with what she's done and whatever happens to you for the rest of her life."

෩෩෩

As Charlie drove the rural back roads toward home, he observed Ben surreptitiously as the boy scrutinized the documents stacked on his lap. Abruptly he looked up from the promissory note, batting it with his hand.

"How could they do this to me?" Squinting while narrowing and widening his eyes, Ben adjusted the pages. That caught Charlie's attention. Most young children with eye problems, including his girls, were nearsighted. Ben held the pages eighteen inches from his face, moving them as if trying to focus.

"Can you read it?" Charlie asked.

"It's just fine print—like at the bottom of ads. I can make out my initials and name."

"When was the last time you had your eyes examined?"

He looked up. Thinking. "Um—sixth grade? The doctor told my mom there was something about my eyes that couldn't be fixed with glasses." He shrugged. "I was okay when I was little and the print in books was huge. As I got older, I just listened—hard—in class. I have a great memory. When I got to ninth grade, this one really cool teacher noticed me squinting. That my answers on tests were perfect, but I couldn't finish in the time allotted. We talked, and she'd let me come in after school and finish the test. Then she started printing out a copy, just for me, in a huge font. And she told the principal, the guidance counselor, and the other teachers."

"But you couldn't read the assignments?"

"No, but like I said, I remembered what was said in class and got by with Bs and Cs."

Charlie pulled over into a strip mall's parking lot. "May I?" he asked. With Ben's permission Charlie shuffled the documents into chronological order and began reading them out loud, starting with the official letterheads and ending with the signatures. It didn't take long for the blood to drain from Ben's face.

He whispered, "How could they do this to me? And why? All I ever wanted was a real family. I've worked so hard; done so much for them. And Tori? Why?"

"Think back, Ben. Did you have a fight with them? Tick them off about something? Was Tori jealous or angry? Think! Something must have precipitated such a drastic response."

Head hanging, Ben rubbed his forehead, closed his eyes, and massaged them.

"Migraine?" Charlie asked. Ben nodded. "Let's go straight home. You can lie in the dark, get some rest. It's in Zeke Geoffrey's hands now and I have every confidence that—"

Ben sat abruptly. "I just thought of something. It wasn't a big deal. We had a little foster girl—couldn't have been much older than four—and she was, well, retarded. She barely spoke intelligibly, had accidents, and didn't understand the rules. My mom would get really angry. Whip her bare butt. Yell and scream at her, and she'd hide her face, sobbing. I told Mom that she couldn't help it. That if she didn't cut it out, I'd tell Child Protective Services. I wouldn't have—I just wanted to scare her into leaving that little kid alone."

"And did she?"

"I don't know. I was never home. When I'd get home at night from my job around eleven, everybody was asleep. I'd clean up the kitchen, do my homework, and hit the sack for a few hours."

"Ben, did you know how much they get paid to keep foster kids?"

"Nothing. Sharing the family income, including what I've made since I was twelve. Dad works for the township. Mom does hair. They say it's their Christian duty to help others in need. And those kids, they have nothing."

"Ben—they get five hundred dollars per child per month tax-free for room and board. The kids come with medical and dental coverage, allowances for shoes and clothing, and any special equipment. There's even a small sum for gifts. To put that in perspective, that's thirty thousand dollars a year for four kids, tax-free. If your parents have jobs, that money wouldn't increase their income tax bracket. To clear thirty thousand dollars a year on top of their other income at regular jobs, they'd have to earn about forty-five thousand dollars extra per year to net thirty thousand."

"No! That can't be right."

"It is, Ben. After somebody else told me what foster parents get, I made some calls. Fibbed a bit about considering being a foster parent myself. Then told her I'd reconsidered—that I was too old."

Ben slumped, slowly turning his head from side to side, hands clasping his head. "I never would have told. But maybe if I had, none of this would have happened. They wouldn't have been so threatened by me."

"Ahhh, that might have been worse. They not only

needed to get rid of you, but in a way that would discredit you, so that nothing you said would be credible."

"Do you think they put Tori up to it?"

"Either that, or she was starved for attention. I mean, with all those kids, how much time was available for her personally? It's even possible she got the idea from that foster girl who accused you of attempted rape."

"It's all too much. What am I going to do if she doesn't back down?"

"I have some ideas. But first, I'm taking you home to rest and get rid of that headache. Maybe your blood sugar many be too low. Or some caffeine would help."

Charlie exited the strip mall's parking lot and motored home. Hours later, when he peeked in on Ben, the boy was asleep. Charlie closed his bedroom door and the pocket door at the end of the hall.

Chapter 9

Charlie wasn't expecting anyone. Jonathan was at his friend Alan's house, and Jade wouldn't bring him home until five. Fearing the doorbell might waken Ben, he hurried to open it. From the sidelight, he saw a late model, top-of-the-line Mercedes parked in his driveway.

"Mr. Alderfer? I'm here to see my grandson, Jonathan. Please produce him. Immediately!"

Charlie was too shocked to respond except to blurt, "He isn't here."

The woman pushed past Charlie into his living room, looking around, craning her neck as if to see around corners. "Jonathan?" she called, her voice echoing into Charlie's deserted home.

Charlie recovered, an adrenalin rush snapping him to attention. That woman. Yes! He remembered her from her visit to Jade at the VA's hospice where Jade's father was dying. She was Jade's late husband's mother—the one who tried to prevent, then ruin their marriage. Who wanted Jade's husband to rise in the family law firm and politics, not to pursue a career in photojournalism. She wore elegant clothes and what his daughters would call major jewelry. No one could criticize her fashion sense—if she were dining in Paris or with nobility. But here in rural Pennsylvania?

She turned on Charlie, manicured hand on her right hip.

"How dare you expose my grandchild to a child molester? You didn't think I'd find out, did you? Well, I'm hiring the best legal minds to get custody of my son's only child. And you can't stop me."

Charlie tried not to laugh, but couldn't help a snicker. "Madam, Jade and Jonathan do not live in this house. They live in an apartment, which I own. And your attorney will tell you that in Pennsylvania, grandparents cannot demand visitation, much less custody of a grandchild, unless the courts so rule. Google it yourself. It's a parent's right to choose who may or not see their child. So get that attorney, but I'm ordering you off my premises or I'll call the police and have you escorted. Do I make myself clear?"

While not intimidated, she merely sniffed her displeasure and, with a jerk of her head, stalked out the door to the Mercedes. The driver, a man who Charlie couldn't make out beyond a bald head and white beard, eased from the driveway and coasted down the street. Through the driver's window, Charlie could see the woman's angry face, finger-jabbing points toward the driver and talking nonstop. Charlie hurried into the den. Firing up his computer he Googled *Grandparents visitation rights in Pennsylvania*. Sometimes eavesdropping in public paid off. And he knew he was right.

☙❧

The following morning, Charlie fed both his boys a hearty country breakfast and sent them to their respective schools—Jonathan on the bus and Ben in his car with a bag of nourishing snacks. Finally the adults had a chance to linger over coffee in Jade's apartment kitchen and discuss her former monster-in-law. Much to Charlie's surprise, Jade merely shrugged. "If push comes to shove, I'll get a restraining order. There's nothing that witch can do to me now that she hasn't tried in the past."

"But if she sincerely wants to visit her grandson…"

"Ha! She'd parade him around like a designer pet and fill his ears with nonsense about the family business. And put ideas in his dear little head that I will not permit."

Charlie smiled, relieved. Attila-the-mom had met her match in Jade Kepley.

Jade asked, "How's Ben?"

"He's all right for now. If his attorney, Zeke Geoffrey prevails, things could end quickly. He phoned last evening that he's set up a conference with the Olingers' attorney about suing the parents for support and expenses, which includes back payment—as much as they get for the foster kids. Says he'll welcome the opportunity to size them up, which will help him plan his strategy. And speaking of strategy, I have some of my own."

Chapter 10

When Charlie asked Ben with whom he could share the polygraph report, he had shrugged and said, "Anyone—it's the truth," a note of resignation having crept into his voice for the first time.

At nine o'clock, Charlie started dialing, lining up appointments at one-hour intervals that covered most of the day. After minor rescheduling to accommodate all targets, he showered and dressed in his best slacks, a white oxford cloth shirt, and a navy V-neck sweater. Aware of the run-off from the spring thaw, he chose wool socks and his high-top waterproof dress shoes. Into his gray lined raincoat's deep pocket, he stowed the stuff he used to ask Emma to put in her purse.

Into the computer bag his California daughter had insisted he needed, he put multiple photocopies of the polygraph report to use in the court of public opinion. He'd start at the high school—the principal and guidance counselor—then work his way to the minister, swim-team parents, his eye doctor, and finally to the agency that licensed the Olingers as foster parents.

Energized, he met the principal and Ben's guidance counselor together. They listened attentively as he ticked through his points that started with Ben's adamant denial of harming his sister; of the police mistreatment: bullying, threats, coercion to confess; and Ben's misguided belief they were truthful and that he had no choice. He mentioned the depth of Ben's predicament and despair. With a flourish, he presented each with copies of the polygraph report. He watched their eyes, carefully, as they turned to page three. Their eyes swept line three and then froze on the fourth line. Both gasped simultaneously, their faces betraying their stunned reaction.

"Is this right?"

"According to the polygraph expert, he answered truthfully."

"But did he ever say that his father actually did—it—with that tool?"

"He told me he was taken into a closet, his pants pulled down, and the metal touched, to which he was threatened that if he ever got out of line, he would do…ah…*it* with the pliers. He was about twelve. But then Ben shot up, started lifting weights, and let the old man know that if he ever came near him again, he'd be sorry."

The pair exchanged hard looks. "And he's a foster parent? Can anyone connect that to the case Ben faces now?"

"He told me his father never touched him again. That, of course, wasn't asked on the test. He says his dad even helped work on his car. Ben rationalized that it was his father's way of keeping boys under control. That maybe his father's father had done it to him. While Ben will stand up for himself, I think he's incapable of lying or exaggerating." Charlie shook his head. "He doesn't realize that everyone's not as honest as he is. That sometimes a little skepticism is healthy."

"You believe this?" the principal asked of the report.

"I'm realistic and not easily fooled. But I've checked out every fact he's ever told me, and it has always proved to be true. He does not lie. He doesn't even exaggerate. But that mother. She lies."

"Well!" the principal said to his colleague. "We'll do whatever we can to help him." The counselor nodded agreement. "Tell him to stop any time and tell us what he needs."

"I think just hearing that you believe him will go a long way. Oh—would you mind checking about his meal plan? Just in case it's been cancelled?"

"Of course. Right away. And thank you for getting involved. Most wouldn't be bothered or would have feared repercussion."

Two down and a whole list to go. Charlie entered the Olinger family's church where he was met by the pastor. They shook hands and settled into his cocoon of a study. After preliminary chitchat about the pastor's fine bookshelves and his extensive collection of leather-bound volumes, Charlie repeated his story. This time, however, he did not mention the closet incident. He just let the man read.

Charlie admired the emerald green Persian carpet and stroked the silky arm of his cherry Queen Anne chair, glancing casually at the collection of framed diplomas, religious paintings, and icons. He thought he could write the great American novel in a study like this. He timed his wandering eyes to study the pastor's face when he flipped to page three and had time to reach sentence number four. His eyebrows lifted with an intake of breath. "Good Lord!"

Charlie remained quiet until he had finished. "I personally took Ben to that professional who was recommended by a close friend—an attorney and a decorated vice-admiral. I saw an impressive collection of commendations from law enforcement entities in multiple jurisdictions. I have every reason to believe that statement faithfully exonerates Ben."

"Of course, as soon as we heard about this, we began praying for the entire family. It's the least we can do in tragic situations."

"Pastor, you can do more. Please make an appointment

to sit down with the mother. Tell her what you have learned. Ask her to question her daughter again. Perhaps if you were present and the child was assured that she wouldn't be punished, she might tell the truth. Can you do that?"

"I'm sorry. I can't use my office to insert myself into a legal dispute. Of course, our congregation will continue to pray for the family. And I will reinforce to the parents that I'll always be here for them if they feel the need to talk. But this report—I can't use it the way you had hoped."

"I wasn't going to ask you to foist this revelation upon them. In fact, I can't let you keep that copy. Hopefully, I haven't made a mistake by presuming that all ministers keep confidences. There's explosive information about the father that could put Ben in danger. Let me leave you with this thought—what's going to happen to Tori as she goes through life knowing she has committed the grievous sin of breaking the ninth commandment unless she tells the truth before it's too late? It could eat her alive, especially if Ben dies in prison, as the police threatened would happen to him if he didn't plead guilty—" And he made air quotes. "—*to something.*"

Charlie rose, shaking right hands with the man of God while collecting the report with his left. "Thank you for seeing me. I trust you'll do what is right."

Interesting. That could go either way, but that man of God has feet of clay, enjoying cheap grace while sequestered in luxury.

ভেওভে

Next, he called on the neighbor who had befriended Emma when they first built the house. How grief-stricken she had been, having claimed Emma as the poster child for breast cancer survival, only to have it return and kill her, just shy of five years. The neighbor had downsized when her husband had passed, now living a few blocks from the Olingers' church.

As he parked, he noticed her watching from her living room window. She opened the door, laughing in delight as she threw her arms around his neck. An ancient Cavalier King Charles Spaniel waddled to greet him with earnest eyes and a wag, her tan muzzle now white. Charlie trailed the pair and the scent of banana bread into her tidy country kitchen with matching maple cupboards, table, and chairs.

"I remember that you like a trace of cinnamon in your coffee, is that still true?"

He grinned his appreciation to this lovely old woman who had cared so much for his Emma.

"Can't believe it's been so long. Tell me all about the girls." Swapping stories, Charlie feared, could derail his schedule, but the dear woman seemed to sense his urgency. "You said on the phone that it was important. About a young man who's in trouble? I'm sorry Emma isn't here to help you—she always had such perspective. Could make sense of anything from obscure snippets of information."

Charlie's executive summary was getting shorter and shorter. While he explained the situation, about which she'd already heard rumors, he merely told her about the charges, Ben's polygraph test, and the overwhelming proof of his innocence. And that an exceptional criminal lawyer had been retained.

She sighed. "We're told, as we taught our children, to believe that police are our friends. If they'd only dealt with him honestly, given him that test in the first place, this farce would have been thrown back at the family. How disillusioning. And disgusting. How can I help?"

"Do you still go to the same church?"

"I do."

"What's the little girl, Tori, like?"

"Oh, she's a sweet little thing. Always eager to talk with everyone who will listen. She sops up every little bit of attention she can get." She darkened, rubbing her knobby hands that she had clasped in her lap. "But that mother. Never a smile or a kind gesture for the child, let alone a hug or a pat on the back. Stern. That's the word."

"You're a mother and a grandmother—you've had lots of experience with kids. Does the little girl exhibit any strange behavior? Act out aggressively, tattle, or act too suggestively for a ten-year-old?"

"I know you won't betray me by repeating this to anyone. I'd feel awful if it got back to the family or my church. One day, about a year ago, we were having social hour after church. The kids, ready to blow off steam for behaving so long, started playing tag. One boy was just watching, and Tori sat down on his lap. He gave her a little shove, but she wasn't discouraged. She sat back down on the edge of his chair.

"He was distracted until he realized she was rubbing up and down against his leg. 'What the hell? Get off me!' he screamed and dumped her on the floor. The kids who noticed laughed then resumed playing tag until parents put a stop to the shenanigans. I saw it myself. Tried hard not to be judgmental about those kids' inappropriate behavior. And with all those foster kids of all ages, and the turnover, I couldn't help but wonder where she had learned it."

Where indeed? Over the next half hour, they sipped coffee and ate delicious hot banana bread that she'd slathered with cream cheese. He hated to leave, promising to keep her informed. Perhaps invite her over to meet his pal Greer? All seven billion of us humans need friends.

⌒⌒⌒

Next stop, the VA. Charlie parked near a small building on the northeast corner of the campus and made his way through connecting corridors to a back office facility. Finding Michelle Clark's door, he knocked on its inner-office doorframe, not wanting to startle the woman. She was multitasking at a desktop computer while eating peanut butter stuffed celery and a carton of low-fat yogurt that sat nearby, a spoon stuck in its depth.

"Oh! I didn't hear you come in," Michelle said, dropping the celery onto a paper plate and covering her mouth with a napkin to finish chewing and swallow. "I was expecting you."

"I'm interrupting your lunch. If later is better, I can run other errands first."

"Nonsense! I need a break from this project. It's making me crazy. What can I do for you?"

"As I said on the phone, the chaplain told me you know all about printing. That you do extensive preparation of materials for the VA. I'm hoping you can identify a particular typeface for me."

"I can try. There's better light in the outer office. Let's have a look." She had a gentle voice and a kind face, framed with a pure, thick silver bob that moved in the air current. Her startlingly blue eyes almost clashed with her pink and white complexion. A perfect, pointy nose made her look cute, even in middle age. With a wide gold ring, she would be married. And no wonder. She was lovely in spite of her simple attire—a long denim skirt, canvas flats, and a man-tailored white shirt, sleeves rolled to the elbow with an upturned, white collar, its open V-neck exposing a carnelian cross necklace.

She led Charlie past tables on which were stacked educational brochures, pamphlets, and flyers of all sizes and colors. She motioned to the clutter, sweeping her arm like a tour guide gesturing to the Grand Canyon. "Our national office produces generic information on a plethora of health-related topics for our doctors' offices, wall racks, and public areas for educational purposes. I also write, edit, proofread, and submit our own internal pieces, which are specific to our VA. A compliance officer circulates them and either approves them or sends them back for revision."

Charlie pointed to cartons, stacked against the wall, onto which were affixed an exemplar of the contents. "Requests for inventory come from designated personnel all over the hospital for replacements from National, for our in-house publications, and requests for new literature. The latter I research, write, design, do a mock-up, and follow the same review process."

"That's a tall order. Do you work alone?"

"I have two volunteers who pull outdated material, note when current supplies are running low, and help track the status of the new projects."

She opened a wall-to-ceiling cupboard that stored art materials. "We don't do paste-up any more—computers are the best. When they work." They chuckled in agreement.

"Where did you learn your job?"

"I was a graphic design major in college and then a military wife. Moving frequently didn't let me launch a career in advertising, which had been my dream. Then I got a job at a VA. And loved it—the veterans, the work ethic, the staff who could work elsewhere for more, but choose to stay. And the VA appreciates military families."

"Bet you've seen great change, thanks to computerization."

"True. But knowing the basics will always be essential. You see that brochure on the table with the bright blue and orange stripes? What I see on the screen will not necessarily be those exact colors on paper. I have to compensate when I choose colors that match what is intended."

"Without taking up too much of your time, I'm hoping you can identify a typeface by its name and size." He gave her a copy of the *Rights Warning and Waiver*, which he'd photocopied after obliterating Ben's and the trooper's names.

"Hum. Haven't seen this in a while. It's a very old style that looks like handset type. Either Franklin Gothic or News Gothic." From the cupboard she extracted a small metal ruler and handed it to Charlie. "As for its size, there are seventy-two points in an inch. Think of a newspaper's blaring headline. *War Ends. Markets Crash. Pope Elopes.* That's seventy-two-point type. The body copy on your piece is eight point, which is nine times smaller," she said referencing the tiny lines on the ruler. "And much smaller under the signature lines. I've seen larger print on legal disclaimers."

"Would you be willing to testify to that in court?"

"Just on that one point? To identify the type and its size?"

"Exactly. That's all. I can't tell you what it's about, except that I need an expert witness."

"Okay. I'll do it. I'll need a subpoena to get out of work."

"I'll make sure it happens."

Chapter 11

If Charlie was right, he'd found a way to get Ben's Miranda Right's document tossed. Forcing his exuberance to chill, he followed the receptionist into his family's ophthalmologist's office.

"Charlie Alderfer! As I live and breathe. They told me you were dead." Dr. Mohr pumped Charlie's hand. "VA not treating your eyes well enough? You've got about two years until I retire, and I'd love to have you until then." They shook hands, exchanging claps on the back, the doctor then ushering Charlie to a leather armchair in his private office.

"My family will always be grateful for your kindness to our daughter."

"I remember her well. She was six and needed glasses. In a year, with those lenses, her vision had decreased from twenty-twenty to twenty-seventy. Next year, same thing. Such a bright little thing who could grasp complicated information way beyond her years. She was scared, trying hard not to cry, fearing she was going blind. Where do kids get these ideas?"

Charlie remembered and smiled his appreciation. "You told her she had fine, healthy eyes that were oval, not round. You showed her a cross-section drawing of a normal eyeball with a < shape representing light entering the pupil and touching the retina. Then you showed her a picture of an oval eye, like hers, where the < didn't reach the retina. You insisted that she had perfect, healthy eyes that just needed glasses to direct incoming images onto the retina. Her prescription was changing because she and her eyes were both growing.

"She was so relieved. By now she's gone through generations of lenses and contacts with advancing technology emerging every time she couldn't achieve twenty-twenty."

"You sounded worried this morning on the phone. What's up? Fill me in."

"I'm hoping you would examine the young friend I mentioned—Benjamin Olinger. It's obvious to me that he needs glasses, but he doesn't have money, family support, or public assistance. I want to pay for his examination and glasses."

"I found a file on him after you called," Dr. Mohr said, tapping it with a finger. "The name sounded familiar. In fact, I'd seen him myself years ago. He was a skinny eleven or twelve year old. The school said he had trouble reading. I examined him and recommended a course of treatment, but we never saw him again."

"I understand about privacy issues. I have documents for your records, giving us permission to talk on his behalf. I have an important question to ask." He slid a copy of Ben's permission form and the *Rights Warning and Waiver*, with the blacked-out modifications, across his desk. "If he didn't have the glasses he needs, and never had treatment, could he read this?"

The doctor opened Ben's seven-year-old file and riffled through the pages. "Absolutely not. I diagnosed Ben with *extreme convergence deficiency*. The boy couldn't cross his eyes."

"Why is that important?"

"Let me demonstrate." He picked up a pencil and held it arm's length from his face. "Watch my eyes as I keep focusing on this pencil." He moved the pencil closer and closer until he was cross-eyed. Charlie laughed. "To focus, our eyes must be able to cross to keep the image intact. Now watch. I'll be Ben." Again, he repeated his hand's motion, while continuing to stare straight ahead, even as the pencil approached his nose.

"What does that mean?"

"Convergence deficiency, in the extreme, means Ben sees straight ahead. It's about his eye muscles, not his ability to see. It's probably congenital."

"Can this be treated surgically?"

"No. What he needs is intense therapy in the form of eye exercises while using special prism glasses that force the images together. The exercises are painful—imagine crossing your eyes and holding it for X-many minutes while wearing strange glasses. He'd start at arm's length then move the pencil a bit closer in a prescribed progression of days and weeks."

"Is it too late? He's eighteen by now."

"No."

"Then my mission? Second, when he's free to pursue it, will you treat him? And most important, will you testify in court that without treatment he could not possibly have read a typeface this small last December?"

Charlie then slid the *Rights Warning and Waiver* across the desk.

The doctor frowned. "Without intervention, he could not."

"What he'll need is only your expert testimony. Period. Anything else would be irrelevant."

"About Ben's lack of insurance—my office still had his parents' billing information on file. Let's see if it pays. And, in the meantime, I suggest you take him to Public Assistance and apply for relief."

❦❧

When Charlie phoned swim-team mom, Ellen Quillen, he was overwhelmed by her eagerness to help. Swept up by her enthusiasm, he detailed the results of the Snyder Bureau of Investigations report, hoping for her help in convincing other parents of Ben's innocence. His goal, beyond expanding Ben's *village*, was to ferret nuggets of truth from a landfill of lies, unrolling the truth like a kitten playing with a loose ball of yarn. No institution as large as that high school could keep gossip from leaking forever.

Ellen's family had uncompromisingly supported Ben ever since the first hint of trouble and had never wavered. And Charlie remembered how infuriated she was when Ben's mother threatened to sic Child Protective Services on them if they allowed Ben to stay at their house. Ellen Quillen was geared up for the fight, her plan of action in hand, even before she seated Charlie in her private home real estate office.

"I've printed the team's contact information by the kids' names, their parents, their addresses, phones—landline and cell. Then I sorted and printed them—not alphabetically—but by the order I feel most illuminating." She tapped several red lines that divided the information into groups. "Start here at the top of page one. These are the mothers who should be supportive and relieved to hear the good news. Their disapproval of the Olingers' treatment of the foster kids in their care has been vocal from day one."

"And the second group?"

"They are most likely to be overextended with careers and family demands. The ones who only show up for meets, but who have nice kids who attend practice, participate in meets, and usually find rides. Not your soccer mom or fund-raising types. Good mothers, but overwhelmed and least likely to be tuned into community scut-tlebutt. I predict they'll be polite, but unaware of the situ-ation. You'll have to decide how to fine-tune your approach.

"The next group are newbies—freshmen parents whose kids just joined the varsity team. I've added, as noted, new transfers and first-timers to the list and those who are new to the sport. They wouldn't have been around long enough to become ingrained in the culture. These parents might not know each other yet, much less know what goes on."

"What's the deal with the X beside this last name?"

"A friend of Ben's mother, who I hear grew up in the coal region with her. On the rare occasion when Ben's mother comes to a meet, they sit together, paying no attention to the swimmers."

While Charlie studied the names, Ellen excused herself to make coffee. In spite of residing in the community for decades, none of names was familiar, these kids having entered school after his own had graduated and left for college.

Charlie took a sip of his fifth cup of coffee. "I'll be cold-calling people whom I don't know. And times have changed since my daughters were in school. I don't want to blow this by saying something inappropriate or that might be misconstrued or make matters worse. What approach do you think I should take?"

"First, I'd ask to talk to the mother by title—I've noted Mrs., Ms., and Miss where applicable. Introduce yourself by name as a long-term resident of the community who is interested in responsible law enforcement. That you have information that swim-team member, Benjamin Olinger, has been wrongly accused of a crime. That you were personally present when XYZ agency concluded that he is innocent. And that while the report is confidential, they can check the credentials of XYZ agency on its website to verify its credentials."

"Should I mention all those plaques of appreciation hung on his wall?"

"Not necessary. The Snyder Bureau of Investigation will undoubtedly include that on their website's home page."

"And what's my sales pitch?"

"That depends upon what you're hoping to accomplish—leads for his personal welfare, such as medical referrals, cheap housing, transportation, etc. Or, if you're getting a really good vibe, if they've heard in the community or from their kids what's going on with Ben's family. Be sure to give them contact information. Since you've caught them off guard, they may think of something after they've digested your news."

As his gaze swept the papers laid out on her desk, an unintended sigh escaped. "I sure hope I'm doing the right thing. Or at least, not making it worse."

She reassured Charlie with a tap to his forearm. "Stay the course. Your persistence will prevail in the end."

❦

Charlie agonized over the nuances of contemporary phone etiquette. Was it still rude to call at dinnertime? Did people even sit down to dinner at six anymore, much less together? What the hell—it was better to apologize than to lose the opportunity.

Mentally, he bracketed six to eight o'clock, but restrained himself until after seven. He could barely contain his excitement when the first four mothers and one father sounded downright euphoric about Charlie's news. While nobody had new information to share, each begged time to grab pencil and paper to jot down his name and the polygraph expert's website address. And yes, they'd be in touch if they heard or remembered anything germane.

He heard the scarlet tanager chirp eight times and glanced at his watch. That was fast! As he worked the list, subsequent results were all over the planet. Two were hang-ups—not unexpected. Three listened politely, thanked him, but declined to take his contact information, even when gently coaxed. One screamed, "This is a National Do Not Call number. If you call it again, I'll report you!" *Click!*

Ellen Quillen had been right. It would have been a terrible idea to visit these families in person and let them read the report. However, everyone seemed to believe him—to take his word at face value. Maybe it was his age, or having no financial stake, his military service, or his passionate plea for justice. Two fathers recognized his name immediately as the VA patient who had stopped a killer. Veterans said they'd welcome meeting him at the VFW to swap war stories and buy him a beer. As Charlie delivered his evolving pitch, based on the others' reactions and unsolicited advice, several listened politely then said they did not want to get involved, said goodbye, and hung up.

One mother mentioned younger children and her fear that her family would be labeled *troublemakers*, which would negatively impact teachers' attitude toward their kids. Until that moment, Charlie hadn't considered the far-reaching possibilities of community polarization if his campaign was sufficiently controversial to fracture the district. Tongues would be wagging by this time tomorrow.

It was time, he thought, to convert his copious notes to computer documents. He opened two files, labeling one Ben's Support and the other Ben's Defense. Into the first, he'd record everything about the young man's well-being—keeping him alive and healthy. And in Ben's defense documents, proof of his innocence while placing the blame where it belonged.

Blame. *He said-she said.* Humm. An idea sprang full-blown in his mind, flourishing like desert flowers following a downpour. He'd write to the Olingers! He'd have to word it with extreme care—not tick off Zeke Geoffrey, Ben's legal defender. The Olingers knew nothing about the polygraph report, its contents or implications. He could offer to share it by meeting with them. Get the shock value. A letter would test them. If they really had chosen their sweet little daughter over a much older brother and that now was in question, they should be eager to learn the truth, however they chose to deal with their daughter. Unless, they knew all along that Ben was the victim.

He opened a new Word document and let months of pent-up frustration flow through his fingers, exhilarated by forward momentum for the first time since undertaking the lie-detector test and hiring Ezekiel Geoffrey. It was time to test the parents themselves. He began:

> *Dear Mr. and Mrs. Olinger,*
>
> *First, I'd like to let you know that our congregation is praying for you and your family. There's nothing any of us would rather see than to have a family reunited and their troubles put to rest.*
>
> *I can't imagine having to choose between my children and realize how hard all of this must be for you. I believed that Ben, even without the lie detector test, was innocent of all charges and was coerced by overzealous police who need to close ninety percent of criminal cases without a trial. Had they proceeded with their polygraph test, for which he had volunteered,*

this matter would have been resolved immediately.

By now, you may have heard via the grapevine about the polygraph test he did take. While it isn't admissible in court, the testimony of the professional who administered it is. The expert formulated questions based on the Arrest Warrant, Probable Cause Affidavit, and an intensive interview with Ben. I personally was present when the pronouncement was made: he passed, he is innocent of all charges, his coerced testimony is negated by this test.

The professional conducting the test is a 20-year leader in his field, whose work is trusted by law enforcement in multiple counties and jurisdictions who hire him to get to the bottom of their cases. I personally read his plaques of appreciation on his office walls. His equipment is state-of-the-art.

I believe Ben was brought to our doorstep for a reason and, with prayer, we will all be guided to the right decision. If you'd like to read the polygraph report yourself, please let me know. I'll meet with you at your convenience.

Chapter 12

Charlie was flooded with relief the minute the mailman extracted his letter to begin its journey to Ben's parents. It was out of his hands. He'd have to wait. How many people had he involved? Surely someone would offer a solution.

As Charlie was pulling a tray of granola and a pan of nutritious nut-laden brownies from the oven, Roxie, who had been napping, shot from under the table, tail wagging half her body, yipping with excitement. Three-thirty. Right on time. The clever little dog had quickly learned which door brought her little master home. She looked like an oversized black and white rabbit, hop-hop-hopping, eyeballing Charlie to hurry with the door. He complied.

Over snacks, Jonathan chattered nonstop, Charlie paying attention to every word, knowing that if he were caught daydreaming, there would be a quiz. "There's this kid in my class whose brother got in big trouble. He copied another kid's homework. The other kid got mad and told the teacher. Papa, Ben says, 'winners never cheat and cheaters never win.' That's right, isn't it?"

"Absolutely."

"And telling the truth is good, right?"

"Always. Lying gets people in all kinds of trouble, especially when they have to cover up their deception, and then can't keep it all straight. Better to just tell the truth in the first place."

"What if you don't know the answer?"

"Then say, 'I don't know.'"

Jonathan chewed a bite of brownie and took a sip of milk. "Papa, why are people telling lies about Ben?"

Oh, brother. The inevitable question Charlie had passionately hoped would never be asked. "Have you and your mom talked about it?"

"I asked her, but she keeps saying, 'Don't worry. The grownups are sorting it out. Everything will be fine.' But Ben seems so sad. And somebody hit him in the nose."

"When? What are you talking about?"

Jonathan jumped down from his chair and led Charlie down the hall into Ben's room and into the bathroom. "Look, Papa!" The wastepaper liner was stuffed with blood-soaked tissues, traces of dried blood remaining in the sink. Noticing that the shower curtain was pulled outside the tub, he stepped closer. Towels and pillowcases soaked in pale brown cold water.

"Nobody hit him. Ben gets severe nosebleeds. In case he doesn't want us to know, let's not say anything to him. I'm guessing he'll use the washer when he gets home. It might embarrass him to think he's made work for me. Now—about homework."

Fortunately, Jonathan had forgotten all about people lying about Ben. Charlie and Jade should talk right away. It wasn't his place to co-parent, and he needed mom-approved answers to Jonathan's grown-up questions, especially after reinforcing the evils of lying. He couldn't rely on *ask your mother* forever.

"Ben told me a secret," Jonathan said with a conspiratorial giggle.

"Is it a good secret? If so, did he say not to tell?

"It's a good one. And he didn't say do not tell." He hopped off the chair and approached Charlie's ear, as if to prevent nefarious eavesdropping. "Ben has a girlfriend!"

Charlie was stunned. With Ben's nonstop schedule, when had he found time to date? Jonathan rapid-fired the details.

"He says she's really pretty and really, really nice. They eat lunch together. She reads him his homework from English class. And she helps him some more during study hall. What's study hall, Papa? He says she has pretty long hair and is from somewhere else."

"That is a nice secret, but I suggest we let Ben tell other people. Sometimes we have to respect people's privacy."

"Like in the restroom? My teacher says that's really important."

How many such questions had Emma fielded when their girls were little? At least she lived to raise them. As Charlie sipped coffee, he added a decision to his *Ben's Support* list. Take him downtown to Public Assistance immediately and initiate the paperwork for medical care. That should include welfare until graduation or until he was established. The high school secretary, still working until five, agreed to process Ben's excused absence for the following morning.

At a little past seven that evening, Ben's jubilant voice boomed through the phone. He remembered his girls' calls home from college. "Dad?" was a problem, and "Dad!" prefaced great news. Ben's greeting was "Mr. A! Dude!" followed by "I have great news."

Could it be? Could the charges be dropped? Surely he would have heard from Ben's attorney. "I got this great new job, and it fits perfectly between school and my fast-food job. I'm going to deliver pizza for that trendy new shop on Main Street. I know what you're going to say— it's too many hours. But I can ask everyone I know to order their pizzas from that shop during my hours, then I'll get lots of business, to say nothing of tips."

"Do they supply a delivery car?"

"No. But mine gets good mileage, and the territory's a tight grid—lots of homes in a high-density neighborhood."

"Well then, congratulations." Charlie rattled off the particulars of the next morning's mission to get public assistance, to which Ben promised to be outside the admin building on time.

⌁⌁⌁

The county's public assistance office essentially duplicated the facility where Charlie had interviewed a social security professional to coordinate his parents' death benefits. Their deaths had predated computerization, and face-to-face appointments were the norm. Today, rows of new institutional chairs seated dozens of clients who ranged in age from infants through extreme old age.

"Pssst!" A middle-aged man in shabby work clothes identified Charlie and Ben as newbies. "Take a number off the hook over there then find the right papers on the table along the wall. They'll call your number—eventually."

Ben did as instructed, nodding his thanks, while Charlie scrutinized the scene.

On average, these applicants looked much happier than the polygraph clients. Two-thirds were women, many with small children, interspersed with knots of girls who couldn't be out of their teens. The latter chattered merrily among themselves. With few exceptions, the single adults wore ear buds. A huge man with skin as black as his hair was soothing a distraught mother whose child had just thrown up on the floor. Attacking the puddle with a string mop, he repeated his joy at having a job and keeping *his* floors spotless.

Seeing Ben struggle with his forms, Charlie offered to read the lines under which Ben should enter his answer. To his relief, Ben agreed with his usual calm. "Can you see what you're writing?" Charlie asked.

"Dude!" Ben responded with a smirk. "I can remember what I just wrote."

"Keep the form. Take it in with you," the friendly expert said in a gravelly voice that wafted booze and cigarette breath. They settled to wait. And wait. Ben drew a burgundy device from his jacket and inserted ear buds.

"A friend lent me her Kindle. She downloaded *Crime and Punishment* onto it then passed it along."

Charlie grinned, mentally scratching from his *Ben Support* list *flunking English*.

Three hours later, his number was called, and they scurried to the reception desk. A civil servant asked pre-interview questions and directed the pair through a maze of gray fabric cubicles to an intake officer.

He was young—late twenties at the most, short hair and clean-shaven, wearing a long-sleeve white dress shirt and tie, but no jacket. Smiling, he dispensed with the pleasantries and got down to business, opening a document and typing the information from Ben's form. Unhurried, he gave Ben ample time to explain his situation, particularly his need for medical care. Charlie resisted the urge to jump in.

The interviewer relaxed his hands from his keyboard and, in a calm voice, explained that Ben had two issues that first needed resolving. "As long as you're in high school, regardless of age, your parents are responsible for your support. If *they* need assistance for your care, *they* need to file for support. If, as you say, they are foster parents, it doesn't sound like that's the case. Perhaps legal aid can help you prove that you're emancipated? That might take some time."

"What's number two?" Charlie asked.

"You need two forms of government ID. I see you have your driver's license. Another could be a passport, social security card, birth certificate—there are others. I'll give you a list." He pulled a sheet from a Pendaflex folder. "As soon as you resolve these two areas, come back, and I'll be glad to get you some help."

"So—this is a bust?"

"No. We've started your record. I'll print you a copy." He entered a command and his printer hummed to life. From his belly drawer he withdrew two business cards that bore the Commonwealth's seal and his name printed in blue ink. On the back, he added his office's direct extension and an email address. "I'm trusting you not to share my email address. I can tell your situation is pretty bleak. If you get desperate and are tempted to harm yourself, don't. Call nine-one-one or call me directly, and I *will* find someone to bypass the red tape."

✐✐✐

As Charlie entered his tomb-quiet home, a pall of depression threatened to settle. Ben had such a light heart and seemed able to live in the moment. But just how much more could he take? There must be something else Charlie could do. He hadn't heard from the minister—no surprise there—the team parents, legal team, updates from the school—except for their concern about his grades. And he'd told everyone who would listen to him about his young friend's predicament, hoping that someone knew something useful.

Someone claiming to be one of the Olingers' neighbors had called anonymously, complaining that *those people* didn't belong in their community. She'd gone on and on. Charlie let her vent then politely brought the conversation to an end. He couldn't help wondering how she had obtained word of his mission and his contact information.

Click, click, click, click. Doggie toenails announced

Roxie's greetings, as she had mastered the doggie door that was cut into the privacy door at Jade's level. The little dickens had even figured out how to manipulate the mechanical latch. That she would come and go as she pleased was becoming evident to both families. Charlie's spirits rose like a phoenix as Roxie worked her head under his hand, beseeching him with soulful eyes. If only people were as loyal as dogs.

"Treat?" he asked, marveling at how Roxie could run straight forward while looking over her shoulder and never run into anything. He looked at the clock—too soon for Jonathan, and Ben wouldn't return until eleven that evening. That new pizza job seemed to be going as expected, enabling him to buy a few things. "It's just you and me," he said to the dog, who cocked her head knowingly. An idea popped into his head. Maybe he could beg a medical referral to an ear-nose-and-throat specialist through a dermatologist he knew from church. Someone who might do a little pro bono work.

Pulling out the church directory, he dialed her home number, intending to leave a message. To his surprise, the physician picked up on the first ring, having taken the day off to tend her sick daughter. She sounded genuinely pleased to hear from him, being delighted that his recovery enabled him to attend Sunday services. Succinctly, Charlie pitched young Ben's medial plight. Perhaps even she, although in an unrelated field, might see him herself.

"I'm sorry, Charlie. It would be unethical for me to treat someone outside my specialty. His parents could sue me. And I can't recommend a friend on whom I could prevail. Most physicians do volunteer work, but within the auspices of nonprofit organizations, such as emergency shelters. I know two doctors who load their personal vehicle with medical supplies and make rounds in parks and under bridges, treating homeless people who refuse to come in.

Your best bet for him is to follow up on public assistance's recommendations. And Charlie—thank God for people like you who are willing to get involved."

ଦ୬ଦ୬

It was time, Charlie realized, having procrastinated too long, to visit the agency that licensed the Olingers. The director's name sounded vaguely familiar, although he couldn't attach any association to the VA, his church, his neighbors, or professionals with whom he had crossed paths over the years. What Charlie had in mind went way beyond exonerating Ben. If he were honest with himself, he was on a mission to rid the foster care system of predators. A couple who used homeless kids as a paycheck and were guilty of child abuse—physically, mentally, emotionally, or in combination. Who knew how many little children's lives those people ruined?

He approached the building, which resembled a cobbled-together strip mall's collection of former businesses, located a mile from a defunct steel mill. He noticed the current mission, evidenced by signage and mottos on a red brick addition that read, *A Happy Childhood Lasts Forever*. From a nearby building, happy youngsters spilled, freed from their classrooms to romp in the April fresh air. He wondered where the kids came from—locally or far-away city ghettos. He refocused on the building that bore the official nameplate and tugged open the heavy steel door. Tall windows beamed sunlight across a receptionist area.

"I'm Charlie Alderfer. I have an appointment with Mr. Watkins?" He hated how that sounded like a question, as if he were a beggar which, in a way, he was. Responding to the receptionist's page, an interior door was flung open, and a slender, smiling man approached Charlie, leading with his arm fully extended. He pumped Charlie's hand.

"It's a pleasure to meet you again," the man said.

Charlie wracked his brain for a prior connection.

"I was hoping you hadn't changed your mind, or had too many demands on your time. Our high school kids would love to meet a real war hero and hear about careers in the military. Few have the resources for post-secondary education. In the Army, they could learn marketable skills and later, take advantage of the GI Bill."

"I apologize—please refresh my memory about our last meeting. So much has happened since this time last year, and I've met so many people."

"The awards ceremony, when our congressman presented citations from the governor's office. We spoke at the reception about your giving our fine young people a presentation on heroism."

Of course. That's why his name was familiar. A hero? He'd been inordinately lucky to stop a killer—it could easily have gone the other way. And the Vietnam War? He had been shot all right. After six months in basic and advanced training at Fort Jackson, his boots were on the ground in Nam for all of three weeks before he got shot. After recuperating in Germany, he had finished his tour behind a desk at Fort Lewis, Washington, having achieved a rank of E-6 and saved enough money to marry his sweetheart. Some hero.

"Mr. Alderfer?"

"Yes. Of course. I'd be happy to participate in your program. Are you planning to include other veterans as well? Perhaps men and women representing all branches of our armed forces? Widen the perspective? The VA could suggest names. But, Mr. Wilkins, that's not why I'm here today. Can we sit down for a minute?"

"Of course. I apologize for keeping you standing. Please. Let's step into my office." He motioned Charlie toward a pair of matching wingback leather chairs that fronted a floor to ceiling glass wall that reminded Charlie of an auto dealer's showroom. Traffic buzzed by on the adjacent highway.

After they settled and chatted entirely too long, Charlie's patience was shot. "Mr. Watkins, I'm here on behalf of a young friend who is in need of compassionate intervention. In researching his plight, it came to my attention that a foster family you license may bear closer inspection."

"Whom are we talking about?"

"The young man's name is Benjamin Olinger, the fosters in question being his parents."

Watkins stared, his jovial manner darkening, like easing a dimmer switch. He offered no comment.

Charlie stumbled to fill the awkward void. "I've uncovered a grievous miscarriage of justice as well as questionable treatment of vulnerable foster children."

"That's a pretty serious accusation if you're talking about the Olingers. I understand that young Benjamin has confessed to a crime—"

"That he did not commit. A confession perpetrated by overzealous police making threats, which led to his being homeless himself."

"His parents had every right to expel him from the house."

"I'm asking you to re-evaluate the Olingers as suitable foster parents. Talk to the kids. Have an unannounced inspection. Ask the neighbors if they have, in fact, seen abuse."

"Mr. Alderfer, we've never had a single complaint about that family. They take kids nobody wants who have come from horrendous circumstances. We don't care if their home isn't Martha Stewart perfect. Those kids get to live in the suburbs, away from the gangs—to attend a public school with an impressive graduation, college prep, and job placement record. We don't care if the pretty police don't like the height of their grass or the bikes on their lawn or the volume of their music. If you have a legitimate complaint, prove it."

Charlie opened his satchel and pulled the polygraph report. "You may read this, but I can't let you keep it. Of course, you can take notes about the professional's website to verify his credentials. Is that agreeable?" Charlie could tell by the look on his face that he was dying to read it while trying to act nonchalant.

"I agree."

Charlie handed him the papers. Watkins affixed cheaters to his nose, settling deeper into his chair, and began to read. If it hadn't been so damn serious, this routine would be hilarious, Charlie thought, as he followed Watkins's eyes as they swept every line on page one. Watkins licked the tip of his thumb, then flicked page one behind the others, and squeezed the stapled corner to align the three sheets. He read, and then flipped to page three, his eyes sweeping line one. Line two. Line three. And then—his eyes shot to Charlie's. "What the hell?"

"I was present to hear the conclusions of Ben's polygraph test." Charlie expounded on the conclusions, unloading his expanded repertoire of the whole story in mind-numbing detail. Watkins wasn't listening. He just kept rereading page three and jumping to the expert's conclusion and the recommendation about the father.

Watkins sighed as he handed Charlie back the document. "When it comes to tweens and teens, I'm pretty shock-proof. By thirteen, they're beyond 'show me yours and I'll show you mine.' You can't erase years of dreadful parenting, or lack thereof, by plunking them down with nice wholesome families and hope they'll seize the lifestyle, morals, and opportunities. We try—so hard—but many count the days until they age out of the system or can run away."

Charlie re-evaluated this man, whom he'd pegged as a smug bureaucrat but who now looked diminished. "Can you at least keep an eye on that house? As a special favor for the kids? And, on a happier note, I'll be happy to speak to your kids in whatever way you think would help."

"Could you meet with our board members who are plan these events?"

"It would be my pleasure."

Good-byes and handshakes completed, Charlie traversed the reception area alone, meaning to thank the receptionist who, by now, was missing. From the empty hook where a lady's coat had hung, he deduced that she had left for the day. It was, after all, after five. He grasped the door's handle but paused as an afterthought occurred him. He'd forgotten to ask an important question. Reversing direction, he approached Watkins's door. As he did so, he heard the director's voice. Glancing at the receptionist's desk phone, he noticed a red light. He halted at the sound of his name.

"He just left. He's going to be trouble unless you make your mess go away." A pause. "He knows nothing about that. But don't make me warn you again. Make nice with the neighbors. Get that lazy wife of yours off her fat ass and spit-shine the house. She's got nothing else to do." A pause. "I know! I know! Just do it." Watkins added, "I'm sending you two little kids, but this time they're staying more than a few days. How long? As long as it takes. You have to fill up those beds you're paid for." A pause. "I do not care if that eats into the profits. You get paid for a month, for three days work, as long as the kids are too young to trigger the schools to ask why they aren't attending." A pause. "Leave the paperwork to me. You work the plan."

Charlie scowled in concentration. What on earth? Were the Olingers keeping kids on paper that didn't exist? Or who left shortly after arriving to be placed with another such family? What was the incentive? To earn stellar marks as excellent placement professionals? What was in it for any of them?

The director's voice turned angry. "Never, ever threaten me. You're on the hook for the kids whose paperwork went missing, even if they're safe and sound in another county. You kept the money. And anything you paid me was cash under the table, for which there's no record. It might be leaked that you're trafficking." Another pause. "Of course that's ridiculous, but you do not want to risk messing with me."

Fearing his eavesdropping might be discovered momentarily, Charlie crossed the outer office with long, silent steps, eased the door open, and shut it. He chose the sidewalk that did not pass beneath the director's expansive glass windows. Once locked in his car, he dared a peek at the structure's front door, half expecting to see the director looking left and then right. Nothing. He sighed, not knowing what to make of this revelation. He'd sort it out later.

Suppose it wasn't just the Olingers? That other foster families were involved? Little kids being moved through a succession of houses while each one claimed $500 per month per child, with a fee being paid, in cash, to the director?

Chapter 13

Charlie auto-piloted home, his mind weighing Ben's criminal versus his civil cases in terms of their progress or lack thereof. He'd better update both files, refresh his perspective, and streamline what research to share with Ben's attorney. So many details; so little time. With the trial date looming in less than two months, he had no time to lose.

He pulled into the garage and, before entering, retraced his route to his mailbox, the flag having been lowered. He extracted a large white envelope from his bank, bent around rubber-banded correspondence. A *Consumer Reports* and his *National Geographic* he pried from the back of the box. Several business envelopes would be bills, as would the robin's egg blue love note from the power company.

Walking his fingers through the collection, he hoped one might contain new drawings from his little grandsons in Atlanta. He grinned at the prospect—until his eye lit on the return address from an unfamiliar law firm. Jade's ex-monster-in-law, making good on her threat? He'd open it later, perhaps in Jade's presence. One more battle to fight.

He texted Jade, *A legal matter needing two heads.* She responded, *Nine p.m. is good.* Ah, no little ears on adult conversations.

That evening was uncharacteristically quiet, as Charlie annotated Ben's files. He edited, streamlined, and spell checked each document, saving and printing three copies of each. He addressed a large manila envelope to Ezekiel Geoffrey, Esquire, and one for Ben. He stretched three trails of documents on the living room carpet, setting three file folders near each envelope and then laid out the pertinent documents in chronological order. He'd leave the trails on the carpet, adding more pages as they became available, and enclose a summary sheet later. The legal documents, which everyone had, would be appended for reference as would a detailed list of resource people including their contact information.

The Audubon clock's scarlet tanager chirped nine o'clock, blending with his iPhone's text from Jade. *Come on down. J sleeps.* Charlie collected the law firm's envelope from the kitchen counter and crept downstairs, his soft-soled moccasins soundless on the wood.

After a quick hug and brief exchange of pleasantries, Charlie handed Jade the sealed envelope. She studied the return address and shrugged. The name meant nothing to her. "Don't look so worried, Charlie. There is no way they can get custody of Jonathan, especially since they live out of state. I'll hire an excellent lawyer and take them all the way to the Supreme Court if I have to. They will never take my son away from me."

"With their wealth and connections, is there a possibility they might try to kidnap him? Take him to Europe or some place that doesn't have extradition treaties with the US?"

"And leave her high-society friends and political connections behind? No way. She'd be more likely to bury me in money—lawsuits that won't go away."

"But you have your husband's insurance and control of Jonathan's trust fund."

"With her kind of wealth, it's a pittance." For the next twenty minutes, they kicked around possible plans of action. "I knew this day would come," she said, eyeballing the envelope. "Let's see what the she-devil has in mind."

Sniff.

Charlie and Jade simultaneously spotted Jonathan, cowering in the hallway. His little red face betrayed that he'd been crying for some time, sobs stuttering with each breath. He clung to Tow Truck, his well-loved teddy bear, burying his face in its fur.

"Jonathan! What's wrong?"

"Don't let that bad woman take me away."

"Of course not. Never. No way. Come here, darling. Have you been listening to what Papa and I were discussing? Come here, baby."

"I'm not a baby. I know what she wants. Please, Mommy, don't let her get me."

Jade drew him onto her lap, rocking him gently. "Can you put on your big boy ears for a minute? I'll try to explain." When he nodded, however doubtfully, she continued. "We live in Pennsylvania. Here, as in most parts of the country, parents decide who may and may not see their children. If she bothers you, I'll call the police, and they'll stop her."

Charlie dug a clean tissue from his pocket and put it in Jonathan's hand. "We shouldn't have been talking about grown-up things when you could hear us. Do you trust us?"

The child bobbed his head.

"Then remember we've had our whole lives to learn how to handle difficult problems. We can and we do."

"And people?"

"Sometimes them, too."

"Like Ben?"

"You let us worry about Ben."

"But why?"

"Because it's our job, not yours. But you can say a

prayer for Ben. He'd like that."

After Jade settled Jonathan and Tow Truck back in bed, sang his special song, and said a prayer, Charlie was beckoned for a quick kiss. To his vast relief, the little guy was smiling around jaw-splitting yawns."

"G'night. Papa. I love you."

"I love you too, buddy, this much!" he said, spreading his arms to their limit.

Seated in the far end of the great room, Jade slit the lawyer's envelope and extracted a single sheet. "Huh!" she said. "Unimpressive." She pointed at the blank margins that should have shown a lengthy list of partners' names. "It's addressed to you, Charlie." She handed him the single sheet of letterhead.

> *Dear Mr. Alderfer,*
>
> *I am writing on behalf of my clients, Leroy and Jane Olinger. It has come to their attention that you have been engaged in slandering their good name and threatening custodial interference in the matter of their foster children. Please be advised that if you do not cease and desest all such actions immediately, civil and criminal charges will be filed against you on their behalf.*
>
> *I trust that you will take this matter seriously and proceed accordingly.*
>
> *Very truly yours,*

Jade laughed. "Hey, Charlie! You rattled their cage. Guess they're finally coming to the conclusion that they're under the microscope. I wonder who told them."

Charlie decided to keep the overheard conversation to himself for the time being. "I'd put money on that man

Watkins who places foster kids with the Olingers. Bet he called them as soon as I was out the door. Warned them to clean up their act or he'd pull the kids. He's got as much at stake as the foster families if anything happens to the children he's placed in their care."

"Let me see that letter again." Jade held the letter to the overhead light and squinted, then flicked on her task lamp. Rummaging in her desk, she located a magnifying glass and scrutinized the paper. "Ah ha! Look at this. No water-mark—unheard of on professional stationery. And if my eyes don't deceive me, the font used for the letterhead and the body of the message are identical. And he misspelled *desist*. The return address is in the city of Philadelphia, but the zip code is wrong."

"You know that how?"

"Endless trips to the City of Brotherly Love in pursuit of my medical education. But let's take a peek at the American and the Pennsylvania Bar Associations for this dude and his firm." Charlie watched as Jade's fingers flew, opening screen after screen, ultimately proclaiming, "Nope!"

"So it's a fake?"

"I'm guessing someone wants you to back off. The work of an amateur and a dumb one at that."

"I'd better fax this to Ben's lawyer. See if he thinks I'm going too far."

એજ

Charlie saved his documents, shut down his computer, and walked his nightly circles throughout the house. How could it be midnight? Across the street, silhouetted behind sheer curtains, Charlie could see that Old Mr. Greer was still reading in his favorite swivel rocker by the window. As was their custom, Charlie double-clicked his living room light to which an identical signal responded good-night through the darkness. All was well in the hood.

In spite of the Olingers' legal threats, Charlie felt remarkably calm as he climbed into bed. Zeke would know what to do. All these years and he still missed Emma's *cold clams*, playfully tickling his back to see if he'd shriek at the touch of her icy toes. He mounded several pillows and opened Jeffrey Deaver's latest thriller, realizing how little time he spent reading these days. It had been his salvation during his months recuperating at the VA. He forced his eyes to reopen—twice—before admitting defeat. This day was toast.

Chimes. Was he dreaming? Like a cathedral on Sunday morning, its notes enticing congregants to worship. He jerked awake—his iPhone. Where was it? He had neglected to set it on the nightstand as his daughters had lectured so many times. In his office—of course. He looked at the clock—one in the morning. Nobody called at this hour unless it was an emergency. His daughters? Their families? Mr. Greer? Jonathan or Jade? Ben! As possibilities sluiced through his mind, he hurried down the hall, his moccasins half on, half off, until his toes wriggled them into place. Not his cell—the landline. He grabbed, but it had stopped ringing.

Redial. He hit it, immediately recognizing Ben's numbers. By the time he'd processed that information, Ben had picked up. "Mr. A?" A question, not a greeting. That sounded like trouble. "I'm sorry that it's so late. Could you come get me? I've had an accident with my car. I think it's totaled."

"Are you hurt? Do you need an ambulance?"

"No. I'm okay. I was hardly moving when I hit the guardrail. I'm on the main drag, two blocks east of the pizza shop."

"And the car?"

"A buddy of mine has an automotive shop a few blocks away. He said he'd give it a tow. That we'd figure out what to do with it tomorrow."

"I'm on my way."

Charlie threw on his jeans, a long-sleeved tee, a rain jacket, and waterproof boots. Storm clouds had overtaken the area, threatening a deluge as he eased the Buick from his garage and accelerated up the street. Wind and rain lashed his windshield, nearly obliterating the landmarks, his tires sending waves in either direction. As he pulled onto the main drag, he was relieved to have the road to himself. With no impatient drivers honking behind him, he inched toward the intersection where Ben would be waiting.

Streetlight illuminated torrents of water, blowing in waves like a nor'easter blizzard. Ben huddled under a store's metal awning that threatened to be torn from its moorings any second. Charlie pulled within inches of Ben's protection and beckoned.

Upon spotting Charlie, he dashed toward the Buick and threw himself into the car. "Hey thanks, man. I'll mop up the water tomorrow."

"What happened? Was it the storm? It must have reached here sooner than home."

"The weather was fine. It was the car. It was overheating. Steaming. Dad and I had worked on the radiator…"

"When? When did you see him?"

"During Thanksgiving vacation. The radiator had a hole, so he patched it. Honest, Mr. A., he does fine work. Didn't have anything to do with what happened."

"Which was?"

"I finished my run and pulled into the lot. The engine was running hot. So I got a big can of water and filled the reservoir. The manager had several orders ready to deliver, and I was the only guy working late."

"When was that?"

"About ten thirty. Anyway, I made the run, and the radiator was still steaming. So, I did it again—filled the radiator to the top, and went in to grab the orders. By the time I got out, there was this humungous puddle under the car."

"Had it started raining?"

"No, but I could hear thunder and knew it was coming. I went back into the store and told the manager that my radiator was shot. Leaking like a sieve. He says, like I'm really dumb, 'Well put some more water in it, and get these pizzas delivered while they're still hot.' So I said, 'It'll overheat and seize up the engine.' So he says, 'If you don't get these pizzas delivered, you're fired.'

"Honest, Mr. A., I'd have run them around on foot if the addresses were nearby or taken a bike if there was one. So I loaded the pizzas, topped off the radiator, and started the run, praying I'd make it. That guy owes me a week's pay. In no time the gauge went nuts, steam everywhere, stinking hot metal, the engine froze up, car wouldn't steer, and went into the guardrail. If I'd been on the highway, I would be dead."

"Let's get you home. We can worry about this tomorrow."

"What am I going to do without my car? I need that car or I can't work. Dad says I still owe him six hundred dollars for it, but I paid for it myself and still have the receipt."

"Is there any chance your father tampered with the car?"

"No. He wouldn't do that. Besides, I would have noticed."

"If you could prove that he did…"

Ben was shaking his head. "That would be lying."

The following morning Jonathan was thrilled to find Ben at the house. As they ate pancakes and Canadian bacon with cinnamon apple wedges, he peppered Ben with questions about what games he could play. "Can you teach me to win at checkers? How about gin rummy? Or Sorry?"

"Sorry is pretty much a game of chance—perhaps with a little strategy. But checkers and rummy take some planning. I can teach you some moves."

Jonathan jumped down from his seat and, rummaging in his backpack, produced a Rubik's cube. "This is Alan's. I told him you'd know how to put the sides back together. He can't figure it out. He said his big brother said to remove the stickers and put them back by color. Alan thinks that's cheating."

"He's right. Let's see." Ben's hands flew, turning and twisting the cube until all six sides had one uniform color. He handed it back. "You tell your friend, 'Cheaters never win and winners never cheat.'"

"No. You said it backward. It's 'Winners never cheat and cheaters never win.' That's the way you always say it." He popped the Rubik's Cube into his backpack. "Will you teach me the trick someday?"

"It's pretty difficult for a six-year-old."

"But I'm almost seven."

Charlie grinned. The boy had been saying that since they first met—nearly nine months ago, only then he was barely five.

Chapter 14

Old Mr. Greer was puttering around his front yard, looking for signs of spring. His snowdrops and Lenten roses had finished blooming, as had his forsythia hedge and a swath of early narcissus. To Charlie's eye, he seemed overly interested in Charlie's house. Sidestepping lingering puddles, Charlie crossed the street, Roxie at his side. Mud—Roxie would have to tolerate footbaths in the laundry tubs if Charlie hoped to save his carpets.

"Saw you come home late last night—or was it this morning—with our young man. What's up? And where's his car?"

"You don't miss much, old man." Charlie shared an edited version of the auto's demise. He sagged, slowly shaking his head. "That poor kid. Just when I think things couldn't get any worse or we make a little bit of progress—POW! Something else hits him. Why he's still vertical I'll never understand. Just how much more can he take? I keep waiting for him to break down."

"You can't be driving him everywhere, that's for sure. That will take over your life. I've got something that might work better."

Charlie followed Mr. Greer into his kitchen, which was immaculately clean.

He caught Charlie's admiring gaze. "The kids said I only needed one set of dishes. That I could hand wash them after each meal. Ha! I kept all twelve place settings. Run the dishwasher once a week. The wife used to say, 'Never do anything a machine can do for you.' Smart woman."

In his built-in kitchen desk drawer he found a small note pad and pencil, then opened his scrap box of miscellaneous information. He chose what had once been a fancy green notecard, repurposed for handwritten messages. He copied an address for Charlie. "These folks are old friends. Live on the main drag. Can't drive any more. Take the bus or a cab. They have a spare room and are looking for a live-in student in exchange for helping with repairs and household chores. If you think Ben would be interested, I'll give them a call. They've already heard me brag about him."

From another drawer he extracted a local map and spread it on the kitchen counter. "See? Here's Main Street, the school, their house, and the bus stop."

"And there," Charlie added, "is the fast food joint where he works after school. Even if public assistance comes through, it could take months and he cannot afford even a flophouse. And he can't stay out here in the country without transportation."

"What about a bike?"

Charlie shook his head. "Weather, books, school projects. He won't accept any more charity from me. I've got to respect that. My biggest fear is that he'll drop out of school without graduating."

Later that day Charlie met Mr. Greer's friends, the Fiorelli couple who lived on Main Street. Delighted with the satisfying exchange, Charlie had to work up the wrath of god before tackling his next mission. He barged into the pizza shop where Ben worked. "You the manager who was on duty last night?" he asked the older employee who looked like a kid himself. A young girl, perhaps fifteen or sixteen, made herself scarce.

"That's me. What's the matter? Your pizza was cold?"

"Were you the only manager working last night at ten-thirty?"

He nodded, rolling his eyes in the bored expression that dull teenagers use when dismissing their elders and betters.

"You sent your employee, Benjamin Olinger, on a pizza run with full knowledge that his vehicle was disabled. That if he didn't make said run, you would fire him. Does that sound about right?"

"Hey, dude—I'm not responsible for these kids' cars. That's on them."

"In case you haven't heard, on that very same run you insisted he take to keep his job, the engine blew up, and the car careened into a guard rail. Didn't you hear the sirens?"

"Is he dead?"

"Would you care?"

"I, ah, not my fault. When these kids apply they are told that they must have reliable transportation to make the deliveries."

"Including gas and repairs?"

"Hey, that's the deal. Take it or leave it."

"Oh, we're leaving it all right. With a capable attorney. I need your name. And the owner's."

"Huh?"

"The person who signs your paychecks—dude."

The kid riffled for a blank piece of paper, finally settling on an old order form. He scribbled.

Charlie took it. "Have a nice day."

☙❦❧

Before that day, Charlie had never heard of *Calendar Call*. Once a month at a specified time, everyone out on bail or on their own recognizance had to show up with their attorney to prove that they hadn't skipped. If an individual didn't show up, the judge would issue a bench warrant. The skip would be tracked down, arrested, and thrown in jail.

With bail revoked, the accused would remain locked up until his day in court. That could be months. Missing calendar call was never an option.

Ben had just lost his car, there was no public transportation, he couldn't afford cabs, and his buddies were in school. With great relief, he accepted Charlie's offer to accompany him to the courthouse. Charlie dropped him off, parked, then wended his way through security to the vast, ornate courtroom. Outside, dozens killed time, milling around, waiting for their people. As Charlie opened the massive door, he was stunned to see hundreds of people packing all available seats. More lined the perimeter walls. They reminded Charlie of the sad-looking lot in the public defender's office. The only professionals had to be attorneys, whom Charlie could subdivide by the quality of their suits.

He slipped into a bench beside Ben. At ten a.m. sharp, the judge took the bench, an officer of the court intoning, "Hear ye! Hear ye! The court is now in session, the honorable…" Someone whose name Charlie didn't catch "…presiding. All those having business with the court…" The last time Charlie observed a multitude that quiet was in church.

"What happens now?" Charlie whispered.

"Zeke will meet me in time for my appointment and I'll join him at the front of the courtroom when they call my name. After they verify that I haven't skipped, I'm free to go." He pointed to the right-hand wall on which several doors were located. "When I came to my first calendar call, I met with my public defender for a few minutes in a little side room. He told me when my next call would be and left. That was it."

Charlie was taken aback, considering the lengthy meetings Zeke had invested in Ben's case already. The PD's strategy was to simply show up for calendar call and his sentencing. Those in the courtroom, previously silenced, resumed whispering to one another, their voices slowly growing in volume. Rap! Rap! Rap! "Silence in my courtroom!" the judge demanded.

That quelled the commotion momentarily.

It didn't take long for Charlie to realize the names would be called in alpha-order. Given that Ben's surname started with an O and the size of the crowd, he realized they could be there a very long time. "I hear a baby!" the judge screamed. "Is there a baby in my courtroom? Court is no place for a baby! Take that baby out immediately!"

The squalling infant was plucked from his mother's arms and toted toward the door by a woman who might be the young defendant's mother.

Someone then called Albert, James, its name holder and his suit meeting at the front of the courtroom. Charlie couldn't see or hear what transpired but in ten minutes the pair exited the courtroom together. Two by two, the process continued, until one defendant approached without an attorney. That infuriated the judge. With her mouth over her mike, she spat instructions to the bailiff, who guided the defendant to the jury box. How that was dispatched, Charlie never knew, as the young man, who looked no more than eighteen, was still waiting nervously after Ben and his attorney completed Ben's obligation.

Ben handed Charlie a paper, which he'd already

scrunched. Charlie smoothed it, noting the instructions amounted to *same time, next month* with paragraphs of legalese warnings.

Guilty or innocent, the criminal justice system left no doubt that degradation was intended for all caught up in a crime. Poor Ben. He couldn't get him out of there fast enough.

☙❧

"You're not going to like this," Charlie launched as soon as Zeke Geoffrey came on the line.

"Uh oh. What have you done now?" He sounded merry. Downright entertained.

Charlie hadn't realized until that moment how much he valued this man's calm, jovial attitude and his compassion.

"I faxed you a letter from a law firm requesting my head. I thought you should know."

He laughed. "I just saw it. Sounds like you're making them nervous. Ignore it. The last thing they need is your response to any lawsuit, which would enable public disclosure of the polygraph report and what that father did. I'm betting the Olingers haven't read what's on the report yet or they'd be less inclined to poke you. Why don't you bundle up your research, and we'll sift through it. Separate the dejeuner from the debris."

"Should I bring Ben?"

"Not this time. Put him to work on a detailed list of his expenses from the time he was expelled from the house to the present. I mean everything, even if he doesn't have receipts. Meals, clothing, toothpaste, 'rent' foregone by people's generosity. For the latter, have him get the average rate of a cheap motel or rooming house. Travel expenses: car, gas, repairs, parking tickets. Tell him to use his imagination."

"Um—about his car…" Charlie gave him a three-minute summary of the pizza shop of horrors.

"Great! Ask the repair shop for an estimate. And the bluebook value of comparable wheels. Don't forget the tow truck's bill. I'll send a letter to the owner of the franchise."

"How much is left in the escrow account?"

"Not to worry! You're doing the lion's share of the legwork. We won't start burning a lot of hours until we're prepping for trial."

∽∾∽∾

Charlie had no sooner disconnected than the phone rang again. The caller ID showed a woman's name and a local exchange. Giving the caller the benefit of the doubt, he picked up. "Hello?"

"Mr. Alderfer?" A woman's pleasant voice. "I understand through a neighbor of a sister of a high school swim-team mother that you've been looking for me. You probably don't remember me. We met in the produce section of the new Giant Grocery shortly after it opened. I was chatting with a friend when she spotted you and introduced you as the person who had helped her select her appliances. Her contractor needed her to make up her mind. She thanked you for being a big help."

"I remember! It seems like a lifetime ago. But how did you get my name and number? I no longer work at that store, that is, if you're looking for appliances."

"Word's gotten around that you're trying to help Benjamin Olinger. My son was one of the seniors at the lunch table when that Hispanic foster girl bragged about getting Ben into trouble."

Charlie came that close to blurting out, *There are three*

races, and one of them is not *Hispanic! That's a bean counter's term for people who come from a country whose native language is Spanish—except for Spain.* He forced civility and concentrated on why the woman had called.

"When I heard through the grapevine about Ben—and I don't believe it for a second—I called my son. He's at Penn State now on a swimming scholarship. He remembers the incident well. He said if you'd like to talk with him personally, you can call. That I should give you his cell number."

"Did you talk about Ben's situation?"

"I didn't know the details, except—you know how it goes—some really good kids come from really bad families, and vice versa. Those Olingers—how they mistreat their fosters!"

"Have you *personally* seen them abuse the foster kids or their own? Reported them? Or know anyone who did? If so, would you be willing to testify about what you saw?"

"No. And I can't get that involved, not with my own kids coming up through the schools. I can't risk the teachers' wrath. But I'll pass along whatever I hear, if you wish."

Charlie thanked the woman and hung up after jotting down the son's number. If she truly had seen abuse, she could have reported it anonymously. He brushed it aside and dialed her son's number. He answered on the third ring.

"Ben was one really cool dude. Awful how his folks treated him. We were his family—the swim team, that is. Mom says you're interested in that foster girl's story."

"Will you tell me what you remember?"

"Sure. Izzette—Izzi. Guys called her 'Izzi the lizard' cause she had reptilian eyes and flicked her tongue with multiple piercings. Guys said she offered to do cool things with that tongue. Anyway, one day she just plunked down at our table and started chattering about the hilarious stunt she had pulled. In this little girl voice, she replayed what she'd told the cops about Ben's attempting to rape her. She even worked up a few tears then laughed hysterically. Man, that chick was scary! We found out through a foster brother who was a junior at the time that the Olingers not only believed her, but kicked Ben out of the house with no plans where he could stay. Just dropped him off on a friend's lawn. When her story was ruled *unfounded*, he was allowed to go home. But get this—no apology. No sorry we didn't believe you. Just 'don't get into any more trouble'"

"Does anyone know whatever became of Izzette?"

"Last we heard, she'd pulled the same prank on the next foster family. They tossed her out on her sorry ass. That's what the Olingers should have done."

"What about the foster teen who witnessed what happened in the house?"

"Social worker located his bio dad, who got custody around Thanksgiving and took him home. Somewhere out west. Bio dad seemed like a good guy—hikes, camps, fishing. We kept in touch for a couple months. Kind of a foster kid's dream."

"Do you still have his contact information?"

"Sorry. No."

Charlie sighed. It would have been amazing to find a witness who overheard the parents telling Tori to lie about Ben. "If you hear from him, would you please call me with his contact information? It would mean a great deal to Ben."

Charlie cast his mind back to another fact gleaned— that the girl had a pattern of prior bad acts—and wondered about the agency that placed her with the Olingers. Did they tell foster parents such details before placing homeless kids in their homes? Could the agency now be in legal jeopardy? Might that be why Mr. Watkins brushed Charlie's information under the rug? "Do you have any idea where we could find Izzi or know anyone who could?"

"Haven't seen or heard anything since she was expelled."

Despondent, Charlie thanked him, wishing him luck with his Olympic dream, and disconnected. Another dead end.

Chapter 15

Days, while seeming to drag, moved inexorably toward Ben's day of reckoning. The trial date was set for mid-May. The wealth of information Charlie had accumulated should, in all fairness, have exonerated Ben—but proving it legally remained elusive.

Charlie was wracked with worry. And guilt. What was he missing? What route unexplored? And through it all, had his battle for justice on behalf of another caused inevitable damage that might have been resolved had he left it alone and not exposed the Olingers to public ridicule? Might the ten-year-old have come clean anyway?

Lives beyond Charlie's walls were moving forward. Even Ben's most stalwart supporters couldn't make his problems their highest priority. Swimmers and their families, having accepted college scholarships, were awash in plans for post-graduation changes. Juniors' families were scrutinizing colleges and making out-of-state recruitment visits. Ellen Quillen, chairing the spring banquet to honor seniors, kept Charlie abreast of the details while caring for her kids and old parents alike. Someone even started a Go Fund Me defense fund for Ben to which many donated generously. The great *in between* time was compressing like an Edgar Allan Poe chamber of horrors.

Feeling forward momentum stalled, Charlie knew it was time to lay out his research on Zeke Geoffrey's desk. He made the appointment for an April morning that made him dizzy with springtime's exuberance. How could anything be wrong when the Bartlett pears were blooming up a snowstorm along city streets, and flowering bulbs rioted in profusion in parks and pedestrian islands. Someone should paint Charlie's name on that parking space in front of Zeke's law firm.

Charlie lugged two fat folders—his originals and copies—into Zeke's office. This time a stranger rolled to greet him in a sleek wheelchair, his tan, well-muscled arm extended to shake. "This is Brownie, my private investigator," Zeke said. "He'll question our witnesses and serve the subpoenas for their court appearances. I wanted him to hear what you've learned to date that might help plan Ben's defense."

Charlie willed his hands not to falter as he dealt the gleanings of many weeks' work. Brownie skimmed the polygraph report with nary a flinch at the top of page three. Obviously, he'd seen it before, and everyone understood it wasn't admissible. And he'd read the appended documents obtained during discovery.

Document by document, Charlie added new information to what they already knew—the events at the state police barracks and the officers' lies, their bungled Miranda, their refusal to halt questioning when Ben asked for a lawyer, their lying about what he was signing, and the actual time it ended, as sworn by a witness who met him two hours after the session supposedly had ended.

"And there's proof that she lied," he said, directing their attention to Tori's statement. "She said she knew it was around Christmas because 'there was a tree.' I was in the house four days before Christmas, and there was no tree. This humungous train set ran all over the first floor. There was no place for a tree. Ben said they never had one." He stabbed an explanation point at the document with his index finger.

"Sorry, Charlie," Zeke countered. "Read it again. She said there was a tree, but she didn't say *where*. It could have been in City Park, at their church, at a friend's, or the mall. She doesn't say 'there was a tree *in my house*.'"

Charlie steamed ahead. "Statements from witnesses who will testify, to my detailed research from the ophthalmologist, to the graphic artist, and the falsified end to his interrogation. And why? What was the big lie really about? Money! His parents, who felt threatened by Ben's accusations of abusing foster children, about which Ben must be silenced. The threat to their income and reputation."

He paused for a breath and a sip of water. "An ugly campaign to destroy Ben physically, mentally, emotionally, financially, and spiritually to hide their profit-making schemes that used foster children as collateral. They'd deprived him of his IDs—a birth certificate, SS card, and medical insurance. They'd emptied his savings account, leaving him penniless, living hand to mouth on others' charity. They couldn't just silence him—they needed to discredit him. Destroy him. And what better way than the accusation of a sweet little ten-year-old girl, who was either put up to it or starved for attention."

He didn't realize how long he'd been pacing, the room deathly silent as he finally sank into a chair.

"If these parents were on trial, I'd hire you to do the summation. They'd convict in five minutes. Charlie, I'm sure Brownie will agree that you've done a yeoman's job of fact finding and exposing what this ugly mess is really about. That will be useful in planning our strategy. The only problem, however, is that the parents are not on trial. Ben is. With charges brought by the district attorney, based on the police investigation. It's the word of a ten-year-old girl against a grown man. Even the parents can't pull the plug now. What else was going on in that household is irrelevant to Ben's case."

"Then you ought to question his little sister. Doesn't Ben have the right to confront his accuser?"

"A child that young cannot be intimidated. No judge would allow it. Her parents convinced the court that she was in danger from Ben, and, thus, a restraining order was issued to protect her."

A thought caught Charlie from out of the blue. "Wait a minute. I just remembered something that might explain why Tori was selected to tell the big lie. A year ago, our Jonathan participated in a lineup to identify a stranger he saw in his grandmother's sick room. Turns out, in Pennsylvania a child has to be ten years old to testify in court. And, no, a younger child can't testify privately in a judge's chambers because the defendant has a right to confront his accuser.

"Tori was ten. And the Olingers are her birth parents. They couldn't have planned it any better. Old enough to testify. Young enough to be an innocent little child." Charlie stilled, his energy drained. "So—where does that leave us? Ben absolutely will not take a plea, even if one is offered. But he says he will not go to jail for something he didn't do. Nobody should."

"What Ben has," Zeke said, "is a slew of character witnesses, but it's still her word against his. If I try to poke holes in her statement and she cries, the jury will crucify him."

"What if she recants? Takes it back?"

"They won't let her do that, not at this point. There's too much at stake. And it's the Commonwealth of PA versus Benjamin Olinger. They might try to proceed without her. Or her parents could tell her that lying to the police was a crime. They can lie to her, just as they did to Ben, only she's just a little kid. They'd tell her it's too late for a do-over. That she'll go to juvi until she's eighteen or end up in foster care herself if she doesn't follow through."

Zeke gestured to the documents Charlie had presented. "Brownie and I will review your research, we'll discuss it, and then he'll talk with the witnesses. Have Ben flesh out his whereabouts around the time of the incident. Expand the two-page document, last appended, of witnesses and their contact information. Add additional names that he might recall."

"Maybe they'll mention something I missed. And everyone said that they'd be willing to testify."

Forty-eight hours later, Charlie got the call. Rather than Zeke shooting down his hypotheses, he requested a conference with Ben alone.

"It's his life. He has to make decisions that will govern the rest of his days. He'll need to make them himself. Alone, he may speak more freely. And, Charlie, it is my duty to protect his interests. You needn't worry—I will do that." Zeke sighed, as if reinforcing his plan of action. "Bring him in. Brownie will drop him at school after we're done. Brownie wants to get the lay of the land anyway. In the meantime, I'm insisting that you leave potential witnesses alone. I can't risk having them testify that they felt compelled to say something—anything—in Ben's defense out of respect for you or pity for him."

❧❦❧

When Charlie responded to his doorbell and peeked through the sidelight, he glimpsed a pale blue VW bug parked in his driveway. Puzzled, he opened the door to a beautiful young lady whose sweet smile turned up at its corners, reminiscent of Christie Brinkley's iconic face.

"Mr. Alderfer? I'm Claire, a friend of Ben's. I have something for you—actually it's for him. He didn't want me to get involved, but I just couldn't help myself."

"C—Come in! Come in!" Charlie stammered, taken

aback by his unexpected visitor. She stepped onto the living room's slate entryway clutching the straps of her backpack. "Please, have a seat. May I take your coat?"

"Thank you, but I can only stay a few minutes."

At his direction she crossed the living room and sat on the edge of the very couch cushion where Ben had unfolded his terrible story.

Charlie thought before he spoke, having almost blurted, *I didn't know Ben had a girlfriend.* "I wouldn't have thought Ben would have time to socialize with such a demanding schedule."

She nodded then got straight to the point. "I wanted so badly to do something—anything—to help with this terrible injustice. We've known each other since ninth grade when we were lab partners in chemistry. We became friends in tenth grade after my father died in a house fire. Being an only child with an overwhelmed mother, my friends were my support system. You know how it is when somebody dies—at first there's an enormous outpouring of help from compassionate people. But in time, that dwindles as people must refocus on their own lives.

"I tried to be my mom's advocate. Dad's family was brutal, blaming her for 'letting' Dad smoke in bed, even though they had separate rooms and you did not 'let' or 'not let' Dad do anything. He had come home late from a business trip, had a few shots to unwind, and fell asleep. The smoke alarm woke us, but it was too late. Dad was trapped. He died of smoke inhalation. His family demanded everything that could be rescued, from family antiques to his share of the family trust. Fortunately, Mom's attorney protected our interests and prevailed.

"My friends were great, but, in time, it got awkward. They became impatient, thinking I should get on with my life. After one of them said, in front of everyone, that I was being silly. 'Get over it. Live goes on.' I exploded. Then everyone avoided me, except Ben. As others faded into the background, he kept checking on me. Called to see how I was doing. Did I need a ride? Help with my homework? Someone to listen? He'd say, 'let's go for a ride,' and pull into a diner, insisting I eat, if only some soup. Our relationship was one-side. He was my rock. The brother I didn't have. My best friend. I was an anchorless victim.

"Even my mom depended on him—he's so practical and full of ideas. You see, when someone dies in a house fire, there's a world of problems beyond grief. Insurance, contractors, legalities, living arrangements, and water damage to valuables, like antique samplers. What's salvageable stinks of smoke. The electricity and water were shut off, and there was no light with windows boarded up.

"Ben to the rescue, from day one, armed with a humongous mag light. Taking Mom to the car rental dealer, the laundromat, finding a storage facility, hauling stuff. Through it all, he was calm and patient, not degenerating into platitudes and lame advice. Always quick with an irreverent joke that made her laugh.

"Until this awful thing happened—which I cannot imagine—our relationship was all about me and my problems. I believe he's in denial. Thinks that his sister will feel guilty enough to confess that she lied. Trouble is, it's way past the point of no return. When I coax him to face that reality, he says 'It will be all right. Nothing bad will come of it.' Or 'You worry too much.' He's such an old soul—bet he was a Dalai Lama in a previous incarnation. He cannot see that some people are evil."

"He told you that?"

"It's his philosophy of life. I have no idea where he gets it, except that some very good people have influenced him along the way."

Charlie thought of people Ben had mentioned in his stories over supper, probably intended for Jonathan's ears.

The Sunday school teachers; the guidance counselors; teachers and coaches, Scout, youth group, and 4-H leaders; and his friends' parents who grasped that his chaotic home life and parental neglect, however benign, begged remediation.

Claire slipped off her backpack and dug into its depth, producing a white number ten envelope. "I wanted to take Ben to the County Services Building after convincing him he needed financial assistance if only to get a medical card. That did not sit well—taking charity. I explained that he already paid taxes to the government to support such programs, and would for the rest of his life. Reluctantly, he told me he'd already started an application. That you and he had sat among ragged mothers with dirty kids in soiled old clothes. Homeless men. Dejected old folks. That he would be taking resources they needed more."

Charlie said, "I encouraged him to get a copy of his *lost* Social Security card, but for that he needed two forms of ID. I thought an insurance card might suffice, but he said his parents removed him from their policy when he turned eighteen."

"Right," Claire said, scowling. "How could they…!" She trailed off in thought for a moment then snapped back. "Then I had an inspiration—birth certificates are public record. One more easy quick errand, I thought. But I was wrong. Not only had Ben been adopted, but he'd have to apply to have his records opened, and that would take time that he doesn't have. Complicating the search, his surname had been changed, but he remembered his birth name. He had been told he was born in Ohio, but he had no idea in which county. Now, I have a pretty good ear. And coming from the mid-west, I realized his accent didn't sound like Ohio. He'd once lived in Schuylkill County. So I tried the Pennsylvania Bureau of Vital Statistics."

From inside the envelope she withdrew several

documents. "This certificate was issued from the hospital where he was born, stating that an official birth certificate would be filed in Harrisburg, the state capitol, and that the parents should send for an official birth certificate. I paid a nominal fee and sent for three official copies in his name. With that, he can request his adoption records that will include his legal name. Now he can get medical assistance and replace his Social Security card."

Charlie mused, "Do you realize how many times you need two forms of ID to get anything? Bank accounts, a passport, driver's license…"

Her countenance darkened. "How could someone as good as Ben come from such a terrible family?" She flicked a glance at her watch. "Gotta go. Thank you for everything you're doing for Ben." As tears welled in her eyes, she hurried to the door, waving over her shoulder.

"Claire? If Ben says it's okay, I'll take him back to Public Assistance and complete his application. It's scary that he has no access to medical care."

"I'd like to take him myself. That is, if you don't mind."

Charlie smiled, remembering his earliest dates with his Emma. How intoxicating it was to have her choose him. His gorgeous young lady whom everyone wanted for their girl or best friend. "Of course, Claire. Let me know how it turns out." Charlie watched from the storm door as Claire maneuvered her VW into the street, sending him her electric smile. He waved, glimpsing Ben's future traveling down the road.

Chapter 16

A glance at the clock told Charlie he had a full hour before Jonathan came home from school. Cookies—he'd bake chocolate chip. He grinned. What else? Hearing a car approaching his driveway, he thought Claire, Ben's girlfriend, might have forgotten something. And he'd neglected to give her his numbers.

A flash of light, bouncing off Charlie's living room wall, drew his attention to an approaching car much larger than Claire's swinging into his driveway. Sneaking a peek around the drapery, Charlie recognized it from its previous visit—the Mercedes belonging to Jade's dreaded ex-in-laws. The driver was alone. Cautiously the driver unfolded an arthritic body, steadying himself on the car's frame while plotting the journey to Charlie's front door. Deliberately, he stepped onto the front porch, three-footed cane at the ready. By the time he reached the bell and was poised to ring it, Charlie had the door open.

"Mr. Alderfer? Might I have a word with you please? It's important."

Without opening the door farther, Charlie scanned the driveway for that awful woman who had demanded to see Jonathan and threatened Charlie with lawsuits—and worse. No one appeared to be accompanying him. "What's this about?"

The man, his head slightly bowed, was fingering the wool tam he had removed from his bald head in spite of the chill. "If I can come in for a minute, I'll explain. My wife isn't with me nor does she know that I'm here."

Charlie realized he'd seen the man before—a lifetime ago. While struggling to regain his strength in the VA's hospice ward after nearly dying, Charlie had just befriended Jade and her shy little boy. Mother and son had been keeping a vigil as her dying father lost ground. Jade's husband's parents had blindsided her with an unannounced visit, lobbing their first volley to gain custody of Jonathan. Jade's shock had been multi-faceted—that her husband had not deserted her but had died when the photographer's little plane had crashed into the Alps. And these people could use their vast wealth to steal her little boy.

Now Charlie remembered that the ploy had been Jade's mother-in law's, and this gentleman had been silent throughout the ordeal. The show had been all hers. Charlie sighed—whatever the pair was up to, he could handle this man, although he eyed his cane warily, prepared to jump aside if necessary.

"I'm hoping you would give Jade a letter for me," the man said, extracting a cream envelope from his breast pocket. "In it, I'm not asking to see her or Jonathan. I'm hoping she'd be willing to let you act as a conduit for memorabilia that Jonathan should have when Jade feels the time is right. No little boy should grow up without a sense of his father. I know my son would have loved him dearly."

"Mr. Kepley, I've seen your wife in action—twice. So, of course, I'm suspicious. Please come in and lay it out for me. All of it. Including every little string that's attached."

The man sighed. Try as he could, Charlie couldn't see any resemblance between this man and his grandson. "Mr. Alderfer, at this late stage of my life, I've grown a backbone. Something my wife would insist I never had. Ours wasn't a marriage—it was the merger of our ambitious parents at a time when adult children were expected to obey. Her blue-blooded, connected but impoverished gentility with my immigrant family's new money.

"Our fathers envisioned a political dynasty, but the ambition gene missed me entirely. Even as my wife's stock rose in society and my father's law firm thrived, nothing was ever enough. It's amazing how strategically-placed philanthropy sterilizes new money and wins influential friends.

"She had great plans for our son. Congressman. Governor. Vice president and so on. The best schools, the right friends, and, yes—the right wife. Then her dreams went terribly wrong. My father died of a massive heart attack on the golf course. Our son fell in love with wildlife photography and Jade, rather than the socialites she and her friends kept throwing at him. My wife thought she could bring him around since she controlled his trust fund. He refused. She boycotted their wedding, which was a simple affair in Jade's parents' back yard. I witnessed it—I'm ashamed to say—hiding behind the neighbors' hedge.

"Had our son known they were expecting a child, he never would have taken that assignment—to go to a war zone to capture Pulitzer-quality photographs. He didn't leave his itinerary with anyone. It was to be a surprise— his big break in his chosen profession. When he never returned, Jade thought my wife had won. That her husband had abandoned her. And all the time he was dead, which nobody knew until five years later when an unusually warm spring thaw exposed that little plane and hikers discovered the wreckage. Evidently, they'd been flying under the radar and failed to see the mountain, notorious for its fickle, dense fog."

"Mr. Kepley, Jade shared these particulars, including the financial arrangements your son made for his family in the event of his death. And the family trust fund that passes over your son to Jonathan. If you want to fight over Jonathan, Jade is prepared to mount a fierce battle, although the law's on her side, especially when it comes to grandparent's interference."

"Not my intention at all. I'm here because I'd like to give Jade a photo history of our son's life as well as the mementos and clippings I've saved."

"And your wife's going along with this? Won't she put up a howl and demand that priceless family records be returned, if only for spite?"

"This is my personal collection, many pieces of which she's never seen or prefers to pretend don't exist. My family's history predates the 1800s, Welsh coal miners, and the potato blight in Ireland. Handwritten diaries detailing births, deaths, and hard-fought survival. Jonathan's father came from sturdy stock, which my wife chooses to bury. Given our history, I am honored by my parents' determination and pride in their heritage."

"Mr. Kepley, I cannot risk that woman's wrath, the prospect of repercussions or violence. I will not—"

Kepley jumped to his feet. "Violence? Surely you don't think my wife is dangerous. Why, why—that's preposterous! The only way she hurts people is with her mouth and her checkbook."

Charlie held up his hands in surrender, urging the man to sit down, the color having risen in his face. "I'm sorry. So sorry." Charlie hurried to the kitchen and returned with a glass of spring water.

Mr. Kepley took a sip. "Here. You may read the letter yourself. And, if both you and Jade are in agreement, we'll figure out what comes next."

"And your wife?"

"I...um...about that backbone. I've had enough. The divorce is in my lawyers' capable hands. My wife can have whatever she wants, but I'll keep the cottage in the Adirondacks. I have sufficient personal resources to live in peace."

Charlie turned the envelope over in his hands. "I don't need to read it. I'll give it to her right away. She'll be home this evening—its movie and popcorn night."

That image brought a smile to the old man's face. "Thank you. I've included my contact information in the letter, but perhaps it would be better if you reached out to me?" From his wallet he produced a business card, his personal phone numbers having been added to its reverse. "Please tell Jade I'm sorry about—everything."

I'm betting she will want to hear that herself.

⁂

Charlie and Jonathan enjoyed Friday night pizza at Jade's kitchen table, a change of venue for Charlie. "Mommy has a date!" the child confided before taking another bite of his sausage, pepperoni, and olive slice. "I told Mommy I thought it would be nice if she had friends she could do special things with. I get to go to my friends' houses. She just goes to school and comes home."

"What did you say, if you don't mind telling me? It's okay if you mind. If it's confidential."

"Confi what?"

"Personal. Private. Something that's between just two people."

He shrugged. "It's okay. We were talking about my birthday party. And my friends' birthday parties. And how Callum's family has horses and he has a pony and he asked me if I'd like to go see them. Mommy said it was okay. But…"

Charlie held his tongue. "But what?"

"I told Mommy I thought she should have fun too. She

said, 'I have lots of fun.' And I asked, 'Doing what?' and she said, 'Enjoying my classes and spending time with you and Papa.' I said, 'But where would you like to go to have grownup fun?' She said, 'Well, I'd have to think about that.' So I said, 'Papa and I could have Friday pizza and movie night while you have grownup fun.'"

"And how did she respond?"

"She did this goofy smile thing that she does when she's feeling silly. Then she said, 'I'll give that some thought.' She usually says that when I want to do something that bigger kids do. Like when I wanted to take the baby wheels off my bike. It was like that. Did I do okay, Papa?"

"Perfectly."

"Want to know where she went?"

"She left her contact information on the bulletin board for me, including who she'd be with and when she'd be back. But she didn't give me any details."

Jonathan bounced in his chair, unable to contain his exuberance at being the one in the know. "She went roller skating! There's this big place where you skate indoors, and she never got to go as a kid. She told me not to worry. That she wouldn't fall down and get hurt. This really nice guy from school is going to meet her there and teach her how. She said, 'Don't save me any pizza.' She said she and this friend are going to eat something later. And she said I'd be asleep when she got home, so she'd tell me all about it tomorrow."

Charlie's mind morphed into father mode, remembering his daughters as teenagers. Jade was a grown woman and a mother, determined to earn her degree. She'd tried not to jump to conclusions about which profession, but she knew law, politics, criminal justice, teaching, art, or business were not for her. It haunted her that no one could cure either parent—one stroke and one heart disease—which made her respect how fragile life was and the importance of skilled professional intervention. Whether that took her into research, nursing, medical or pharmacy school, it was too soon to decide. She needed to muddy her feet in many curricula.

Yet Charlie's instinct was to profile her date. Did he come from a nice family with good values? Did he like children? Did he have a lurid past? Could he pass a criminal background check? Was he solvent? He whisked those thoughts aside. She wasn't his teenage daughter, but she was blended family. His being Jonathan's Papa would bind them forever.

Jonathan had hopped down from his chair. "Papa, I need to tell Mommy something. It's about something I did. If I tell you, will you tell her for me?"

"Well, I don't know. We've talked a lot about honesty. If you did something you're not proud of or broke a rule or whatever, you shouldn't be afraid to man up. Tell her the truth. You'll feel a lot better."

"No. It's not like that. It's com…com…"

"Complicated? And you'd like me to run interference for you? Soften her up a little? Why don't you just tell me what this bad awful thing is, then we'll figure it out. Did you rob a bank?" Charlie stifled a smile. *How much trouble could an almost-seven-year-old get into? It had nothing to do with school—like cheating or fighting—that would have reached home before he did.*

Jonathan reverted to his much younger self, hands clasped behind his back, one toe touching his sneaker's other toe. An image of Jonathan, a sad little five-year-old, was burned in Charlie's memory. A mute little boy with a terrible secret, *knowing* he'd killed his grandma. To an adult, that was silly, but to the child, a traumatic misunderstanding. A dead grandmother, a dying grandfather, a stoic, determined mother. "What did you do?"

"I listened."

Charlie was taken aback. "Well, listening is a good trait. To your teacher's lessons, your mom's rules, letting others take a turn talking."

"No, Papa. Not that kind of listening." He took Charlie's hand and tugged him toward his bedroom and circled the bed. "There," he said, pointing to his end table. Charlie saw nothing of importance. "Behind it. I can hear things."

"That's nothing unusual. All houses have peculiar sounds. The rattles and clicks when the heat comes on. The siding on the house makes popping noises when the sun heats it."

"No, Papa. I hear people talking. And I know stuff Mommy doesn't want to tell me. But I already know."

Charlie sat on the edge of the bed and circled the child's shoulder, drawing him close. "Tell me. What did you hear?"

"That I have another grandfather. My grandpa died, and you are my Papa, and, and, and—is the new grandfather going to try to take me away like that mean woman? Don't say 'ask Mommy.' Please. If I have another grandfather, will you still be my adopted grandpa?"

"First things first. I will always be your Papa. You chose me, remember? And gave me my name. You told me about the little friend who was adopted and asked me what adopted meant. Do you remember what I said?"

Jonathan grinned. "It means *chosen*. We chose each other."

"Families happen when a child is born, when a child is adopted, or when families choose to blend together. That's us."

"I was scared that I'd have to move away."

"That's not going to happen." Charlie refrained from even a hint that someday they might all be elsewhere. When his time came, Jonathan would be itching to fledge.

"But what about—him? And please don't say to ask Mom."

"No, I won't as long as you tell her what we talked about. Let her adjust the words, tell you more, or correct what I misunderstood."

Jonathan nodded his head then searched Charlie's eyes, as if imploring him to explain.

"All right. You're turning seven. Some people believe seven is the age of reason, so I'll tell you some reasonable things." Charlie picked up the framed photo of Jonathan's father and they looked at it together. "Your father had a father who is still alive. He has lived far away for many years and didn't even know about you until very recently. He doesn't want to intrude on your life, like that woman who scared you so badly."

"Is she—that woman—coming back with him?"

"No. They are divorced. Do you know what that means? It means they got *un-married*."

Jonathan was silent, studying a loose thread on the hem of his shirt. "I have a friend. His name is Luke. His mom and dad are getting divorced. Luke lives with his mom and stays with his dad some Saturdays and Sundays. His girl-friend lives with his dad. Luke hates her, says she's real mean to him. And his mom cries all the time."

"That's too bad. How's Luke doing?"

"Okay, I guess. We guys make sure he gets picked first for the teams."

"About your dad's father—I think your mom just doesn't know how to explain him to you. If you tell her everything you've overheard, she'll make sense of it for you."

Should he tell him that Mr. Kepley came to meet Charlie and asked him to intercede with Jade on his behalf? Wasn't that exactly what the child was now asking him to do? "If you still want me to, I'll tell your mom that you've

overheard things you don't understand about a new grandfather and that you're concerned."

"That's okay, Papa. I'll tell her. Do you think she'll be
mad that I've been snooping?"

"That's not snooping, which is sneaking—like looking
into people's private things without their permission. You
can't help how this house is built."

"I don't like hearing voices. They're all worry-like."

"I'll talk with my contractor and see what we can do
about that."

Chapter 17

Charlie pulled up to Zeke Geoffrey's office first thing Monday morning, thinking he should bring paint to embellish his name on the curb. "Wait here a minute," Charlie said to Ben, who released his grip on the passenger's handle. "I'll just be a minute, then you can go in."

At seven-thirty, his secretary had not yet arrived, and Zeke's interior door stood ajar. Ben's attorney motioned him to enter and take a seat. "What's on the agenda?" Charlie asked Zeke.

"I want to bring Ben up to date on my decision to sue his parents for financial support. That should shake them up a little. Besides, it needs to be done. An eighteen-year-old high school kid with affluent parents cannot finish his education without shelter, food, clothing, medical expenses, et cetera. Besides, it will give me an opportunity to get a read on the parents as well as their lawyer. He's new; I haven't seen him in action yet, and I need to get a sense of their game plan before trial."

"Then the case is going to trial?"

"They're not blinking. It might even be a pet project for the DA. Prosecuting child abusers is a sexy issue and a career maker. And we already know the police have their asses to cover, having messed up the initial investigation. The stakes are too high to back down."

"Do you need any more money?"

Zeke flicked his hand. "We've barely dented the retainer. The case for support is on me because I'm fascinated to know what makes these people tick."

"Greed. Money. People say 'money is the root of all evil,' but the exact quote is 'The love of money is the root of all evil.' It's not the same thing."

"How's Ben doing?"

"Floating above it all. He's the poster child for denial. He loves working hard. Crams every minute of his waking hours with meaningful activity, to earn a living, be a good student, and help others. He has internalized Christianity the best that I've known. Still, I'm waiting for this atrocity to hit him—and then what?"

"Keep a close eye on him for shifting behavior. Get counseling if you feel he's breaking. Might not be a bad idea anyway. And if he ever mentions anything about harming himself, get help."

Charlie nodded. "But first, he needs medical insurance. He will not take any more charity from anyone. Whatever his pain, it's buried and guarded in his head. He is not sharing. What bad things he has revealed are said nonchalantly or are a slip of the lip. But I will be vigilant."

"Thanks for the list you emailed about his past, present, and anticipated expenses. I'll ask Ben to provide dollar amounts."

"Thank you." Charlie rose and shook Zeke's hand and started toward the door. Pivoting, he added, "It's not lost on me that you're throwing in some pro bono time. That isn't expected."

"I know a miscarriage of justice when I see one. And this must be squelched before a jury decides that he's guilty."

"Do you really think that could happen, knowing what prompted this case?"

"I cannot emphasize enough, Charlie. Are you

listening? The parents are not on trial. It's the word of a sweet little girl against a grown man. The jury, even if undecided, could convict 'just in case' to keep society safe."

"What are the odds?"

Zeke shrugged. "Truthfully? We just don't have enough at this time to mount a serious defense."

Through the exterior door, Charlie beckoned Ben into the office. "Remember, Ben, your lawyer cannot repeat anything you tell him in confidence, so you can complain about my rules all you want."

"Thanks, man." Ben gave Charlie a playful knuckle bump to his shoulder.

As soon as the outer door latched, Ben took the guest chair Zeke indicated.

"Did you bring the list of your expenses?" Ben fished a tri-folded lined yellow paper from his jacket's inner pocket and placed it in Zeke's outstretched hand. He watched while Zeke skimmed the content. Paused. Turned it over, then back again.

"This will do nicely for a start. I will, however, add a few things from my personal experience when I lived on my own that you wouldn't consider. Like utilities, renter's insurance, dental care, and so on. I'll fill out the paperwork, file it, and get the lawsuit under way. Any questions?"

"I'm eighteen. Can't they kick me out if they want?"

"Yes. But not without paying for your livelihood. In Pennsylvania, parents are responsible for their children until they turn eighteen or graduate from high school, whichever comes last. As a legal adult, you can sign yourself out of school, sign contracts, go and do whatever you choose, in which case, their obligation ends. But if you wish to finish high school, they're on the hook."

"Who decides what I get?"

"The court. And I'm sure a judge will take a dim view

of parents who neglect their own kids while taking money to support others' children."

"They're going to be furious."

"Let's hope so! If they started all this to discredit you, now they'll know that they're in for a fight, and their suitability for being foster parents will be scrutinized publicly. You okay with that? It's going to get nasty. If you feel compassionate because they're your parents or you're being disloyal, you must put that aside. You can deal with your feelings when all this is over. In the meantime, it's war. Shall we proceed?" Ben nodded consent.

"Now tell me about your new home."

Ben grinned. "They are this really neat old Italian couple, who came to America when they were teenagers. They speak English with a thick accent, but Italian to each other, loudly with lots of hand gestures. First thing Mrs. Fiorelli said when I walked in the door was, 'You're too thin. I will cook for you.'"

"And does she?"

"Oh, man! Everything's homemade. And she's teaching me to make pasta from scratch. But you would not believe how many things need fixing in that old house. I'm on it."

Chapter 18

The following evening, Charlie's phone clamored for attention. He realized, as he hurried to snag it, how most calls announced Ben's newest problem. He was starting to dread its ringing. With the trial seeming distant and with Ben settled with the Fiorellis, life had settled into a semblance of normalcy. But tonight, Charlie could barely understand what Ben was saying. He got the idea on Ben's third attempt. "He's going to kill me! He's going to shoot me!"

"Who, Ben? Who's threatening you?"

"My father. He's got a rifle. He said he's coming over here—right now! I've gotta get out of here!"

"Stay put, Ben. I'll call 9-1-1 immediately and have them send the police to the house. We'll figure it out."

The suit for support! The Olingers must have received the bad news from their attorney, the effect like poking a hornet's nest. Charlie aimed the Buick through the gathering darkness toward town, plotting plans of action. He had to stay calm while snatching Ben out of the house. Take him to safety, but where? And what of the Fiorellis? Having no recollection about how he got there, Charlie skidded to a stop in front of their 1920s red brick house and thundered up the steps onto the porch. Without waiting to be admitted, he flung open the door and barged in.

The scene inside astounded him. A cacophony of Italian voices emanated from dozens of people with similar

Mediterranean features, obviously family or countrymen. Three generations from teens to seniors all shouted at once. One wore a priest's collar, another a military uniform. Ben cowered in a corner, protected by his landlady. Somehow these people must have beaten the 9-1-1 dispatcher's request for assistance.

The commotion stopped as soon as Charlie entered the room. "What happened?" Charlie addressed Ben through the sudden quiet.

"I don't know how he found this address. I didn't tell them where I was living."

"Maybe he still doesn't know. Did he call on your cell phone?"

Ben looked sheepishly at the device he clutched in white-knuckled fingers. "Well. Yeah. I haven't changed the number."

Thud! Thud! Thud! "Police. Open the door."

Mr. Fiorelli, short and fierce, elbowed a path through the mob while everyone froze. He opened the door to a sole police officer. Had Charlie expected a SWAT team or at least multiple cops, he would have been disappointed. Mr. Fiorelli admitted the officer while scowling left and right beyond his front porch, then snapped and locked the door.

"What seems to be the problem?" the new arrival asked with a bored expression as if he'd been summoned to settle a playground squabble. The room exploded in a multi-lingual torrent about the terrifying event that had been perpetrated against these old, law-abiding citizens.

Charlie caught the officer's name on his uniform, instantly recognizing it from the documents Zeke had received during discovery. This was one of the same guys who had responded—twice—to the Olingers' complaints, first about Izzi, the foster girl, and then their own daughter, Tori. He was one of the trio who had tricked Ben into making a false confession. Charlie felt his anger rising. His face redden. His heart rate take off. He took a half-step forward, prepared to give this lazy SOB a piece of his mind. But he caught himself.

It was conceivable that by now the local cops knew their hapless victim had help, and a lot of it. Many community members were in an uproar about police brutality, no doubt complaining to the police who then interfaced with the DA's office and learned that an excellent lawyer, not a public defender, was handling Ben's defense. Charlie stepped back, turning his face, hoping he hadn't been recognized. Having solved the murders at the VA, newspaper coverage had been intense. He wasn't anonymous. And police were not fond of civilians who solved major crimes for them.

A young, smartly dressed man in a well-cut suit, white monogrammed shirt, and silk tie stepped forward. He seemed taller than the officer when he tilted his chin and looked down his nose when he spoke. "We know who made that call. I insist you arrest him."

The officer took a step back. "We will investigate."

With Ben's phone in one hand and a notepad in the other, the man scrolled, located the last call received, and jotted the number. The screech of the page being ripped from the notepad reverberated in the now-silent room. "I fully expect your next call will be to my family's tormentor. Let him know that charges will be brought against him immediately if he ever pulls that stunt again."

The officer took the slip from the attorney. "I'll follow up." As he pivoted to leave, he spotted Ben in the far corner. He squinted, recognition dawning in his previously bored eyes. He smirked at Ben.

As soon as he'd left, Charlie approached the young man, whom he surmised was the family's attorney and spokesperson. "I'll understand if you fear repercussions

should Ben stay any longer. I can make other arrangements."

"Nonsense! My dear aunt and uncle will not hear of
such a thing. They don't let any of us do anything for them.
They are so proud. But they will let Ben help them, since
it's a reciprocal agreement. We all sleep better, knowing
they're not alone in this old house." He shook Charlie's
hand. "Besides, I pride myself on being a pretty good
judge of character. Ben is a *keeper* and my aunt adores
him."

⌘

Zeke Geoffrey's terse greeting put Charlie on high
alert, even before the attorney said another word. "I met
with the Olingers and their civil attorney to discuss the
case for support. The event proceeded as an exchange of
paperwork. I gave them an embellished list of Ben's expenses, debts, and pending obligations to which their attorney didn't respond. His attitude reflected that he sees
this kind of thing all day, every day. The Olingers said
nothing. Didn't make eye contact. When the meeting
ended, I was the last one to leave. The Olingers' financials
were still laying on the table, so I gathered them and
brought them to my office."

"Any surprises?"

"Just an ordinary lower-middle-class family that pays
their bills. Interestingly, they didn't include child support
payments for the fosters. I guess for tax purposes that's not
counted as income."

"That's not right. If they're good money managers, they
could cover many of their own bills at the expense of the
fosters. And their house is appreciating as we speak. Is any
financial resolution pending? Did the attorney make an offer? What's your read on these people and the case?"

"First, this attorney has nothing to do with the criminal case, although he did state that the judge, in his experience, would rule for the parents, due to the sexual nature of the case pending against the son. The judge, who I've heard is old school, would rule that the parents acted in the best interest of the family to expel him from the home. The most he could get would be for the time he was out of the home before he pled guilty. A date has been set for the support hearing, but that's months away. He will have graduated from high school by then."

"Months! What's he going to live on in the meantime? His eyes need remedial treatment, his nose needs attention…"

"I know. I know. He does qualify for public assistance, which will give him a small paycheck and a medical card. And he can work. But, Charlie, please be prepared. In spite of the fine research you've done getting to the bottom of this, there's a better-than-even chance he will get nothing. While seeming dull, the parents exude an evil undercurrent. I suspect you're right—there's more going on than the potential loss of their foster parent status and income."

"Have I done a terrible thing, getting involved? What if I'd left it alone? Let the matter run its course. With his perfect record, community support, and sterling reputation, couldn't he be given probation? Community service? Maybe counseling?"

"Not for this type of crime. And he could be labeled a sexual predator, which would follow him the rest of his life. Any time something happened in his neighborhood—assuming the residents didn't run him off—he'd be the first person the police would question if he remotely resembled the perp."

"There's got to be something we can do. She lied. What if she comes to her senses? Recants?"

"I believe the Commonwealth would go forward,

claiming she felt sorry for him or her family. Perhaps intimidated her about lying. But, Charlie—keep being supportive. In the meantime, if you find anything new, Brownie will investigate. If there's more to the story, we need to find it."

ℰℴℰℴ

Charlie was exhausted. For once, there was nothing to do, but he couldn't rest, in spite of the late hour. Old Mr. Greer had signaled goodnight and he had responded. He had forced himself into his pre-Ben routine, accepting what his daughters were saying about his being obsessed with a situation he could not control. His life should revolve around his recaptured health, a peaceful retirement, time spent with Jonathan and Jade, volunteer work, and frequent communication with his family. What was that old Army saying? *Hurry up and wait.* Yeah, that fit. He admitted he couldn't even plan activities, fearing he'd be summoned any minute by phone.

Needing distraction, he flipped through *National Geographic*, finally settling on Emma's scrupulous records of their gardens, recorded from their first spring in residence until her health failed. Gently, he unfolded graph paper on which she had designed their rose and perennial garden, each plant labeled in Latin. A parchment paper with her free-hand drawings of evergreens, rhododendrons and azaleas for their shady islands made him smile.

He had planted the foundation with a line of what she called *his little soldiers* that now reached the front windows. And trees—the weeping cherry that she had proclaimed way too expensive with which they'd surprised her that first Mother's Day. Now it towered elegantly, unfurling a snowstorm of pink blossoms. He replayed the old song in his mind: *See The Tree How Big It's Grown.*

Bobby Vinton sang it, he recalled. Sometimes he was blindsided by how much he missed her, even after fifteen years, the number at which he'd stopped counting.

The scarlet tanager on the Audubon clock chirped twelve times. Best try to sleep. All his married life he'd tossed his clothes on the armchair beside the bed, intending to deal with them in the morning. Emma always beat him to it, scolding that he *needed picking up after*. He toed off his shoes, starting a pile with his socks to which he added more laundry. The dress slacks he'd worn to impress his subjects he hung neatly in the closet, folding his sweater and placing it in the armoire. He pulled on jammies that matched his Atlanta daughters' *jammies for your families*—how they'd laughed at their Christmas group photo. If only—Emma would have loved it. It wasn't just about how much he missed her, but about how much she was missing that hurt.

As Charlie sank into the armchair, he wondered what she would contribute to Ben's defense, given the chance. For all her kindness and gentle nature, she was practical and plain spoken when dissecting problems. After her death, their daughters convinced him that poor women would benefit from Emma's clothes. He agreed, but hid while they gathered her things into bags. He did insist, however, that they leave her bathrobe—the soft velour that she called her *housecoat*. The favorite she'd snuggle into the moment she could shed her street clothes.

He settled deeper into the armchair, covering his lap with her robe. He imagined it still held her scent. He stroked its soft fibers, letting his mind wander. He tried to connect with her mind, letting his thoughts drift. *Emma— what would you say?*

He dozed.

'He was never at home.'

Charlie awoke with a jerk, still hearing Emma's voice

in his mind. What was it she said? He concentrated and then remembered. *'He was never home!'*

He jumped from the chair, realizing by the clock's illumination that he had slept several hours. Nearly tripping on Emma's robe that lay at his feet, he hurried barefoot into his study. Grabbing a pen and notepad, he began scribbling the names of people who had said that very thing. Their oft-spoken words: "How could they say that about him? He was never at home."

So where was he? And could it be proven? He couldn't have been two places at once. With devilish glee, Charlie formulated a plan—to construct an alibi defense for Ben. Not just the days around Christmas when, according to Tori's statement, there was a tree, but for the entire month of December—from the time he got up in the morning until he went to bed at night. Six a.m. until midnight. He counted back the time—over six months ago. Would records still exist? Would witnesses remember exact dates and times? First, he'd hit Zeke with his brainstorm. At last he had a plan that might convince a jury.

❦

Charlie was lying in wait when Zeke approached his office's door, old-fashioned keys in hand. Charlie trailed Zeke into his office, fearing that the attorney might laugh or dismiss his plan out of hand. But he didn't. In fact, he sounded intrigued. He chuckled. "Do you think you can do it?"

"I do! Anyone like Ben, who's in constant motion, leaves a trail. Picture this—a huge poster of the month of December, drawn with big blocks representing the days of the month. Each activity that can be proven is written in its square. School should be easy since they keep attendance records. Now, picture this—each witness takes the stand as he or she accounts for a category and its date and time while you, standing beside our calendar, tap with a pointer. Get it?"

"I gotta tell you—that would get old fast with the jury."

"Here's what I'm thinking, if it's okay with you. I'll make a list of anyone who told me that very thing—that Ben was never at home. I'll have Ben make a list of all his activities, then we'll talk to the witnesses who can verify it."

"Better let Brownie talk to the witnesses. You just gather information from them informally and let him pin down the facts. He'll be able to distinguish what's admissible. And he can eliminate guesses or well-meaning attempts to embellish the truth. And lies. You never want to lie to that man."

"Did he think Ben was honest?"

"Of course. But we can't rule out that Ben may have convinced himself in some areas."

"But not about the big stuff."

"That's why a professional needs to interview potential witnesses. We cannot risk being blindsided in court."

Charlie jumped from Zeke's visitor's chair, eager to tear into the task.

"One hurdle to face first," the attorney said, making a calming motion with his hand. "I must enter an alibi defense, which should have been done five months ago."

"Do you think the delay in timing will be a problem?"

"Don't worry. I'll make a case for new evidence. You concentrate on that calendar."

Chapter 19

Ben surprised Charlie, Jade, and Jonathan with a homemade dinner of his own making. "Did you know shrimp aren't always pink? I never saw a raw one before. And are they good!" he said, chatting happily about the first thing he loved that loved him back—food. Ceremoniously, he set plates, salad bowls, silverware, and napkins on Charlie's dining room table and placed his creation within reach—a huge bowl of homemade pasta with meatballs and red sauce and a salad of mixed greens. "Help yourselves, everyone."

"What's the funny curly one that looks like a dandelion?" Jonathan asked, having stabbed a sample from his bowl.

"That's endive. It's full of vitamins. Eat lots of leafy green stuff and, before you know it, you'll be strong enough to mow Papa's lawn all by yourself." Ben passed the platters, and each filled their plates. Silence reigned as the feast was dispatched. "Save room for dessert. Mrs. Fiorelli taught me to make pizzelle from scratch. It is so easy."

"Anything's easy if you know how to do it," Charlie interjected.

"She makes it from memory, but I found a recipe on the internet. We mixed sugar, butter, milk, vanilla, anise—that's an extract that tastes like licorice—and eggs in a bowl, then added flour, baking powder, and salt. Stir it until it's smooth. We let it stand for an hour—something the butter requires—then she heated a thing called a pizzelle iron that looks like a waffle iron with round designs." He produced a plate, covered with a tea towel, and set it on the table. "Ta! Da! Her prize recipes are locked in her memory from her ancestors in the old country. And she's sharing them with me."

"Does she miss it? Her homeland?" Jade asked.

"No," Ben said. "For as long as she can remember, her family was planning to come to America. Her extended family preceded them, had settled, and found a church."

"Does she ever eat American food like pizza?" Jonathan asked. Everyone laughed.

"My dear boy," Charlie said, smothering a smile. "American soldiers brought pizza to America after the war. And spaghetti, but never this good."

Half comatose from stuffing themselves, the diners grew drowsy. Jonathan's eyes drooped, even as he nibbled his third pizzelle. "Come on, kiddo. Tomorrow's a school day. Thank Ben for a great supper and say goodnight to Papa."

"Ben and I will do the dishes. We have a few grown-up things to discuss."

"Aw," Jonathan protested. "That's what you always say about interesting stuff." With prodding, Jade shepherded Jonathan down the interior staircase.

Roxie, on high alert, didn't budge from under the table. Jade gave the Sheltie the eye, which brought her slinking after them. "No fat dogs," she admonished the little beggar. "You'll have to settle for a frozen carrot slice."

Having reduced the dishes to what wouldn't go in the dishwasher, Charlie washed while Ben dried, his impressive wingspan enabling him to return serving platters to the top cupboard shelf. Charlie waited, suppressing the urge to tear into his plan until he could present it succinctly and calmly.

While coffee perked and Ben used the restroom, Charlie fetched the folder labeled *Ben Legal* from his office. Riffling through the contents, he chose and unfolded a seventeen-by-eleven inch paper titled *Ben's Calendar*, which he had constructed by taping together two sheets of duplicator paper. In preparation for their meeting, Charlie had drawn the month of December, its thirty-one squares delineated with a fine-pointed marker representing every day. These squares would receive the whereabouts of Ben's waking moments that entire fateful month.

Beside it, he set another document onto which he'd listed each date and day of the week, separated by triple spaces. Rather than start with the graph, he could sort each day's activities in ascending order of time. His blessed computer could rearrange the entries before he copied them onto the chart. He set a legal tablet and pen nearby, onto which he had already started a skeletal list of potential witnesses.

Ben sat down, eyeing the documents with intense concentration. Charlie began.

"Have you ever noticed how you can hear something, over and over, without it registering as something important?" Ben's eyebrows lowered as he digested that thought, digging for the significance of what Charlie was saying. "Do you know how many people have said, 'Ben was never at home'"?

Ben shrugged. "Many. I guess. 'Cause it's true."

"Ben, nobody can be two places at once. If you were, as everyone said, 'never at home,' then that begs the question, *where were you*? Well, we're going to find out and take that information to court. We're going to construct a month of your life and leave nothing out.

"We'll start with the easy stuff—the school keeps attendance records—and every job and activity for which records are kept. The tough part will be verifying your social activities. It won't be good enough for your friends to say, 'he was with me.' We'll need the testimony of responsible adults, like a parent, coach, or youth leader. And if there is time missing at critical junctures, between three and eight p.m., we'll have to track down where you were."

"But it's been half a year. What if…"

"I know it seems like a daunting challenge. But it's the best shot we have. We'll flesh out the calendar, and then Brownie, Zeke's private detective, will verify witnesses' statements and issue subpoenas for them to appear in court. All records will be subpoenaed as well."

"Do you really think I'm going to be tried? For a crime I didn't commit?"

"I certainly hope not. But we'll hope for the best and plan for the worst. Now, let's begin with something easy."

Ben squinted at the boxes. "December twenty-fourth and twenty-fifth. Those are easy."

"Were you ever alone with Tori on either of those days, even for a few minutes? Remember, it was Christmas break, and school wasn't in session."

"Christmas Eve day, I worked from nine to five. Then there was this humongous group of my dad's family over for dinner and present exchange. After everyone left, the family went to late church."

"Did you go to church with them? Did Tori?"

"No. And yes, she did. By the time they got home, I'd washed the dishes and cleaned up the kitchen—that was my job—and gone to bed."

"And Christmas day?"

"Hysteria. Kids ripping into presents by seven o'clock. We had a special brunch my mom makes for Christmas, then the house filled up with her side of the family. Same deal."

"And that evening?"

"I went to my buddy's house, but my mom's family was

still there, snacking and drinking when I got home around eleven."

"And Tori?"

"All the kids were asleep."

"The twentieth is easy," Charlie said. "It snowed a foot. You did Mr. Greer's and my drive, had lunch with us, then you took Jonathan sledding."

"Right. Then I changed clothes and went straight to work." His enthusiasm for the project was telling.

"Three days down, twenty-eight to go. Tomorrow I'll stop at the school to request a copy of your attendance records. And the guy you work for at Burger King—is he the same guy you worked for in December?"

"Yeah. And he's a really good guy. Appreciated that I was always on time, worked hard, was nice to the customers, and never called off for no reason. I'll give you his name and number."

಄ಌಉಌ

The next morning, as soon as Charlie knew the high school would have finished with the start-of-day drama, he spoke with the principal's secretary. "He's off campus for the day, but I'll be happy to give him a message when he checks in."

"It's important. It's about Ben Olinger. Would you please ask him if he could supply me with a copy of Ben's attendance record for last December? The originals will be subpoenaed at a later day, but for now, if he could just give me a list by the date and the times. And tell him it's confidential."

She agreed. Charlie was relieved when she didn't probe for details. Even though she was a consummate professional, he couldn't risk his request getting back to the prosecutors and revealing their strategy or key witnesses. They'd know soon enough.

Since Burger King had been open forever, Charlie took a chance that Ben's boss might be on duty. He blanked on the name—Bryan or Ryan. The boss, who turned out to be the manager, was not only working but wore a nametag. Ah. Ryan. Brightening at the sound of Ben's name and that his help was needed, Ryan ushered Charlie to a table in the corner away from the morning regulars. He listened intently as Charlie explained.

"This is bad shit, ah, excuse me sir. I mean, how could anyone do something this evil to Ben? He's Mr. Dependability and makes my job bearable. I have a wife and two little kids, and I'm trying to go to community college at night. I can absolutely count on Ben to be on time, take extra hours if I'm in a bind, fill in for others, do his job well, and be honest to the penny with the restaurant's money. And when business is slow, he takes it upon himself to wipe floors and tables without being asked. He even washes the windows. I used to dread pop-up visits from the franchise's owner, but Ben takes such pride in keeping us ship-shape. It's as if he owned the damn franchise. How can I help? You needn't ask twice."

"Your testimony to his character is greatly appreciated, but what we need is your timecards—exactly when he worked last December. A record that can be subpoenaed and about which you'll testify."

"Sure. That's easy. I think. I'll check my calendar and see what I can remember. He had continued his regular hours during the school break then filled in some hard spots to fill—like Christmas Eve. I mean, the day of Christmas Eve. Never know what to call it exactly. Anyway, he was here from nine to five. I remember because I was able to spend time with my family."

"A list would be great, but I need the physical

timecards."

Ryan shook his head, frowning. "That paper's long gone. We have no place to store old timecards. As soon as the bookkeeper records the dates and hours so the kids can get paid, we shred them."

"Would the bookkeeper's records include the exact times?"

"'Fraid not. Just the hours. But I can fake you some duplicates that coincide with the dates and times you need. It's the least I can do."

"I appreciate that you'd stick your neck out for him, but I can't let you do that. Your information must be honest and accurate. If anyone raised conflicting times, and it could be proven that he wasn't here, Ben's whole case could go down the drain. Besides, lying under oath is a felony. For your family's sake, you couldn't risk it. If you could just reconstruct his records to the best of your knowledge, we'll see how it fits. Maybe he signed off on incoming orders or something …"

Ryan's head drooped. "Honestly? That's a tall order, after six months. But I'll try." Charlie left him his contact information and returned to his car. Only then did he realize how hungry he was.

享愛

The minute Jonathan emerged from the school bus, Charlie sensed something was wrong. Instead of two-foot hopping from the last step onto the grass, then rebounding as if on springs, the child disembarked slowly. He dragged his backpack by one strap rather than wearing it, as was his habit. As Charlie approached him, he could see that Jonathan's face was red and his nose had been running.

It had to happen sooner or later—the nasty school germs made a direct hit on the little fellow. Not surprising, since he had spent his early years sequestered with adults, not a sitter or preschool. Play dates had been a foreign concept. Jade's minister's wife, who kept him occasionally, wouldn't if anyone in her household was sick. "You feeling puny?" he asked.

Jonathan shrugged.

"Come on. Let's go into the house and sort you out. I baked banana bread with walnuts, the way that you like it."

Rather than being happily distracted, the boy trudged behind Charlie, dragging his backpack.

Wait. He'll explain when he's ready.

Roxie trotted beside Jonathan, looking expectantly at his face, as if she too needed an explanation for the unusual departure from the child's jovial disposition.

In the powder room, Charlie wrung out a warm washcloth and handed it to Jonathan. "Can you manage it yourself?"

The child nodded and did a reasonably good job of cleaning his face. Then he pushed his sleeves above the elbow, ran water in the washbowl to the line Charlie had painted for reference, and lathered his hands. He did not sing happy birthday. He swished his hands in the water, momentarily captivated by the circling ripples. Finally he depressed the plunger and pulled his towel from its special ring beside the sink.

"Do you feel sick?" Charlie asked after settling Jonathan at the kitchen table. He shook his head no. "How about at school?" Another no. "Then would you like to tell me what's wrong? Did something happen at school?"

It all came out in a torrent. "My friend Alan said his big brother said that Ben did something awful. He called it something I can't remember. That the cops will take Ben to jail and lock him up and keep him there forever and ever where he'll die for the awful thing that he did." Tears spurted off his lashes and ran down his face, dripping off his chin.

Dear God. Where to begin? Charlie dabbed Jonathan's face with a napkin. "Police do not put people in jail unless there's a good reason. Like they stole a car or robbed a bank. If there is a good reason, a judge and jury decide if it's true. It sounds like someone heard about a minor situation involving Ben and blew it all out of proportion."

"I hear you and Mommy talking about Ben. Sometimes you take Ben to see a judge. If you don't, they'll throw him in jail."

Ah, they'd become lax in their conversing, as if children only hear what they should. There was nothing wrong with the little guy's ears.

"Please don't tell me to ask Mommy. She'll say, 'Everything's fine.' Or 'Don't worry.' Or 'The grownups will take care of it.' But I want to know."

"Okay, I'll try, but only if you tell your mom what we talked about. Is that a deal?" He bobbed his head. "What have you heard Mommy and me say about Ben?"

He thought a minute. "That some bad little girl said Ben did something bad and her mommy and daddy believed her. So you gave Ben some test. He didn't do it, but they don't believe him."

"That's about right. Do you know what a judge and jury do?" He didn't wait for an answer. "They listen to both sides of the story then decide who is telling the truth."

"Like when two kids get in a fight on the playground and they get sent to the principal's office?"

"Well, something like that. What you need to know is that very good people are working on Ben's behalf. They'll sort it out and prepare Ben's story for the judge."

"Will it make him sick? Like Grandpa? Is Ben going to die too?"

"No. Of course not. Unlike your grandpa, Ben is young

and has a healthy heart."

Charlie hoped that Jonathan had forgotten all about it, being only four at the time, but evidently he hadn't. What an awful episode in this small child's life. His invalid grandmother murdered by a serial killer in her own home. His grandfather, known by nosey neighbors to yell a lot, arrested and hauled off in handcuffs then released on bail. Jonathan was told that his mom made the police give him back.

The grandfather, having had a massive heart attack at his arraignment, ended up in the VA's hospice ward—down the hall from where Charlie was recovering from his ruptured aneurism. The VA was where he, Jade, and Jonathan had bonded. At least the grandfather lived long enough to be exonerated and for his wife's killer to be apprehended.

"If the little girl lied, why doesn't she say so? Is she scared they'll punish her?"

"I can't answer that because I don't know the girl or what she's been taught about telling the truth. That's the bad part about lying, Jonathan. Sometimes the person who lies has to tell another lie and another and another to hide what she did to avoid being punished. And the lies get so big that she can't confess. If someone makes a mistake, it's best to say they're sorry, ask for forgiveness, and then not do it again."

Jonathan hopped from his chair and hugged Charlie. "Thanks, Papa." He stepped back, giving Charlie his earnest look. "What should I tell Alan at school?"

"I suggest you say nothing. Pretend you didn't hear what he said. By tomorrow, everyone may have forgotten all about it and have moved on."

He brightened. "Yeah! Tomorrow we're going to the zoo."

"Let's sort your backpack. See if there's any homework

for your mom to return. And there's banana bread we should eat. Let's package a hunk for your mom's snack when she gets in from class."

Chapter 20

Charlie studied the list Ben had supplied of his life's activities that December. It didn't take Charlie long to realize the enormity of verifying each segment of every day.

School

His job(s)

Swim team practice & meets

Diving practice

Youth Group

Church

Hanging out with buddies Dan, Don, Dave, Eric & Steve at various homes

One day at home, parents out, but piano teacher Magda was there for the fosters.

Time with estranged former girlfriend

Time spent with Charlie & Jade. Jonathan was too young to testify.

Charlie decided the school's attendance records could wait and, in the meantime, he'd visit the swim team's coach. Charlie remembered their meeting in the school's parking lot after the athletic banquet. Coach had been so concerned that Ben not quit the team, entreating Charlie to discourage that decision. Ben, he insisted, was college-athlete material and should be applying for scholarships. Coach's impression of Ben's parents was downright negative. Charlie phoned the school office, requested and received his schedule and was pleased to learn it included a free period that day.

Rather than trying to schedule an appointment, Charlie located the coach at poolside. The hot, moist air smacked his face as he entered the natatorium. Had it not been for the smell of chlorine, rather than dead fish and rotting vegetation, he could be back in the Mekong Delta. The coach, crouched at poolside, appeared to be taking water samples, filling test tubes, corking them, and arranging them in a holder. *Complicated business*, Charlie thought. Not wanting to startle the coach and cause him to break the glass tubes, he waited until the coach looked up.

Charlie moved toward him, extending his hand. "We met after the athletic banquet last fall. Ben Olinger is a special friend of mine. You were concerned that he might quit the team."

Rather than break into wreaths of smiles as Charlie expected, the coach's countenance darkened, no hand extending to welcome his visitor. "What is it you want? If you're here for a character reference, I can't get involved. I've heard all about Ben's predicament, and I'm sorry for your misguided loyalty. I've got to say I'm disappointed that a role model like yourself would take the side of a confessed child molester."

Slowly Charlie recovered from his surprise. "I won't take up your time explaining why the charges are bogus, which they are. I have proof. And I'm not here to work the court of public opinion. What I want, simply, is your December attendance records for both practices and swim meets, including transportation time to and from away meets. Ben's attorney will subpoena these records. You will be asked to testify about them in court. I'm hoping you will cooperate with the request and give me a copy."

The coach stared, speechless. Charlie continued. "I

mean by tomorrow. Please jot a list from your records. Then preserve the original records with whatever means are available to you. I'd suggest giving them to the principal, who is up to speed on the legalities." Charlie stared until the coach broke eye contact first.

"All right. You'll have it. But if Ben tries to add to or embellish my records in any way, I'll tell the court that he's a liar."

"About diving …"

"Not mine. You'll have to talk to the diving instructor separately. He keeps his own schedule of practices and competitions."

"Who is he and where can I find him?"

"Ask in the athletic office."

Charlie left, not bothering to thank him. Following the signs, he located a person who could help him. She pointed down the hall to an open doorway where a young man with a blond buzz cut was hanging up the phone. "I'm Charlie…"

"I know. Coach just called. I'll photocopy December and jot down the hours Ben was here when I saw him with my own eyes. I can fax, mail, or leave an envelope at the office for you."

"Thanks. Fax is fine. I'll give you my number. And please, in case coach didn't tell you, safeguard the originals. You and they will be subpoenaed in a couple of weeks."

The diving coach shook his head. "I find this hard to believe. Ben is so *even*. Placid. Kind. Never takes anything the wrong way. Goes out of his way to help others. If tempers are frayed, he gets everyone laughing." He shook his head. "I hope you'll get to the bottom of it."

"We're trying. And your records will help. But coach, no embellishing, editing, no manipulating the data. Just the truth."

"Yes, sir." He took Charlie's card and nodded his thanks. As Charlie was rounding the doorway, the coach called after him. "I hope you're right. That kid has real talent. I could not believe my eyes the first time I saw that six-two skinny kid execute an Olympic-worthy jackknife."

Charlie sighed, glad that he'd seen it too. Regardless of the legal outcome, sadly that part of Ben's life was over.

⌘

"Yo! Mr. Alderfer! This is Ryan at Burger King. You are not going to believe what I found! You gotta come see."

Charlie's heart jumped into overdrive. "Please tell me it's December's timecards."

"Roger that. Now how does this work, legally and all? Can I lend them to you to photocopy or do you snap them with your phone? Should I keep them or lock them up somewhere?"

"I'll find out. But in the meantime, I'd love to come and copy the dates and times."

Charlie was on his way in five minutes. Jonathan's bus wasn't due for two hours. That should be plenty of time.

Ryan handed Charlie a beat-up cardboard box that looked like it had been used as a French fry tray. Under its flap, once held together by a rubber band that now lay in pieces, was a stack of timecards—the heavy kind that could withstand being inserted and retrieved from the machine many times. "Let's take them back to the office," Ryan said, directing Charlie to a tiny room that held a work surface, chair, a file cabinet, and shelves. Sweeping mounds of papers aside, he set the box in front of Charlie."

"Each kid has a card. Look through them until you find Ben's."

"It looks like he had several."

"That's because the machine malfunctioned, and we had to install a new one."

Charlie was thrilled at the touch of so much information. "Where did you find them?"

"Under some junk that should have been pitched long ago. I got to wondering what might be up there, and voila! Old timecards. How do you want to handle this?"

"I'd like to photograph them for my immediate use. Ben's attorney is sending his private investigator with a subpoena to collect the cards. He'll safeguard them until they're needed."

"Maybe I should shoot them too. So I'll remember what to say in court. This is really neat. I've never been in a courtroom before, much less been asked to testify."

Charlie gave the enthusiastic young man a level gaze, inspired to reveal something he hadn't considered until that very moment. "If I had to choose between a dreaded disease or being accused of a crime I didn't commit, I'd take the disease. At least everyone would be fighting for me."

Charlie snapped several pictures and, having made sure they were sharp, emailed them to his home computer. He thanked Ryan profusely, hurrying home to retrieve the data and enter them on his worksheet by their respective dates. Maybe the swim coach's fax would be waiting for him as well. Charlie reveled in the sense of forward momentum—at last.

⌘

Charlie could hardly stand his jubilation as he entered the swim team and diving practices which Ben had attended—December 2, 3, 4, 5, 6 (break) 9, 10, 11, 12, 13 (break) 16, 17 (break) 19 (break) 21 (break) 24, Christmas, 26, 27 (break) 29, 30, and on into the new year. Some days, like December third, he had school, followed immediately by back-to-back practices that started at three-fifteen and lasting until after eight with a half hour break to grab a snack. Coach noted when he'd stayed later to help clean up, whatever that entailed. Ryan's timecards revealed that he then went to work.

Ben's life revealed a nonstop schedule of school, practices, and work. Friends said he didn't go home until the kids were in bed at which time he cleaned house, did homework, and then grabbed a few hours' sleep. Next day, same drill. Wow! No wonder the kid was so skinny. The challenge might be the weekends.

Charlie nibbled leftovers alone, relaxing. For the first time in weeks, he felt confident that Team Ben would exonerate him. He sipped herbal tea, rehearsing what he would say to the parents of Ben's friends who would verify when Ben was a guest in their homes. Those times typically would start around seven and run until late Friday and Saturday evenings. Then there was an ex-wannabe girlfriend who was making threats to deny Ben was with her. That would take some finesse.

When the phone jangled, Charlie's tea sloshed as he had been aiming for his mouth. Wiping his mouth on a napkin, he leapt for the beast. In broken English, Mrs. Fiorelli half spoke, half cried Ben's latest predicament. "So sad. The poor angel. So much blood."

Panic shot through Charlie's core. "What's happened? What are you talking about? Has Ben been in an accident?"

"No, no, no. He so sad. Went to room. I thought to be by self. I heard big thud. Then too quiet. I check on him. He in bathroom. Blood everywhere! Like a battlefield."

"Did you call 9-1-1?"

"Yes. They come. They do things. Take him away."

"Where? Where did they take him?"

"To big hospital." Charlie lost whatever she said next that was buried in her sobbing.

"Think. Please. Which hospital?"

"Big one. What's its name? Like the city's name. Not far."

Of course. There was only one large hospital near the Fiorellis that had a trauma center. He Googled its name, called information, and asked about a missing family member who had been brought by ambulance within the last hour. He described Ben, and told the woman that he had legal papers to act on behalf of Benjamin Olinger. Was he there?"

Charlie sped to the hospital and accepted the valet's offer to park his car. He'd worry about its retrieval later. At the entry to the ER, he was required to go through airport-type security, complete with wanding, just short of a strip search. They plastered a huge yellow visitors' ID to his shirt, complete with his picture they copied from his Veteran's ID card. How odd, by contrast, that anyone could enter the VA without any of this intrusion. Did he look like a terrorist?

Past security, he approached an information platform with several alert employees who wore packs of laminated cards clipped to lanyards. He presented his photo ID, Ben's authorization, and begged to know where he had been taken. A bored woman listened dispassionately as he described the young man and that he'd been covered in blood. "Have a seat over there," she said without telling him what would come next.

What seemed like an eternity later, although it must have been just thirty minutes, he approached the desk again. "Is anybody going to help me? Tell me where Benjamin has been taken. I don't know if he's dead or alive!"

The woman next to her gave her a nudge, which prompted both women to stare at him. "Aren't you that veteran who's been in the news? The one who stopped a killer at the VA?"

Charlie grinned. *Oh what the hell.* "That would be me." The second woman left her perch and scurried through the double doors that separated the waiting room from the examination suite. She returned in a matter of minutes.

"Come with me, sir," she said. "And thank you for your service."

She left him at the nurses' station where he reiterated his mission. Glancing at her monitor, the nurse rose, circled the desk, and bade him to follow her. The ER was set up with private, curtained bays that circled the room and surrounded a huge nursing station in the vast department's core. Halfway around, and a dozen bays later, she stopped to check. She parted the curtain for Charlie to enter.

Ben's eyes were closed, massive bandages obscuring half his face, plugs sticking out of his nose. Someone had made an attempt to clean up his face, but brown traces of dried blood remained in the creases. This was not what Charlie expected. His worst fear had been that Ben—physically, mentally, emotionally, and spiritually exhausted—had tried to take his own life.

A man in surgical scrubs appeared wheeling a small cart that held a computer. "Mr. Olinger?" he asked.

"No. I'm his emergency contact. I have a copy of his directive if you need it. Is he going to be all right?"

"He was lucky. He lost a lot of blood. The EMT said when he fainted he cracked his head on a washbowl. His skull isn't fractured—just bruised, but head wounds can bleed profusely. We've stopped the nosebleed and packed his nose. That's one hell of a lesion he has near an artery. If he's had it awhile, it may be infected. We'll try cauterizing it if the bleeding persists. An ENT will examine him."

"What caused it?"

The doctor shrugged. "Congenital defect. Old injury. Weak artery wall. Good thing he wasn't driving. We won't admit him, but we'll keep him here in the ER overnight and keep an eye on him." He looked at the screen. "Do you know if he has any allergies?"

"He mentioned penicillin, but beyond that I don't know. Can I stay with him awhile?"

"Sure, but I imagine he'll sleep for some time. By the way, if you have any influence over his dietary habits, encourage him to gain some weight. He's terribly thin."

Charlie sat by Ben's gurney as hours slipped away. He studied Ben's face, battered though it looked, and wondered all over again how anybody could throw away such a beautiful person. He moaned. Charlie jumped from his chair. "Ben? It's me. I'm here."

"Mr. A?" he murmured. "Where am I?"

"In the hospital." Briefly he explained what had transpired. "They've sutured the gash in your scalp and a specialist is going to cauterize your nose. Then you'll be good as new. Maybe better. No more nose bleeds. This one got out of hand."

"You mean 'out of nose.'" Trying to smile at his own joke, Ben winced.

"They'll keep you here overnight, then I'll be back tomorrow to fetch you. Will you be okay by yourself?"

Ben motioned thumbs up. Charlie gave Ben's arm a gentle pat then scurried from the cubicle, a jumble of emotions. A flashback—the smells, the sounds, even the lighting and medical personnel trying to resuscitate his Emma.

Chapter 21

As Charlie crossed the covered walkway that led to the parking garage, he realized the sky had transitioned from pitch to slate. The stars were gone and a slivery moon hung low in the western horizon. He flicked his wrist to reposition his watch. Five thirty. It was morning. Surprisingly, he didn't feel tired, no doubt still pumped on adrenalin and relief. A valet produced a cardboard ticket onto which was written his car's location with an attached wire ring that held his keys. To his request for directions, the valet wouldn't hear of it, claiming he enjoyed having something to do. He strode away to retrieve it.

As Charlie turned the corner onto his street, he was stunned to see a line of police cars bracketing either side of Old Mr. Greer's house. *Oh, no. Not him too. Not now. Dear God, please, please, please.* He skidded to a stop in his own driveway and hurried toward the commotion outside the Greer home.

Encircled with uniformed officers, Old Mr. Greer was holding forth in his pajamas and bathrobe. He punctuated whatever he was saying with jabs of his index finger, entirely too close to one officer's face. Wilting with relief, it finally registered with Charlie that something else had transpired. Had Mr. Greer been robbed? Become ill? Called his daughter cross country then refused help once it arrived? Couldn't be, as no EMT vehicles were on the scene.

When Charlie succeeded in working his way through the knot of officers and neighbors, Mr. Greer stalked forward to meet him. "I saw the whole thing. And they won't believe me." He transmitted his disapproval with an angry squint at the cops.

"What? What did you see?"

"Over there. At your house." He pointed toward Charlie's front lawn where another officer was staring at Charlie's picture window. Even from that distance, Charlie could see it was smashed. Not a small hole, like an intruder might attempt, but a jagged crater in the middle of the expanse. Charlie gasped.

"Got up to go to the bathroom." He pointed to the small window, located between his living room and his bedroom. "Saw lights moving down the street. Not unusual. Then someone turned them off, but the car kept on moving. It stopped in front of your house. When a guy dressed head to foot in black opened the driver-side door, his dome light didn't come on. Now that got my attention!

"Guy walks across the front lawn, looks left and right, then hurtles something at the window. It exploded! Guy takes off running toward his car, jumps in, and splits. No tire squealing or anything, just moving fast."

"Could you see who it was? Anyone from around here? How about the car?"

"I gave the car's description to that guy over there," he said pointing to the officer he had previously been jabbing to reinforce a point. "He doesn't believe me."

Charlie approached the officer. "I can assure you that whatever my neighbor told you will be spot on. Don't let his age fool you. He's smart as they come, and there's nothing wrong with his memory or eyesight."

The officer approached them. "Mr. Greer, I—"

"That's Admiral Greer to you, son. Show some respect."

"I apologize, Admiral Greer. It's just that I find it would be…ah…challenging to catch a license plate from this distance in the dark. Are you sure?"

Old Mr. Greer gave a snort. "I stuck my head out the bathroom window, memorized it, and then wrote it down on my kitchen notepad. The car's rear, when stopped, was angled toward my house since the road begins to bear to the right beyond the Alderfer home. My post light throws a three-hundred-degree arc, low enough to the ground to avoid upstairs windows."

"And you're eyesight is…"

"Twenty-twenty. Now you go find the hoodlum who vandalized my friend's window."

The officer nodded and turned to depart.

"And, sonny? A little white vinegar will take that mustard spot off your right shirt cuff."

The cop reflexively jerked a look at his cuff, laughed, and nodded consent to the old gentleman, who was wandering back to his house.

Across the street, Charlie approached a pair of officers, one of whom was holding an object in gloved hands. "Mr. Alderfer, do you know who might have done this?" he said, extending a brick for Charlie's inspection. On it, white painted letters read *YOUR NEXT*.

"Maybe. I'm a witness in a trial that's coming up soon. The accuser's family must be angry about that. Please. Talk to them. I don't want any trouble. Just the truth."

The officer noted the Olingers' names and addresses. "They've misspelled *you're*."

Charlie left the police to investigate the scene and went inside to check on Jade and Jonathan. He found them unaware of the unfolding drama until the police followed him to sweep for intruders. Cocooned as they'd been in their underground apartment, they were ready to leave for the day. Jade decided to drive Jonathan to school, texting the school's transportation officer to avoid their block. Having confirmed that no locked windows or doors had been breached Charlie called his insurance agent and left the details to the respective professionals.

Midday, while sipping coffee in Mr. Greer's kitchen, Charlie watched a glass company remove the damaged window and install a replacement. "Admiral?"

Old Mr. Greer shrugged and grinned sheepishly. "Served him right. He did take my report seriously then, didn't he?"

"I wish we had a contact in the PD. I'd love to know who owns that car."

"Can't that investigator on Ben's case poke around? Those guys have intel we can't imagine. I'll give you the make, model, year, and plate. Sorry, I didn't get the VIN."

Early that afternoon, Brownie, Zeke's PI, returned Charlie's call. "You sitting down?"

"Always when the landline rings. What did you learn?"

"The car's registered to a kid—a so-called adult by today's reckoning—who has a sealed juvenile record. His physical address is a halfway house in the city. Must be out on parole. A person who shall remain anonymous told me he used to be in the foster care system, and he aged out before getting his shit together. And guess who placed him with foster families?" He didn't wait for an answer. "Your Mr. Watkins. And guess into which home?" A long pause.

"Come on. Come on." Brownie laughed. "Guess."

"The Olingers'? Oh my gosh. Do you think Ben's parents put him up to it? But why?"

A deep sigh through the line. "To rattle your cage for taking Ben's side. Can't think of any other reason except to stop you from poking into the foster care operation. You've hit a nerve. Any idea which one?"

Charlie remembered the overheard conversation at the Home when he'd called upon its director, that man named Watkins. Besides stopping Ben from interfering with the Olingers' ability to make money from the fosters, Ben must have been threatening something more dangerous without grasping its relevance. He'd have to pump Ben for more details.

"Thanks so much, Brownie. Just add it to my tab."

Charlie had no sooner hung up than the phone rang again. The caller ID recognized Ben. "Hey, buddy, how are you feeling? Have they stopped the gusher?"

Ben's voice resembled the world's worst head cold. "I'll live. They'll let me leave if someone will be responsible for me until the ENT can remove the packing and see if I need surgery. That would be outpatient a few days later."

"Just let me know what time they can spring you, and I'll be there. I'll let Mrs. Fiorelli know you'll be staying with me in the meantime."

"Mr. A—I don't know what all this is costing. I was able to get that medical card, but…"

"Don't worry about it. I'll ask a few questions. Unless I'm mistaken, everything's covered."

"That would be awesome. Thank you sooooo much!"

∽∾∽

In spite of telemarketers' nuisance calls, Charlie was afraid not to answer the landline. He'd left such a trail of inquiries, seeking general information from chains of friends to potential witnesses. If the caller ID looked remotely local, he'd bite. He had just hung up on a foreign-sounding young man who was *responding to his inquiry* about lowering his credit card balances. Nice try. His financial plan had been simple throughout his life: pay cash at the point of purchase or pay off his credit cards at the end of every month. He resisted the urge to slam the handset into the cradle.

As he walked back toward his study, it rang again. He crept toward the beast, waiting to see if the caller would leave a message. The number, he realized, was vaguely familiar. "Mr. Alderfer? Sir? I called you once before but didn't identify myself. I was afraid of repercussions or worse. I'm a neighbor of the Olingers."

Charlie snatched up the phone and barked, "I'm here." Then, backing off a little, he added, "What is it you want?"

"I was hoping you'd listen to what I've been seeing. Bizarre stuff is going on across the street with them little kids."

"If you see abuse, you should call the hotline. It's anonymous, and somebody will investigate your complaint."

"It's nothing like that. It's like, well, weird goings on."

"Weird? Like what?"

"I started noticing…well, it was last fall. Before Halloween. These two little kids—they couldn't have been more than three or four—were brought to the door by that social worker woman from that home. I remember them because they had funny matching cartoon stickers on their little bags. About three days later, the same woman collects them. And off they go. I figured their custody problem had been resolved, and they were being returned to their family. About two days later, the woman returns with two different little kids. One was a toddler, the other about three. Same thing. Three days later, she collects them."

Charlie interrupted her. "So the Olingers, in addition to school-age children, take little ones on a short-term basis. Like animal shelters take in runaway dogs until the owners track down their pets. There's nothing odd about that."

"Now wait. Around day ten, the lady returns with a third set of kids. Same deal. And they stay exactly three days until—wait for it—here she comes again and there go the kids. You get the idea? Every month like clockwork. You do the math. But here's the kicker. At the beginning of month number two, here come the first two kids with the same bags with the stickers. Out they go in three days followed by the same second set. I recognized them—the toddler and the three-year-old. She's distinctive with all those red curls. So, on the predictable day, the routine repeats until over a dozen kids come and go. Month after month. And this routine keeps repeating itself."

"Are you sure? How did you happen to notice the pattern?"

"By the third month, I was watching for them. I was afraid to take pictures, sure I'd get caught. I'd been painting my interior with all that wood trim. As dumb luck would have it, my work coincided with the social worker's comings and goings."

"Have your neighbors said anything to you about this?"

"Nah. They think I'm an old busybody and a gossip. Which I am. But I hear plenty about the trash in their yard and how they've let the place run down, but nothing about this. Most of them are at work. But like I said, I even thought it might be about some witness protection program where they need to keep the kids moving."

Charlie grappled with what to do with this nosey neighbor's information. Surely she didn't want him to intervene on behalf of the kids. He'd ask Ben if her account made any sense. "Why don't you give me your name, address, and phone number. And, if you'll trust me with the written agenda, jot it down in the chronology you described and mail it to me, including a brief description of each child."

"You could pick it up at my house."

Terrible idea. The Olingers knew who he was. "That might look like a conspiracy since I understand other neighbors have complained to the director who places the kids. Best I keep a low profile. Just mail it to me."

✺

Charlie settled Ben in his recliner in the study, trying not to hover, which was impossible. Was he in pain? Hungry? Warm or cool enough? Would an ice pack help relieve the pain from the repeated cautery procedures? No, no, no, and no. And thank you. He would be fine. Realizing that he had Ben at his mercy, Charlie fetched his December documents and seized the opportunity to dredge Ben's memory for minute details that might be significant.

"You've got to see these," Charlie said, sliding the contents of a manila envelope onto Ben's lap. "Photocopies of school, swim and dive team, and Burger King timecard records. The originals have been subpoenaed. Lists from your band friends, including some parents in whose home you were a guest. You've been a busy, predictable fellow. We have Christmas week fairly well documented, but we have some holes that need plugging. Do you feel up to searching your memory?"

"Sure. I'll try. I just wish I'd kept my own calendar."

"Thursday, December nineteenth. Coach documents an away swim meet from two to six p.m. Mr. Greer and I attended, and we left immediately afterward. What did you do after the meet?" When Charlie mentioned the meet's location, Ben squirmed.

"I remember. I went to a girl's house for dinner. Her name's Nicolette Van Dyke. I was there until nine that evening. Then she drove me home, and we sat in her car and talked for some time."

"And she'll testify to that? Who was home cooking dinner, a parent? Are you still on good terms with them?"

He sighed. "I doubt it. She was pretty angry that evening. We had a big fight. She wanted a commitment from me. I'd told her before that my life was too complicated for a serious relationship. That there were years to do—that."

"She wanted sex?"

"Well, sure. All her girlfriends were doing it, or so she said. That if I really loved her, I'd want her too. I do not know how I got into that mess. The last thing I needed was a pregnant girl who, I admit, I didn't even like that much. I'd taken her to a couple basketball games, then she started coming to my meets. Syncing her class passing to mesh with mine. Offered me rides to and from school when my car wasn't working. That, I appreciated.

"But she got really, really angry when I started eating lunch with Claire, even though I told her Claire was help-ing me with my classwork. As if I owed her an explana-tion, but I hate unpleasantness. She said she could help me. Yeah, like 'Miss Bottom of the Class.' Don't get me wrong. She's smart. Real popular. A cheerleader, on stu-dent council, and so on. She just doesn't believe in study-ing."

"Do you think her parents would talk with me about that particular evening?"

He shrugged. "The last time she asked me out, and I made a flimsy excuse, she said if I didn't take her to—whatever it was—a movie or party or something—she'd tell her father I'd raped her."

Charlie felt his eyebrows shoot up. "Really! And what did you say to that?"

"I said, 'Do what you have to, but you know it's a lie.' In the end, I gave in and took her out. I was becoming afraid of what she might say. I really liked Claire and didn't want it getting around school that I'd done some-thing that awful."

"So. Was anyone at her house the night you had din-ner?"

"Just her mom and dad. He's real protective of her. Believes anything she tells him. Like when she went to a party where there was serious drinking, and she came home smelling of booze. She told him someone spilled a drink on her, and when she realized what it was, she left and went to another friend's house. Huh! She drinks like a fish. Parties—she wasn't supposed to go unless a parent was home. She always said 'Yes. I asked.' And he believed her without even checking."

"Do I talk to the mother or the father?"

"I'd try her mother when he's at work. But even if she agrees to testify, can't she change her mind?"

"Not when Zeke delivers a reality check with a subpoena, including a stiff warning about committing perjury." Charlie jotted down the parents' contact information and looked at his notes.

"Saturday, December twenty-first. I have you working from nine-thirty to eleven-thirty, then eight p.m. to midnight. What did you do in between?"

Ben scrunched his forehead, then touched it gently when it triggered pain. "I can't think of anything. Wait—there was a party at Burger King for employees that afternoon."

"Okay. I'll ask Ryan about that since there's no timecard. I looked back through Saturdays and see you usually spent time with friends from midday to late evening. What about Saturday the seventh?"

Ben beamed. "That was my birthday. And that was the first time I saw Nicolette. My family had a party for me, and everyone was over. Relatives, the band guys, school friends, swimmers, and so on."

Charlie considered the obvious. "Tori would have mentioned in her complaint if she remembered the date coinciding with your party. And with all those people in attendance, her account would be impossible. Next. Sunday the twenty-second. You worked at Burger King until four p.m. What did you do that evening?"

"I had a big fight with my father. He accused me of damaging the kids' air mattresses, which I didn't. I wasn't even home when they had a sword fight. He was angry enough to beat me up, but I couldn't let that happen—not after Izzi. I hold a weight-lifting record. I could have killed him. So I walked out, left him screaming after me, got in my car, and went back to Burger King. I hung out there until closing about two a.m. Then I went to my buddy's and sacked out on his couch."

"And the next day?"

"My parents came to my buddy's house around ten. He apologized. Said I should come home, which I did. I'd missed diving practice anyway."

"The coach's time sheet agrees. What did you do that afternoon?"

"My band practiced at my house until late afternoon. Mom was home, baking Christmas cookies until late. I remember because she used every pot and pan in the kitchen, which she left for me to clean up."

"Ben, I'll need to know which of your four band friends' homes you're still welcome in. Which parents believe in your innocence."

"I'd start with Steve's mom. I've told her everything, and she lost it. I'll get you everyone's numbers."

Charlie realized he had his work cut out for him. If Ben's band buddies were under age, what if their parents refused to let their son talk with anyone, much less testify? There was only one way to find out. Using Ben's contact information, he'd ask.

Chapter 22

Saturday, the second of May, left two weeks and change to prepare for the trial, which was scheduled to begin the morning of Monday, May eighteenth. It was time. Charlie and Jade launched their plan to construct Ben's visual aid in one marathon session. Ben, taking Charlie's Buick with Jonathan's car seat, dropped the youngster at his best friend Alan's house for the day. Ben then proceeded to work, keeping his cell phone at the ready, lest they need details only he could provide.

Jade's apartment had the perfect workplace—a huge oak surface that had served as a dining room table for Charlie's parents, then a place for his kids' projects and games, and now used by Jade and Jonathan. In preparation, Jade had polished every trace of peanut butter and honey sandwiches from its surface.

"I'm no artist," Charlie confessed as Jade affixed a large piece of poster with artist's tape. "I bet Jonathan could do a better job than I can. He's got the gene."

"He gets that from his father. I'm guessing, with proper instruction, he'll make a fine artist. That little imp was drawing as soon as he could hold a crayon. A lot of babies prefer to gnaw them, but not him. As soon as he discovered crayon-meets-wall, the artist in him was unleashed. My mother would have let him decorate every inch of her walls he could reach, but I thought paper was a better medium."

"Ok. Where do we begin? I have the month of December onto which I've written his schedule. And I printed a word document of the days in order. I'll show you." He unfolded the calendar and the document and set them side-by-side on the table.

"Let's get started." Jade drew a series of dots along all four edges of the poster board, then connected them with faint pencil lines. Determining them to be correct, she used a metal yardstick, under which she had taped pennies to raise the edge, and then inked the pencil grid with a fine-point Sharpie. With each new line, she lifted the ruler by both ends, preventing the line from smearing while it dried. That proved tedious but worthwhile as a perfect grid emerged.

"Dates," she said, producing sheets of press-on numbers she'd found at a dollar store. "Let's put them in the upper right corner of each square. People read English left to right, so we can start writing in the upper left corner." She laughed at Charlie's skeptical expression. "You can practice on duplicator paper, using the letters we won't need. Or you can supervise the numbering so I don't screw up the order."

Charlie concentrated on his seventeen-by-eleven inch calendar mockup and they began. He was amazed how quickly she placed thirty-one dates, perfectly aligned in their respective corners. In ten minutes, they stood back, admiring their work.

"What's next?" Jade asked.

"This could be tricky. Ben's schedule is penciled on my mockup, and also typed in linear format. We should double-check every entry before committing them with ink. Otherwise, we'll have to start over, the prospect of which I don't relish."

"I suggest we pencil them lightly first. I have an art gum eraser that won't leave any *ghosts* if we make mistakes.

When we're satisfied, I'll ink them."

"It sounds too easy."

"You did all the legwork, Charlie. Hours and hours of it. We're just committing research to a visual. Let's get started." She produced a fine-point, soft graphite pencil. "This should do the trick. It makes a fine line without denting the poster board." She taped a one-foot by three-foot piece of tissue paper to the table, covering weeks three, four, and five to protect those squares from stray marks and soil. "Here we go."

"On Saturday, December first, pencil *Burger King 8 a.m. to 4 p.m.*"

"What goes under it?"

"Put *band practice with friends 5 p.m. to 11 p.m.* Put an asterisk after friends. We'll footnote the names of those who will testify. December second is different from any of the others. Put *No School In-service* at the top, then *Diving 9 to 11:30 a.m.* Put *Work Noon to 5 p.m.* beneath it. Finally, print *Piano teacher at house 7 to 9 p.m.*"

"Did you think to subpoena her too?"

"I did. She wasn't happy about it, but when Zeke explained that her testimony was only to confirm her presence in the house, who was there during those hours and nothing else, she acquiesced."

"Where was Ben during that time?"

"Doesn't matter. Tori's statement was very specific about the time of day, and the piano teacher remembers Ben and his car weren't around. She remembered about the car because she parked in his spot."

The pair continued the painstaking process. Some entries became easier, as certain days of the week repeated, especially school hours. Seeing that December third, tenth, and seventeenth were identical, they adjusted the tissue paper, being extra careful not to make smudges. Even the weekends had a rhythm. Wednesdays included school, diving and swim team practices or meets, or a youth group meetings if there was no meet. Charlie began to relax.

"Once we pencil everything in, what's next?"

"I have great markers that are brilliant and distinctive. We can ink matching entries to identify the witness who will testify. For instance, the swim team coach's hours could be brilliant blue. The diving coach's purple. Red for the principal to verify Ben's attendance during school hours and so on."

Charlie struck a statuesque pose and intoned. "Ladies and gentlemen of the jury, as you can see, Coach What's-His-Name puts Mr. Olinger in the pool here, here, here and here… and so on. As Zeke said, this will get old fast. And he'll embellish the alibi defense with testimony from the ophthalmologist and anyone else who can discredit the police and Tori's fabrication."

"Will you be testifying Charlie?"

"I will—for that snow day shortly before Christmas. Ben shoveled, and afterward sledded with Jonathan—we have dated pictures—then he went to work."

"I wish you could sneak in a hint about the polygraph test."

Charlie shook his head. "Zeke says the prosecutor would cry foul, and the judge would declare a mistrial. He might even place Zeke in contempt for *the stunt* or at least fine him. And we'd have to start all over again if the DA refiled the charges. Which he would. More limbo and expense for poor Ben. So no, he will not allow it."

Charlie and Jade were so deep in execution that they didn't hear the doorbell. "Who could that be?" Jade asked, approaching the sidelight and taking a peek.

"Hi, Mommy," Jonathan mouthed, Alan's mother already shrugging an apology with her expression. They stepped inside. Jonathan went straight to the table while Alan's mother explained her dilemma.

"Jonathan no sooner arrived than Alan threw up. He'd seemed fine at breakfast, but—Ben had already left, so I thought it best to bring Jonathan home. I left Alan at home with his dad, so I can drop Jonathan off at another friend's if you like. Or take him to a movie or to the park. I know you have a big project on deadline."

"That's so sweet of you, but we'll be fine. And please tell Alan we hope he feels better soon. These pesky viruses." Jade sighed. "Nasty school germs."

"Whacha doing?" Jonathan asked as he started to reach for the beautiful markers that, fortunately, were still sealed in their box.

Think fast. Think fast. "We're making a special graduation present for someone," Charlie ad-libbed.

"Who? Who's it for?"

"It's for Ben," Jade said in a nonchalant voice.

Silence prevailed as the child thought it over then scrunched his face, perplexed. He trotted over to the wall where the calendar hung, then looked back at the artwork. "It looks like the calendar we made for D before Christmas. But—but this is May. My teacher said so. So why…" He trailed off.

"We chose December because that's his birthday month. He turned eighteen on his last birthday. That was an extra-special December because it meant he is now an adult. A grownup. That happens just once."

"I want to help too. Can I draw some pictures on it?"

"I have an idea. How would you like to make your very own December for Ben? I'll draw the boxes, and you can create anything you want in them and around the edges. How about that?"

"Oh, boy!" Jonathan ran to his bedroom and returned momentarily with the artist's bag he'd been given at the VA. Charlie and Jade exchanged solemn glances. With the help of a child psychologist-artist, Jonathan had drawn a picture of his grandmother's death scene without his ever knowing what he had witnessed. He did not know its significance to that day. He was a prodigy, the artist had proclaimed enthusiastically.

Jade produced another poster board and quickly duplicated the squares. "Perhaps you'd be more comfortable working on the floor?" she suggested. But he'd already spread his crayons in his favorite special order, preparing to create his own present.

Jonathan tapped the first square. "What goes in here? I want to make mine just like yours. But I'll draw pictures."

"Perfect," Charlie said. "In this box with the number one, you need—oh, my—what represents Burger King?"

"I know. A French fry!"

"If we tell you what we'll be printing on this poster, you can think about what to draw? Like what looks like a school? Or Ben swimming?"

The child dug a tablet from his bag, and with his tongue clamped against his upper lip, he drew a yellow circle with interlocking blue scallops under it. "That's his head and that's the water." He grinned at his creation. Next, he drew a brown ellipsis that resembled a fuzzy caterpillar. On it he added white dots then a bright red smudge at one end. "That's a French fry with lots of salt and ketchup. Would you like to know a secret?"

"If it's a nice one and you didn't promise not to tell," Charlie said.

"That's how Ben eats broccoli and other veggies he doesn't like. He said he even puts it on baked beans."

"Sugar," Jade harrumphed.

During the next hour, while Charlie dictated and Jade penciled, their chart soon filled with Ben's December. "I still have some spots to research, particularly on the weekends, but his social life turned out easier than expected. Seems he and some guys had formed a little band and practiced in parents' garages and basements. The boys had high expectations of making some money doing a few gigs. They ran into problems with their favorite songs, however, which turned out to be copyrighted material. Applying to use one song would cost three hundred dollars just to get someone to talk with them. Since none of them writes original songs, they lost interest eventually."

"The houses where they practiced—will a parent testify to their schedule?"

"I can try. Ben says he's no longer welcome in some of the parents' homes. I just hope it isn't the ones where they practiced."

If they thought Jonathan would lose interest quickly and begin pestering for attention, they needn't have worried. His enthusiasm remained high. Charlie appreciated, all over again, the child's excellent attention span that his teacher frequently noted.

Rather than working horizontally through consecutive days, they decided to fill the identical categories as they repeated themselves. From the principal's attendance records, Jade entered school hours, verifying that, by the principal's notes, no classes were cut. During two periods the principal included the nurse's notes when Ben had been sent to her for nose bleeds and returned to class when they abated. Ben never worked before school.

Efficiently, they plotted the days and hours of Ben's work schedule, swim and diving practices and meets, the band gang, and the Saturdays Old Mr. Greer insisted he helped. Charlie himself could account for the twentieth of December, that snow day when Ben cleared everyone's driveway then accompanied all of them sledding. The house! Charlie remembered being in the Olingers' house, the trains and, most important, the lack of a Christmas tree.

"Why don't we go ahead and color what we can?" Jade suggested. "The poster is nearly complete, and the dates that we've entered aren't going to change. Right, Charlie? Each is verifiable with official records and the witnesses who will testify in court."

"Just don't color the entries we still need to verify."

Charlie rose, stretched, and swiveled his neck in opposing directions. It creaked. "If you aren't too tired…"

"I'm afraid that some great unknown will gobble up clumps of time between now and Ben's court date. Best we get as far as we can as soon as possible," Jade said.

"Right. Except for the holes. I'll work on them."

"I've been thinking," Jade started a new train of thought with a quizzical expression that always troubled Charlie. "Our poster really is a work of art, but suppose we could get an artist to duplicate it on, say, a PowerPoint presentation that could be projected on a screen in the courtroom? If Zeke had a clicker, he could make each date appear to jump forward as the witness speaks. Like a technological pointer."

Charlie shook his head. "I wouldn't know where to find such a person, and I wouldn't want to hire a stranger."

"Do you think Zeke could surface someone?" Jade asked.

"A professional would cost the earth." Glad that Jonathan was taking a bathroom break, he unloaded his fear. "If things go badly, or there is a mistrial, or unexpected expenses turn up, I must be prepared for that eventuality. Let's be frugal—let the facts tell the story."

Jade jumped to her feet, so abruptly that her chair nearly toppled backward. She snapped her fingers. "I've got it! Photography, not artwork. The guy I met in the camera shop that sells high-quality equipment. Troy—let me find his card. I've got it here somewhere. Rather than research online, I wanted to get a professional's opinion, but the shopkeeper was engaged in an unending conversation with a man that appeared to be a good friend. He didn't even look up much less tell me he'd be with me in a minute. I was making a big production of looking at my watch—tapping my fingers on his glass case when a nice-looking stranger approached me."

"He said, 'Not very helpful, is he?' I asked him, 'Do you know anything about digital cameras for kids? My son's turning seven, which is too young for a phone. He's heard so much about his father. He was a photographer who dreamed of shooting award-winning photos or working for *National Geographic*. Maybe it's in my son's genes.'

"He asked me if my ex could recommend something. I said, 'If only he could. He died before our son was born.' Not wanting to get into that, I cleared my throat in the direction of the guy behind the counter. 'I'm a photographer,' the stranger said. 'Maybe I could make some suggestions.' And he did. In the end, he offered me his card and said to call if I had any questions.

"I went to his website—gorgeous shots of animals, people, holiday cards. Maybe he could copy our poster."

"What do you suppose that would cost?"

"Don't worry—I'll cover it. Ben's been such a great friend to Jonathan and me. Thanks to my late husband's foresight, I have insurance and a trust fund, although my fellow students, who are up to their eyeballs in student debt, don't need to know that. I was impoverished for so many years, it's easy to fit in."

"Would your acquaintance need to know the purpose of our calendar?"

"Just that it would be projected in a large room. And what equipment would be needed to do so. We'd have to rent that if it's not available at the courthouse."

"We could ask Zeke. Surely he knows what's allowed, what approvals must be secured, and what AV equipment is on hand to borrow or rent cheap."

"Let's work backward. First, you ask Zeke those questions, right down to extension and power cords. Then we can coordinate with Troy, so whatever format he uses would be compatible."

"That is, if he's up to the challenge... But if he's not?" Charlie asked.

"At least we'll have the right information to tell the next person. Maybe a teacher in the school's industrial arts department could recommend a student."

"Or the community college."

"And if high tech doesn't materialize, we still have our beautiful poster and a pointer for Zeke."

As soon as Jonathan returned from his break, Jade cracked open her dazzling array of markers. Jonathan's eyes bugged. "Awesome," he sighed.

"We'll share."

☙❧☙

Charlie could hardly contain his euphoria as the day morphed into evening. They'd accomplished so much! That called for a pizza celebration, which the trio devoured in Charlie's kitchen. "Leave plenty for Ben," Jonathan instructed, dipping his head toward the half-eaten pie in box number two. "He can eat lots and lots and lots of pizza."

Jonathan chewed thoughtfully for a minute then raised his hand as he had been learning in first grade. "Where are we going to hide Ben's surprise?"

"One place he'd never look is in the drawer in my daughter's front bedroom. It's only used when her family visits from Atlanta, and they won't come until summer."

"I know! I know! I'll put my present under my bed. He'll never see it there."

"I have a box that's just the right size," Jade offered.

Jonathan jumped from his chair and ran toward the

stairs. "He could be home any minute. Quick. We gotta hide our presents." Charlie and Jade exchanged tickled smiles. Safeguarding their artwork, and thus their fabrication, hadn't crossed their minds. They could not let the child worry about Ben's precarious legal dilemma.

∽∾

Late that evening, Charlie seized another opportunity to dredge Ben's memory. Exhausted from a double shift at the restaurant, Ben savored reheated pizza and caffeine-free Coke, finally able to eat while breathing through his nose.

"Have you decided what you want to do—about your nose, that is?"

"I'm going to wait. The doc says to call at the first sign of infection, if it bleeds heavily again, or if I have concerns. She gave me a list of what to look for." He looked up, almost imploringly, at Charlie. "I cannot take on one more thing at this time. Claire says to keep my eye on the prize—graduation. She says I must pass every class with no grade lower than a C to protect my academic record should I ever want to apply to college. Besides, studying will keep my mind off the trial."

"Smart lady. Ben, speaking of ladies, do you remember a woman who lives catty-corner to your parents' house? An older woman with grown or no children who describes herself as a nosy busybody?"

Ben grinned at the description. "Oh, yeah. Her, I remember."

"She's called here twice about 'weird goings on' at your house." As succinctly as possible, Charlie described the comings and goings of the pairs of small children with a person she guessed was a social worker. "Do you remember anything like that?"

Ben shook his head as he had just committed to a huge bite. He chewed and swallowed. "I was never home when the kids were dropped off or picked up, which probably happened during school hours."

"Do you remember pairs of little kids in the house for just a few days at a time? Then another pair? And another?"

"I left for school before the little guys were awake, and they were asleep when I got home after work."

"How about a little red-headed girl, about three, with brown eyes and curls?"

"Can't say that I do. Our house was a bit of a zoo, with kids of all ages coming and going if you include family and friends. I was content to clean house, do laundry, or wash dishes after everyone was asleep and it was quiet."

"Did you ever see either of your parents abuse a little child."

"Just that one, only Mom didn't beat her or anything. But she was old school. Thought a *bare bottom spanking* was in order as a last resort. But that little girl—there was something wrong with her. Maybe she'd been a crack baby or had fetal alcohol syndrome. Or was traumatized by her past or was extremely shy. She was about four. Didn't talk much, and wet herself when she was frightened. Then Mom would land on her. I told her to knock it off. That she couldn't help it."

"And you threatened to tell?"

"Well, yeah. Once. But I just wanted to get her attention."

"Would you have? Ratted her out?"

Ben thought about that, took a sip of Coke, and wiped his mouth on a Pizza Hut napkin. "I suppose I might have. But after a while, I didn't see her anymore."

"Where do you suppose she went? That little girl?" Ben shrugged. "And do you remember her name?"

He looked up and to the right, as if searching the left side of his brain, then alerted and snapped his fingers. "Oceana. Oceana Corona. Like the sea and the sun—that's how I remembered it. An awesome name for a doomed little girl."

"And you never saw her again?"

"Nope."

"Were you suspicious that something awful might have happened to her?"

"No. I was used to the kids coming and going. I thought my folks were doing a kind, Christian thing, taking in kids that nobody wanted. That's how I got into the family. I didn't expect the kids not to be damaged in some way. Look at Izzi." He pushed back from the table and stood. "Thanks so much for saving me pizza. It was awesome, and I was so hungry."

Charlie glanced at the clock. "Past my bedtime. Stay up as late as you want. I can't hear your TV from my bedroom. And help yourself to anything in the fridge that looks good. I'll see you tomorrow."

Ben rubbed his stomach and grinned. "I'm good. Thanks again, Mr. A. I can't say it often enough."

"You have and you're welcome."

Chapter 23

Charlie knew he couldn't put it off any longer. Ben's alibi for Thursday, December nineteenth, was riding on the girl's parents verifying his presence at their home for dinner and into the evening. And the girl, Nicolette Van Dyke, was furious with Ben. Charlie considered phoning her parents' home and asking to speak with the mother, but preferred to catch her off guard. Ben mentioned that she worked part time at a consignment boutique that sold local artists' work.

He parked across the busy little town's main drag in a parking lot used by people who patronized the trendy shops. A florist, a pond landscaper, a ladies' fashion shop, a realtor, a Victorian teashop, a jeweler, a redware potter, and other tourist destinations flanked the boutique. Ben had correctly guessed the hours when Charlie might find Mrs. Van Dyke on the job. When he opened the double-glass etched door, a tiny bell jingled somewhere in the shop. Two women looked up smiling and beckoned him to enter.

A pretty brunette, who couldn't be more than her late twenties, approached him, wiping her hands on a rag. Apologetically, she motioned to the back of the shop. "I'm the owner and a painter. I was just finishing framing a watercolor. Please look around. And if you have any questions, we'll be happy to help you. All our giftware is made by local artists and is displayed with the artist's cards. You won't find anything here that's made overseas." China was not mentioned.

Bobbing his head in appreciation, Charlie dawdled his way through the shop, admiring objects d'art. By her age, the other woman had to be Mrs. Van Dyke. He took a deep, four-second breath, held it for two seconds, then slowly exhaled, making his face as placid as possible. A little white lie was in order.

"Mrs. Van Dyke?" he asked.

Caught off guard, the woman gave Charlie a winning smile that said she was happy to be remembered from—somewhere—but her memory was failing her.

"You're one of the cheerleader's moms, right? Those lovely kids do such a great job. We met at a basketball game, but with such a throng of excited students and parents, I'd be surprised if you remembered me."

"Do you have students in our school?"

"Not anymore, but I mentor young people. Your daughter—Nicolette? I hear she's the class secretary besides being a cheerleader. You must be very proud of her. When does she find time to study?"

At his last comment, Mrs. Van Dyke's smile wavered and became fixed, as if from practice. "Her father and I think she'll be a good fit for a small college that appreciates students who participate in leadership activities."

Charlie reflected on his own daughters' applications, their choices of higher institutions having tunnel vision for A's and occasional B's in advanced courses. One admissions counselor even said that extracurricular activities were a *tick mark*. Another said they dismissed them altogether.

He'd better get on with his story. "Quite a coincidence meeting you here. I was shopping for gifts for my daughters, and a young man who knows your daughter suggested I come here. Isn't Ben Olinger a friend of your daughter's?

I met him through a neighbor for whom he does handyman work and now for me too. Ben's quite the hard worker."

Mrs. Van Dyke's face fell. "Shame, all the trouble he got himself into."

"Actually, he was put into that trouble by mean-spirited people with ulterior motives. Can you keep a little secret?" He paused, until it was obvious that she was close to exploding. "I have personally read the polygraph test he passed with flying colors."

"Really! But how…"

He raised his hand to his lips, shaking his head. "Forget that I said that. His attorney would kill me if I let that slip. Besides, it's not admissible in court."

"I never did believe he would do such a thing. When could he? He was never home."

Perfect. "That's what his attorney, Zeke Geoffrey, will be telling the court. During his entire month of December, everyone says he was never at home. That he couldn't have been there when that girl…well, she lied. I had a chance to talk with him about that particular month. He mentioned how grateful he was for the meals his girl-friend's family fed him when he had so little. Was that you?"

She smiled modestly. "We did feed him a lot."

"He mentioned a particular day, the one after what we call *the big snow*. He dug my neighborhood's old folks out, even those who don't drive, in case medical personnel needed to come to their aid." Charlie punctuated that with a nod, as if underscoring the memory of Ben's kindness. "Do you remember the storm? And the evening before, which Ben told me about?"

"Why yes. As a matter of fact I do. The kids had come straight from a swim meet—Ben had set some kind of rec-ord and they were very excited—and starving. The food that young man can eat!"

"Believe me, he appreciated it. You sound quite fond of him."

"I am." She sighed. "I just wish things had worked out between them. Of course they're way too young to form life-long attachments, but…oh, well."

"Mrs. Van Dyke—about that evening after the swim meet. It was, I believe, December nineteenth. Would you be willing to tell Ben's attorney that he was at your house that evening? Not that he really needs to know, but just in case his whereabouts are questioned."

"Why—yes. I'd be happy to do that."

Charlie smiled. "Thank you. Now—about the reason I came. I'd be so happy if you'd help me choose gifts for my daughters. Their birthdays fall in May, which is sneaking up on me. One is a teacher, the other a scientist. And your daughter is such a lovely girl. I bet you know exactly what would appeal to young ladies." He ambled after her, inspecting many beautiful things, ultimately making two pricy selections, even though one's birthday wasn't until September and the other in January. He'd send them now anyway, just because. He practically danced from the store.

That evening Jade gleefully entered the evening of December nineteenth on Ben's calendar while Charlie emailed the particulars to Zeke, urging him to be extra solicitous to this lovely alibi mother. The only remaining date that needed embellishing was Saturday the twenty-first—diving practice from nine-thirty to eleven-thirty, followed by Burger King until five p.m., which morphed into a party for the staff. With all his activities, adults and friends, the calendar looked ready for finishing touches.

 share

That blasted phone. He unleashed a barrage of

expletives in its direction, which he'd learned in the army and had erased from his vocabulary, having lived for decades in a petticoat world with Emma and their lovely daughters.

Tentatively. "Hello?"

The woman's harsh voice prompted Charlie's hand involuntarily to jerk the handset away from his ear. "If you think my daughter, Magda, is going to help that child molester beat the rap, you're out of your mind."

"Please. Back up. What brought this on? I thought you and your daughter understood…"

"You weren't honest with me. I found out that you're using my daughter to fabricate a lie about that dear little Tori."

"Magda will merely testify as to who was in the house while she was teaching piano lessons. Period. That's it."

"Not according to Mrs. Olinger. She says that if Magda testifies, the prosecutor will file charges against my daughter as a co-conspirator. That she's covering up for something she's doing too. She's just starting out teaching piano. This could ruin her reputation to say nothing of getting into a good music college and being unable to teach little kids."

"Ma'am, according to Ben's attorney, Ezekiel Geoffrey, the prosecutor can only cross-examine on the questions that Magda has been asked. Such as, 'Was Benjamin Olinger in the house between the hours of seven to nine p.m. on Monday, November ninth? Was Benjamin's car parked at the house? Why were you there? And when did you leave? Did you see Ben at any time while you were there?' Period. Or words to that effect."

"Well, she said…"

"I'd be careful about discussing the case with Mrs. Olinger because you might be asked at some point if she tried to influence your daughter through you. Both she and you could be accused of witness tampering, which is a fel-ony. I suggest you address your concerns to Attorney Geoffrey. I'll give you his contact information."

"Well…I don't like this, one little bit."

"None of us do. It's a prime example of what can hap-pen when one little lie grows exponentially to cover up a big one. The stakes are huge—the life of an innocent young man whose life full of promise has been compro-mised through no fault of his own."

"What makes you so sure?"

"My instincts, at first. From the time we met, I found him to be honest. But after the case broke, I checked and rechecked every statement he's made. He never lies, even when a bit of fabrication, embroidery, or an exaggeration would benefit his cause. And Mrs. Olinger never tells the truth."

"Is it true about the lie detector test? Mrs. Olinger said that he flunked it."

"My point exactly about Mrs. Olinger. Quite the oppo-site. I read it myself. He passed on every point."

"Then why would she say that?"

"I can't answer that. I wrote Mrs. Olinger a letter telling her about the test, and how I sympathized with a parent having to take the word of one child over another. And I invited her to get in touch with me about it."

"And did she?"

"Nope. I was testing her to see if she already knew, or suspected who was lying."

"Well…I don't know."

"Please. Talk to Ben's attorney. He'll be reviewing Magda's testimony with her before the trial. You both need to be comfortable with him."

"And that dear little girl? Tori?"

"She'll have to live with what she's done, regardless of the outcome."

As smoothly as possible, Charlie ended the conversation. Oh, boy! What next? He went to his computer and relayed the conversation as faithfully as possible to Ben's attorney. He prayed that he'd been convincing and blessed his decision, all over again, to take Ben to the Snyder Bureau of Investigations for that lie detector test. It crossed his mind that it wasn't the test itself that convinced people of Ben's innocence, even without reading it themselves. It was Charlie's passion and unwavering faith in Ben.

໑๑໑

Before ten the next morning, Roxie alerted that fun was afoot. Having wriggled through the doggie door and taken the steps two at a time, she balanced on her hind legs at Charlie's angle-bay window. She was testing, he knew, because with one agile leap she could be on the window seat cushion. He wondered what she did when he was away, but neither was pushing the issue. Still, he had moved Emma's prized figurines to a curio cabinet and installed the cushion, which had been Jonathan's idea. He liked to sit there and read the books the elementary librarian recommended. Charlie was thrilled—always an avid reader, he knew this caring teacher had opened a whole world to a gifted child. Perhaps he should send the figurines to his girls now, knowing they loved their mother's treasures. Maybe it was time to let go.

Roxie heard it long before he did in spite of Charlie's excellent hearing. The dog went nuts, hopping and spinning at the front door, then running to the garage door to be let out. The black and white streak skidded to a stop by the mailbox, stopping inches short of the street. Roxie was waiting, tail wagging her entire body, as the mail carrier shoved the mail into the box, murmuring *there's my good girl* and slipping Roxie a treat. Charlie waved and extracted a plain five-by-eight brown envelope from a huddle of magazines, bills, and junk mail. His name and address were scrawled with smeared black marker. Curious, he tucked the other mail under his arm and opened his mystery mail on the spot.

Neat columns, ruled horizontally on duplicator paper, contained the promised records from the Olingers' nosey neighbor. It didn't take Charlie more than a quick skim to digest the pattern of the little kids' comings and goings in columns by date, time, the children's descriptions and their length of stay at the Olingers' house. The far right column included the key to her observations.

Charlie looked at his watch and compared it to the time and dates when the children were being exchanged. If the pattern repeated itself, at one o'clock today another exchange would be made. He knew he couldn't resist the challenge, but he needed a different car. If he hung around their neighborhood, someone could run his plates, even if he managed to park for just a few minutes. Jade was at home, studying for finals. Perhaps she'd lend him her Civic.

Of course she would, he thought, as he approached the stairway and rang her bell. She opened it before he could knock. Giving her an abbreviated summary of his need, he accepted her keys.

"What's the plan?" she asked.

"I'll figure that out when I get there."

"Registration and insurance are in the glove box. Don't wreck it." They started to go separate ways. "Oh, Charlie? Your keys?" He tossed them to her, glad he had installed a car seat for Jonathan. "I'm not planning to go anywhere, but with kids, you never know."

"Don't wreck it," he said, doubting the old Buick had any bluebook value. No way he was taking the vintage Corvette, which would draw way too much attention.

❧❧❧

At precisely twelve fifty-five, Charlie eased down the Olingers' street. The lovely suburban neighborhood of split-level homes, built in the seventies on quarter-acre lots, was beautifully maintained. Designed with one-car garages at a time that preceded the present-day custom of a car for every licensed driver, the otherwise wide street was narrowed by a continuous ribbon of parallel-parked cars. The Olingers' home was easily distinguishable. A remnant of lawn, scraped to dirt, was littered with children's toys and bikes. A rusting pick-up truck sat on blocks beside the garage, and a picture window displayed kids art projects snipped from colored construction paper.

He circled the block and finding a spot on the opposite side two houses away, he sat, hoping for action. A brilliant sun befitted his disguise: oversized sunglasses, a ball cap pulled low, and a nondescript denim shirt. He'd thrown an old army blanket over Jonathan's car seat—no point in having descriptors—and he'd added strategically positioned mud splatters to a couple numbers on the plate, making a seven look like a one, and an eight look like a three. He'd refrained from drinking anything after making his decision to spy, following Jade's oft-time instruction to Jonathan to *empty his tank* just before leaving.

He waited. And watched. This was insane. He turned on his new iPhone, a Christmas gift from his girls, and tapped the camera icon. Mentally, he reviewed the instructions for zooming an image.

Suddenly a car swooped from nowhere and double-parked in front of the Olingers' house. Charlie held his breath and watched. A somber-looking woman who looked vaguely familiar exited the driver's side, circled the rear of the car, and opened the trunk from which she extracted two small battered suitcases. Switching both handles to her left hand, she slammed the lid and circled to the right rear passenger door. She yanked it open, reached in, and fumbled with…seat belts? She beckoned to someone with a jerk of her head, and a pair of young boys tumbled from the back seat. Younger than Jonathan…three maybe four?

The trio angled across the yard to the house, the social worker managing the suitcases which, by the swing of her arm, must be quite light. The children, dressed in clean but shabby clothes, clutched a pile of folded clothes and well-loved stuffed animals. One toy had matted fur that must have been brown years ago. A monkey?

Approaching the listing front stoop, the woman pressed the doorbell and knocked impatiently when nobody appeared instantaneously. As the door swung wide, Charlie started his engine and eased his car forward until he could see directly into the hall that bisected the house. The social worker, hand on one child's shoulder, urged him toward a couple who loomed at the far end of the hall, side by side. That would be the Olingers.

They did not approach the children. Just stood there. They exchanged what looked like papers. Whoever opened the door had vanished. Woman and children halted, as if frozen, eight feet from the couple. Charlie couldn't see the kids' faces, but couldn't miss that the smaller one's head was buried in his toy's fur. Charlie wiped an errant tear from his own face, feeling the child's sadness.

While apparent negotiations were ongoing within the house, Charlie studied Ms. Nosey's chart and scanned until he found a description that fit these two little children. Huh! If the neighbor's observations were correct, the social worker should be emerging with—and there they were! Two children, a bit older than the newcomers, carrying their own little suitcases. With prodding, they approached the woman's car.

Charlie cracked his front passenger-side window, hoping to hear something useful.

"I do myself!" a child's voice wailed across the distance.

The woman, nevertheless, reached into the depths of the back seat, probably testing the seatbelt.

"Gimme those!" she barked at the children, leveraging their bags with what looked to Charlie like significant resistance. Having won the tug of war, she slammed the rear car door, stomped to the trunk, and popped it to throw in the bags. Behind the wheel, she revved the engine unnecessarily for a late-model car and glided down the street.

Chapter 24

Oh, why not? Traffic was brisk, and having read enough crime novels, Charlie knew to keep two car-lengths' distance behind the getaway car. *Stay green, stay green, stay green,* he willed the lights at each intersection. Fortunately, they did as he asked, having been timed for the heaviest traffic, which seemed to include traffic from his direction. Shortly the woman exited, taking the bypass that routed traffic across town or across Pennsylvania whichever was her intent.

Thirty minutes later, she exited toward the east side of the city, looped several housing developments, and ultimately slowed at a subdivision of modest ranchers. Charlie glided past her, picking up speed as if he knew where he was going. The streets were laid out in square blocks. He made three right turns. A huge blue spruce, planted on the corner perpendicular to the street in question, enabled a good view of the woman's movements while hiding most of the Civic.

It didn't take long to complete the transaction. Charlie captured a shot of the kids entering the house, which he'd missed at the Olingers' house, and the next pair who were swapping places with them. As they got into her car, Charlie zoomed to focus on their faces. The woman settling the kids gave Charlie a moment to study Ms. Nosey's description of the kids that the woman had just picked up. He penciled a checkmark beside both pairs and entered the time.

And off they went, back to the highway and south on an expressway to an exit just north of the turnpike. Again, they looped through housing developments. Something odd occurred to Charlie. If these kids had stayed at these homes before, why wasn't anyone greeting them at the door? At least going through the motions of acting glad to see them and making them welcome? The social worker never stayed more than a few minutes. This was hasty work.

For his own protection, he hung back farther and farther and yet stayed close enough to observe the transaction and snap photos. By the time twelve kids had been rotated through six different homes, he was exhausted and ready to quit. Ms. Nosey's list was complete. But Charlie could not help himself. He had to capture the social worker's identity.

He noted her car's details and photographed the license, something that Ms. Nosey had been unable to provide. He waited until she was well out of sight then guessed where she might be headed. Possibly back up the interstate, away from the turnpike, but he couldn't risk being observed, even though Jade's gray Honda blended with the asphalt. He hung back too long and thus lost her.

As he entered the city, he followed a hunch, exiting in the direction of the orphanage. He circled the block, searching for its employee lot. And there was her car! What on earth? He paused momentarily, but the woman was nowhere in sight. Back at home, he Googled the home's website, where Mr. Watkins's picture smiled. But it would have been too easy to find the social worker's picture among the employees.

After checking emails, he clicked *Photos* and discovered, wonder of wonders, that his marvelous new iPhone had added the kids' shots to his computer as well. Hallelujah! One less thing to figure out how to do. Double clicking, his first shot displayed full-screen with little arrows to view its neighbors. He was thrilled at the quality that he, a fumble-fingered, shaky-handed grandfather, could capture such beautiful pictures.

He opened and saved a new Word document and set up a horizontal table that duplicated Ms. Nosey's columns. After entering her data in sequential squares, he added his own observations beside hers.

Here was absolute proof of the Olingers' duplicity in something related to Ben's case. If he had objected to how they treated little Oceana, he had to go, lest he have also observed the larger part of the entire operation. Sooner or later, something would have clicked in Ben's mind, or he might have been home, nursing a migraine, when the transaction occurred. Perhaps met the social worker and asked too many questions. And being both smart and honest, he would have felt compelled to say something to someone.

Charlie sent three emails to Zeke. In the first he explained his body of evidence and attached the chart. Fearing how much memory photos might take, he divided them between two additional emails. As an afterthought, he shot a photo of Ms. Nosey's handwritten chart and sent that as well.

❧❦❧

Ever since Ben had spooled the story of his family's betrayal, their motive had haunted Charlie. Now he got it. Ben was an innocent witness. Now the little girl, Oceana, preyed on his mind, whispering to his subconscious that she was a link. That Ben's threat to call Children's Protective Services on her behalf shouldn't have motivated such overkill. All his mother had to do was be nice to the little girl while faking compassionate care. Charlie's mind was filled with what-ifs.

By the time Ben returned from work, Charlie had sent his emails to Zeke and was lying in wait for the young man. "Ben—it's important. Will you please look at the photos of these little kids and tell me if you recognize any of them from your parents' house?"

Ben dropped his gym bag, shed his jacket, and took Charlie's offered task chair. He studied each shot carefully, shook his head no, and then clicked the forward arrow for the slide show to continue. By the time he finished the photo array, he had nothing to report.

"I'm sorry, Mr. A. I don't recognize any of these kids. Like I said before, they came and went while I was at school, or they were asleep."

"How about Oceana. Is she among these kids?"

"No. And I would have recognized her. For all her developmental delays, she was a sweet little kid and so easy to please. In the summer, when I worked two jobs and came home to change clothes, she'd be waiting for me. I'd bring her a little stuffed toy—the ones you pick up for a few bucks at a convenience store—and she'd be delighted. Hugged it and cradled it like it was her baby, then hugged me and thanked me. I was ashamed how little it took to make her happy when I had so much."

"When was this, and when did you last see her?"

Ben thought for a moment. "It was the summer I was seventeen. Between my junior and senior years. She was still there on Halloween. I remember how terrified she was of the ghosts and goblins. Mom insisted I take care of her while the neighborhood kids were trick-or-treating. I dragged a rocker into the kitchen and read her stories until she fell asleep."

"How long after that did she leave?"

"I don't remember exactly, but she wasn't there around

Christmas. I bought her a fuzzy white sweater I thought that she'd love. She always stroked soft things while sucking her thumb when she was anxious, and Mom wouldn't let her have her blanket. I don't know what happened to her gift."

"Was that when you threatened your mother?"

"That happened right before my birthday. She started having accidents, and Mom was furious. When I realized Oceana was gone, I hoped Children's Services had located some family or loving people to adopt her. Helping her develop her full potential. She deserved nothing less."

"Do you have a picture of her?"

"When they kicked me out, they kept my camera. I had boxes of prints, but when the constable took me to retrieve my stuff, the boxes were gone. So, no. I don't have any snapshots."

"What about your friends? Did they take pictures when you guys were hanging out at your house? Might she have been in the background?"

"I don't know, but I could ask them."

"Please do. Ask them to email attach them to me. Ask them to include any shots that include little kids in your house, even if the quality is poor."

"Sure. I'll do it right away. But—why? What are you thinking?"

"Something's eating at me—the motive for your parents' over reaction. I feel like it's right there in front of me, and I can't grasp it. Do you have anything that might have Oceana's DNA?"

Ben got a sheepish look on his face. "She had a ratty baby blanket that she couldn't go to sleep without. Mom berated her about it. Had her in tears. She asked me to hide it for her and sneak it to her if she really needed it. When I unpacked the stuff from my house, it was among my clothes."

"Did you keep it? If so, can I borrow it for a while?"

"I guess, but don't lose it. In case she comes back." Ben hung his head. "I know that she won't, but I pray that she's happy somewhere and having a good life."

"Do you have anything else she might have touched— like one of those small stuffed animals?"

"Afraid not."

"Okay. Let's see if your friends' pictures captured her face in the background."

☙❧☙

Charlie stretched out in bed, trying to remember the relaxation exercises he and Emma had attempted to relieve her pain with while waiting for the morphine dose to kick in. Part of her discomfort, she insisted, was caused by the tension with which she braced herself. It wasn't unlike the space between labor pains, only this pain would produce nothing good.

It was no use. Grabbing two extra pillows to position his back, he slid the book he'd been reading from the end table onto his lap. In reading James D. Robertson's *For Good Reason*, he realized, in spite of being wounded, how extraordinarily lucky he had been to escape the Vietnam War in a matter of weeks, never to return. Through Robertson's fiction-based-on-fact novel, he was transported back to Southeast Asia and remembered the stifling heat, humidity, and the smell of rotting vegetation and dead fish. Try as he might, he couldn't remember hearing any birds. Perhaps they'd all fled the death and destruction or been eaten by hungry Vietnamese.

The blare of the landline startled him back to the present. He looked at the clock, which illuminated exactly ten p.m. It wouldn't be Ben—they had just spoken a half hour ago, and he'd FaceTimed with his girls and their families around six. When did telemarketers become so bold? Still, it might be important. He slid from the four-poster bed and paddled down the hall to the kitchen. If he had half a brain he'd install an extension, but then it might scare him to death in the night. Maybe a soundless extension?

A local caller ID looked familiar—one that he'd jotted within recent days but couldn't recall. "Hello?"

"Who the hell do you think you are, bothering my wife at work! She may be gullible, but I sure as hell ain't."

Mr. Van Dyke. Had to be.

"Guess who showed up on my doorstep—a process server! My wife has been subpoenaed to testify at the Olinger trial. Well guess what—that ain't gonna happen. Get this through your head, Alderfer. My wife misspoke. Got her dates mixed up. And I'm going to testify that Benjamin Olinger was nowhere near my home on December nineteenth. I picked up my little girl right after that swim meet and drove her home. We had a quiet dinner. Alone!"

"You'd lie about that? On the stand? Do you know the penalty for perjury?"

"And you're going to prove it, how? My family, including our daughter, doesn't want anything to do with that child molester, especially after the way he treated her. Strung her along then refused to take her to the prom."

"Oh. So the three of you are going to punish him because of something as silly as a prom invitation? You know what this sounds like? The story that girl Izzi told because he refused to have sex with her. Is that where Nicolette got the idea? From that bitch bragging about it at school? I read that polygraph report myself," Charlie shouted over Van Dyke's blustering. "He's innocent. I raised two beautiful, honest daughters, so I can tell you as an experienced parent. If you love your daughter, you'd get a handle on her behavior. And those drinking parties she frequents where parents are supposed to be home? Ask around, Mr. Van Dyke. Clean up your own mess before you start lying and accusing others. I'll see Mrs. Van Dyke in court."

He banged down the receiver, although he doubted that today's technology would carry the *bang!* He counted ten deep breaths, remembering to exhale at the correct intervals. Now what were they going to do about December nineteenth? He'd been at the meet. Saw Ben's magnificent dive. But he and Mr. Greer had departed without even saying goodbye or having the opportunity to ask where or with whom he'd be celebrating that evening.

Chapter 25

Good news!" Jade chirped. "I called the photographer, Troy Rauenzahn, and he's agreed to take a look at our project. I told him I'd seen his website, and that I'd pay his hourly fee, portal to portal, and whatever the work costs. But I warned him that I had no idea what was involved. It might even require retyping thirty-one blocks of multi-line copy into a document that could be projected in a large room. He seemed unperturbed."

"When can he come?"

"Actually, today. Monday is his day off, and he could come around eleven. I'll be here. Jonathan's at school, and I hoped you'd be available too, Charlie."

"That I am. Let's see what we're getting ourselves into. At the very least, we have the original artwork as backup. Your place or mine?"

"Let's have him come to your front door, then just bring him downstairs. I'll have everything laid out."

At eleven sharp, Roxie balanced at the bay window, barked her fool head off. "Enough," Charlie barked back, and the little dog dropped to her belly, giving him a baleful look. "Stay!" She did. Charlie followed Jade to his front door. The young man who entered could have passed for any professional—a banker, professor, realtor, or business owner. Tall and lean with wide-set blue eyes, close-cropped hair, and a winning smile, he beamed a greeting.

"Charlie, this is Troy Rauenzahn, the photographer

who rescued me at the camera shop. He's the owner of Roughtooth Photography. He might be able to help us." Dressed in smart business casual, he looked nothing like Charlie's daughters' wedding photographers, one of whom had arrived in a tux and the other in a Hawaiian shirt, cargo pants, and sandals. From his website, however, they'd learned that Troy did not do weddings. Examples of his work ranged from precious pets to special family moments to an array of marketing possibilities.

"We'll be working downstairs in Jade's apartment," Charlie said, turning to lead the way.

"Give me a minute to grab my equipment, and I'll follow along." Shortly he returned with leather bags of various sizes. "From Jade's description of the project, I brought what I guessed we might need."

They descended the stairs, entering Jade's great room that occupied the width and the core of the seventy-foot wide by twenty-five foot deep apartment. "Great light," Troy said, of the floor-to-ceiling windows that faced the backyard gardens.

"Here's the project," Charlie kicked off their need for a professional presentation. He pointed to the calendar, nearly completed, that lay on the large oak table. "We need to duplicate this calendar and project it onto a screen to be seen by two dozen people in a cavernous space. We have a couple more entries to verify, but we're hoping to have it completed shortly."

"When is your deadline?"

"We need it Monday, May eighteenth, so let's say Friday the fifteenth?"

Troy shook his head. "In the first place, I never trust anyone with my real deadlines. You've got to pad it a little. Stuff happens."

"Oh. Okay. Perhaps you could tell us what's involved and how long it will take."

"Are you familiar with PowerPoint presentations?"

"I am," Jade said. "I have MS Office on my MacBook Pro. I've never had to use PowerPoint, but I've seen presentations many times. The software is loaded on my Mac."

"Great. I can shoot it and download the image into a PowerPoint file. Your Mac, Jade, can be linked to a digital projector to show the calendar on a screen. I'd suggest designing it so that each day in December is a separate document that could be selected individually and enlarged to fill the entire screen."

"That would be fantastic," Charlie said, even though it was over his head.

"You mean you don't have to retype the whole calendar?" Jade asked.

"Nope. We'll take pictures. Technology's grand…"

"When it works!" Jade quipped.

The trio grinned.

"To shoot this, why don't we set your December on the floor away from the windows, I'll set up my lights, adjust yours, and see what we get."

"Then you'll do it?"

"Be happy to."

Charlie thought Troy would snap-snap-snap and the work would be done. Instead, he took his time adjusting lights and a white umbrella, then taking light readings with a small hand-held device. You'd think he was shooting the Mona Lisa, not their homemade exhibit. As if hoping no one would notice, Roxie sneaked along the front windows and edged closer to the action.

"Hey, girl." Troy stopped what he was doing and knelt, extending his hand, palm down, for Roxie to sniff. In a flash, she was licking his face.

"Roxie! Enough! Come here! I'm sorry, Troy. She thinks she's still a puppy," Jade said.

"As she should. And an adorable one. May she have a little treat?" he asked, slipping his hand into the pocket of his blazer.

"You'll never get rid of her. Why don't I put her in my bedroom?"

"She's fine. She can stay. Let's proceed." He resumed working, shooting and reviewing, until he seemed satisfied.

"Um—Troy? About the content of the calendar. It's, um, sensitive material."

Troy raised his right hand. "Eagle Scout's honor. I'll share your documents with no one. Now—one more thing. You said you had additional data to add? That's no big deal, even if I have to reshoot it. Knowing exactly what's involved, it will be a piece of cake. In fact, I can type it into the document with a font that looks like your printing which, by the way, is pretty impressive."

He began packing his equipment.

"It's noon. Can we offer you a bite of lunch? I have sandwich fixings upstairs, and I baked brownies for our little guy's after-school treat. He'll never miss a few."

"Thank you, Charlie, but I have a midafternoon obligation for which I must prepare. Why don't I stop by, same time next week, to review my work? That leaves lots of wiggle room to finish your research."

⌘

The minute Troy's SUV eased down the street, Jade and Charlie high-fived in delight. "Whew!" Jade exclaimed. "He made it so easy. This alibi defense will blow the prosecution out of the courtroom."

"I'd better bring Zeke up to speed."

"And ask him to join us next Monday to view the

presentation. If he can't, maybe Troy could accommodate us at a different time."

"I bet Zeke's secretary knows all about PowerPoint presentations. I can't believe they haven't used it. They probably have the digital projector Troy mentioned or know where to get one. And the screen and extension cords. They've gotta use equipment in the courtroom from time to time."

"All the same—I want to take our artwork, an easel, and a pointer to court, just in case the computer fails us. Maybe a laser-pointer with the red dot."

"Oh! And ask Zeke who should operate the remote. Could one of us assist him?"

"Not me," Charlie said. "I'm a witness, so I'm not permitted to hear others' testimony. But oh! How I'll love being in that courtroom to watch it unfold."

"Maybe Troy could be on Team Ben for the trial. Just a thought."

"Speaking of Troy, how did the search for Jonathan's birthday present turn out? We could be mid-trial on May twenty-fifth."

"I was thinking we'd celebrate Saturday or Sunday—take him somewhere fun. Include a few of his friends." She sighed. "About his present. I'm sure he'll be delighted with the camera I chose, but do you know what he really wants? Pictures of his father, specifically when he was Jonathan's age. He must think there's an album somewhere, but I don't have anything. His folks gave me squat."

"Might your father-in-law have photos to lend and duplicate? Remember, he stopped by, saying he had memorabilia Jonathan should have—someday. I thought at the time he meant for you to safeguard until he was older. He seemed downright contrite. Even telling me about the divorce in progress. I have his contact information, although getting in touch could unleash a host of unsavory problems for you."

"He was never unkind to me. Just trotted dutifully behind her the few times I saw him. What's your read?"

"That he is desperately sorry for how things turned out. He didn't try to wrangle an audience with Jonathan, but rather wanted to give you his personal collection of keepsakes. I don't think it would hurt to meet him somewhere neutral if he promises he'll come alone. I can ask my priest if our church's little conference room could be made available."

"That would be nice, but it's such short notice. You know, Charlie, we're coming full circle—my neglecting my little boy and you finding solutions."

"Ha!" Charlie couldn't stop his reaction. "You are the best mother, and that little guy lacks for nothing. You have weeks to plan his party, which is nothing compared to having your invalid mother being murdered, your father charged with the crime, being broke, and thinking your deceased husband had run out on you, not even knowing you were pregnant. And through it all, you prevailed. If being a bad mother is your favorite miserable feeling, stop! It's time to quit obsessing and let it go, you hear me?"

Jade wiped a tear from her cheek. "I hear you. Now, if you please, give me his contact information. If he agrees to see me, and if everything he says has a ring of truth, then maybe I can get that picture Jonathan wants. I do have time to frame it."

"I'll get his card."

"Charlie? Will you come with me?"

He took a deep breath, considering. "I suppose I could be there when he arrives to make introductions. Break the ice. But you should speak with him alone."

⟨⟩⟨⟩

Jade pulled into the church's parking lot with Charlie riding shotgun. At the far end, the teachers' cars were aligned like pigs at a trough. A mother held hands with a preschooler who appeared to be chattering nonstop, punctuating her monologue with wavy hand motions. A few other cars were scattered in the church's main lot, which gave them hope that they might be alone.

As the newly recruited chair of the property committee, Charlie had a fob, which *thwacked* the security lock on the main door. Inside, the narthex fronted the entire sanctuary's half theater-in-the round, which was separated from the narthex by a series of glass doors. Upholstered couches and chairs formed conversation groups beyond the entry's double doors. Charlie and Jade chose a couch that faced the expansive windows with a clear view of the parking lot.

"I'm glad you decided to meet with him," Charlie said although somewhat conflicted. The reunion could go either way, and Jade had nearly a decade for her anger to fester.

"It's for Jonathan, not me. Now that he's getting older, he needs to know more about his father. He's asking questions that I cannot answer or have forgotten. My husband was a fine, talented, happy man. I'd love for Jonathan to hear that from someone besides me. When I made the appointment on the phone, Mr. Kepley sounded so earnest and determined to do something special for his grandson."

Charlie leapt to his feet when a vintage Cadillac pulled into the lot. "I'll need to let him in," he said, referencing the blinking light on the security system. The elder Kepley carried a cardboard box under one arm. From his halting movements, it appeared to be heavy. Between the doubleglass doors, Charlie greeted him and shook his free hand.

"Nice to see you again. Come in."

Jade eased from the couch and approached her former father-in-law. With the slightest repositioning of his head, Kepley bent to give her cheek a fatherly peck. "You're as pretty as ever," he said of the petite mother of his grand-son.

"Well, let me show you two around a bit," Charlie said to deflect the tension. "The sanctuary is beyond those in-terior glass doors—that's our organist practicing. Re-strooms are off to the left, and our offices are around the corner to the right. I thought you'd find our little confer-ence room, straight ahead and to the right, perfect for your meeting. Here—I'll let you in."

Charlie knew it wouldn't be locked, but went through the motions to break the ice. "We especially like the glass windows. The room is soundproof—inside people can hear the service, like a *cry room*, but noise doesn't travel outside. Can I get you anything? We have bottled water in the fridge, and there's usually coffee in the other wing."

Both declined.

"Okay, then. I'll be around back, checking my mail and other projects that need my attention. Take as long as you wish. I have nothing else planned for this afternoon."

"You're welcome to stay," Kepley said.

"Thanks, but that would change your conversation. I'll make myself scarce." Winking at Jade, he left the little room, closing the door behind him.

Charlie killed half an hour, digesting the minutia in the property committee's mailbox. A drywall seam behind the altar had split. The fire inspector was concerned about car-tons in a back hallway. There was way too much humidity in the choir room, causing the sheet music to curl. A per-sonal thank-you note from a widow for preparing the col-umbarium spot for her husband's ashes. He smiled, reflecting on his own gratitude for those who ministered to him when Emma passed.

Finally, he fabricated an excuse to knock on the conference room door. "How are you doing? Need anything?" Both were beaming. Jade motioned him into the room. Dozens of photos and newspaper clippings covered the large maple table. "Wait till you see this. There are photos of Jonathan's father taken when he was seven. They look identical!"

Kepley reached across the table, giving Jade's fingers a brief squeeze. "I should have kept in touch. Now I can't even remember what I was afraid of. But enough of that."

❧

Jade and Charlie returned home with time to spare before Jonathan's return from school. Jade clutched a bulging manila envelope to her chest, chattering about which pictures to enlarge and how to frame them.

"I invited him to join us for Jonathan's birthday party, but he has declined, feeling that would be disruptive. He wants me to explain—things—to Jonathan before they meet face to face. I don't know where to start."

"You might begin by asking what he's overheard."

❧

A series of *pings!* signaled that Charlie had incoming email. As he opened one after another, he found messages from Ben's band buddies. Each contained a series of attachments. Eagerly he opened them. Photos of varying quality showed the band members in various goofy poses. Clicking several arrows, he was treated to awful renditions of Bob Dylan's *Heaven's Door*. He saved each photo, then opened and zoomed in hopes of finding a child in the background.

Steve, the fourth buddy who would testify at Ben's trial, sent the best batch of photos. There must have been twenty, including the young man's promise to send more if these didn't yield what was needed. When none did, Charlie emailed his thanks and asked for any others that showed a little girl, about four years old.

Bing! A second batch arrived, one capturing a sweet little face, framed with lanky blonde hair and clutching what looked like a worn baby blanket. Charlie saved it to Photos, opened it, and clicked the edit function. He cropped it to include just the child, chose every edit option available, and then saved it to his Ben file. From there he could email attach it to whomever seemed appropriate, especially Ben, who was at work. In a matter of minutes, he responded. "Bingo! That's Oceana."

Thrilled, he phoned Brownie, Zeke's private detective. "Could I hire you for a personal project? I need to satisfy my curiosity—something I can't quit thinking about. It's connected to the Ben tangentially, but not to the criminal case. My gut tells me it involves a missing person's case. A little girl that somehow ended up at the Olingers'. I have her picture and her security blanket, which might contain her DNA. Do you have any connections to data bases of missing or exploited children that could be cross referenced?"

Brownie laughed. "You just can't leave well enough alone, can you! All right. Let me have what you've got, and I'll see what I can find out. Any idea what it's about?"

"She just doesn't fit the other foster children's circumstances. Ben thought she was slow, but it's possible she doesn't speak much English. I wish I had more, like her toothbrush. She's known by the name Oceana Corona—

like the sea and the sun. That might mean something, or nothing at all."

"Her 'blankie' might be enough for DNA. How long since she went missing?"

"Sometime between Halloween and Christmas, last year. I suppose that's too recent to match skeletal remains. Maybe there's a Jane Doe that fits. I just hope she's okay."

"I'll call in some favors. If she's a missing celebrity's kid, I'll split the reward with you as my fee."

"Find her, and it's all yours."

Chapter 26

Jonathan was delighted to help Jade push chairs into a semi-circular theater, their backs to the windows. Shortly after they finished, he raced outside to catch the school bus. Relieved to be spared dozens of questions, Jade concentrated on setting the stage. Charlie returned with Roxie, assuring Jade that Jonathan had waved as the bus rolled away. He'd made it in spite of the last-minute dash. Jade's living room was infinitely smaller than a courtroom, but the distance between the projector and the screen would be similar. They could fine-tune the setup on site.

She set a card table twelve feet from the wall, from which she had removed a collection of artwork. "For once I'm glad we didn't paint it a dark, designer color, like all the magazines depict so beautifully. In the end, I'd have created a cave, since this entire wall is underground."

"Maybe I should invest in special lighting," Charlie mused. "We can make a field trip to that lighting emporium. Maybe Jonathan would like to pick fixtures for his walls. His room really is a cave." He paused. "Ah! There's my doorbell."

Charlie hurried upstairs with Roxie preceding him.

"What should we do with her?" Jade called after him.

"She can stay. Troy seemed quite taken with her."

"I was thinking I'd hire Troy to do family shots of us before Christmas, including Roxie. You and Ben too."

Charlie felt his shoulders sag from the weight of potential disaster. What a difference next December could make—Ben post-graduation, exonerated, launching his life, or locked away in prison. What if…

Two cars converged on his driveway simultaneously—Zeke, his secretary, and Brownie, driving his handicap-accessible van in the lead followed by Troy in his SUV. As they met in the driveway, they seemed to be negotiating with the lady about who would carry a piece of equipment. When it came to being a gentlemen, some things never changed. Brownie wheeled the sloping walkway to Jade's front door, the group converging at the lower level.

Welcoming them inside, and with introductions accomplished, Charlie unveiled Jade's makeshift studio. "Perfect," Troy proclaimed, after considering the possibilities. With minor adjustments to the chairs and the table, he set about rigging extension cords. "Did the PowerPoint presentation and individual documents come through all right on your Mac?" he asked Jade.

"They're great! Nice and sharp. Now, if anyone knows how to connect my Mac to a digital projector…?"

"That would be me," Zeke's secretary said. With quick nimble fingers, she married the equipment. "Troy, would you take Zeke and me through the nuances of navigating the days for best advantage?"

"Sure. Somebody dim the lights." He stepped toward the table, retrieved the remote, then did a quick demonstration. "If you like, I can be in court, just in case it malfunctions."

"That would be great."

Suddenly Roxie jumped to attention and dashed toward the open stairway door.

"Jonathan!" Jade lamented. "I'd forgotten—early dismissal today. I knew I'd be home, so I neglected to make a play date for him. Zeke, how do you want me to handle this?"

"Can he stay?" Charlie asked. "He's been with us throughout the design process. However, we must be careful what we say about Ben's case since he thinks December is a graduation present. We can't talk about the trial. He can have a snack in the kitchen and watch from the pass-through."

Charlie couldn't help smiling as Jonathan offered his hand to shake those of his fellow grown-ups. He wolfed his snack and a glass of milk then claimed a stool in their midst. As soon as December came to life on the screen, Jonathan raced to his bedroom, returning shortly with his own creation. "Show mine too!" he instructed. The group exchanged amused glances.

"I have tape that won't damage the paint. I'll get it." Jade returned shortly with a package and scissors and began rolling pieces, sticky side out, around her hand. "I think it will hold. Jonathan, will you help me position your artwork?"

Jonathan clasped his hands in delight. "I just know he will love it. Papa, can he hang it upstairs in his room?"

Zeke cleared his throat. "Okay, folks. Tick Tock. Let's get to work. Charlie, I want you to pretend to be a wit…ah, the manager."

"You need a chair, yeah, that one will do," Charlie said, pointing.

Troy wheeled Jade's task chair from its spot at her desk on the far side of the room. "Go!"

Zeke began. "Oh! We need Ryan, the Burger King manager's last name. For now, I'll address him as Mr. Whatever."

"On it," Charlie said, nodding to Zeke's secretary. "I'll email it to you."

Zeke got into his role. "Mr. Whatever, will you please refer to Monday, December first. Was Benjamin Olinger working in your restaurant consistently from eight a.m. to four p.m.?"

"Yes. He was," Charlie pretended.

"Did he leave the restaurant at any time for any reason that you observed?"

"He did not. The only breaks he took were to use the restroom and to grab a quick bite at the table by the window."

"Do you have proof of that timeframe?"

"I do. It's on his timecard, which I gave to Mr. Brown."

"Good! No, I won't say *good*. I'll say 'thank you.' And 'your witness.' Troy, do you recommend that I click back to the whole month after I exhaust December first?"

"That's up to you, but of course you can."

Zeke said, "Yes. I want to do that. To refresh the audience's attention."

"What about the original poster—should I stand that on an easel?"

"Why don't you see how the jury's reacting? Whenever they seem confused, toggle back and forth, then go to the next day."

Jonathan crept closer and closer to the wall-turned-screen, backing up each time Jade gently reminded him not to block the projector. He walked to his poster, hung low on the wall, then tried repeatedly to get close to the projected facsimile. Finally, he approached Charlie.

"Papa. What goes in here?" He tapped his own creation's December eighteenth. "You don't have enough sentences."

"Jonathan, hush. It's important that you be quiet," Jade reinforced, tapping her lips with her index finger. The secretary took Charlie's place on the witness stand to play the part of the swim-team coach for Monday, December second. That was the in-service day which, without any school, was especially important to fill.

"Papa," Jonathan repeated. "What goes in here?" He tap-tap-tapped the box for the eighteenth, on which he'd left ample space for another addition. He pointed to the wall, which showed December eighteenth's square looking complete.

Charlie whispered, exasperated, "He has swim team until five—you have that—and his youth group that lasts until nine. Now please be still."

Jonathan squinted at his poster and frowned. "No, Papa. There's a hole. You said we'd fill it in later, 'cause there was no swimming." Everyone paused as Jonathan's voice grew louder and gave the unfolding situation their undivided attention.

"That can't be right." Charlie grabbed his box and unfolded his seventeen-by-twelve-inch hand-drawn calendar, the Word document with numbered lists by dates, and the photocopies of all the witnesses' records. "I'll show you." He shuffled so quickly that several papers spilled onto the floor. "I've got it here. I know that I do."

Troy said, "Why don't we take a break? Maybe Jonathan and I can take Roxie outside. Does she like to play fetch?"

"Boy, does she! Let's go!"

Over his shoulder Troy gave the group a calming motion with his hand. "I have all day," he mouthed.

"I've got it—right here," Charlie insisted. "He always had a youth group meeting on alternate Wednesdays when there wasn't a swim meet." He shuffled though the papers. "Sorry folks. I'm just a little rattled."

"Take your time," Zeke and Jade said in unison.

"Got it." He stared at the paper. "There should have been a swim meet, but I've mixed up the dates." Finally, he dropped the papers, realizing his error. "Looks like we have a problem with the calendar—Wednesday, December eighteenth from five o'clock on. I don't have a record for there being a youth club meeting."

"What's Zeke going to do?" Jade whispered to Charlie.

Zeke intervened. "Charlie, why don't you go through your research? Brownie will review his notes with the witnesses. And, if we do indeed have missing time, then we'll have to find where he was. But first, Charlie, ask Ben if he remembers that day and what he did."

"I'm so sorry," Charlie stammered. "I thought our alibi was perfect. I'll make those calls."

"One other problem," Zeke said. "Mr. Van Dyke was downright nasty about his family being subpoenaed to testify. He's threatening to say that Ben wasn't with them that Thursday after the swim meet."

"Under oath? Still? You gotta be kidding!"

"We'll take another run at the mother and the girl, and remind them about the penalty for perjury or not showing up. But that gap may be an unresolvable problem, unless I successfully bluff that a neighbor saw them sitting in her car in front of Ben's house."

"Will that work?" Charlie asked.

"Brownie can be very persuasive, but if lying is entrenched behavior in the Van Dyke family, we may have a problem."

As Jonathan and Troy returned with Roxie, the others were packing the equipment. Troy and Zeke's secretary exchanged contact information for him to transmit *December* to the laptop she'd take to court. "Just let me have your revisions so that I can update the data. I can add copy or configure a different presentation. That could include selective dates which, instead of following December in order, are a collection of similar days, such as school days."

ↄ৩ৎↄ

"Think!"

"I'm trying!"

Charlie and Ben huddled over Charlie's computer, studying the two documents simultaneously using the split-screen option. One showed the entries by date, which he scrolled to December eighteenth, and the other, the calendar document that he could scroll week by week. He pumped up the View to 400% to help Ben's eyes focus. Ben looked from the screen, rubbing his eyes, then cast his gaze around the ceiling.

"I don't know. I had to be somewhere. I just can't remember. My days were so much alike, and it's all running together."

"Zeke has instructed us not to revisit your friends or their families again. It might creep into their minds that you were at home after all. We don't want to erode their confidence or second guess their recollections."

"How much time do we have?"

"The trial starts on Monday." Charlie feared that Ben might suggest that he ask his best buddy, Steve, to remember *something*. But he didn't. Ben would never do that. "Let's sleep on it. Troy can make additions, even at the last minute. We will be fine."

"What if Zeke has to start my alibi defense without Thursday, December eighteenth? Remember the 'tree?' They show up everywhere right after Thanksgiving."

"Ben, Zeke knows what he's doing. I'm guessing he won't even mention the tree. I have faith that he'll make a wise decision. And, in the meantime, Brownie will continue his investigation. Maybe your family's nosey neighbor remembers something."

"That long ago? I doubt it."

"What if Tori says, 'Wait a minute. It may have happened in November?'"

"I asked Zeke that very question. She cannot change her story mid-trial, especially after giving detailed statements repeatedly."

Having beaten the subject nearly to death and beginning to loop through it multiple times, they said their goodnights. Ben would stay over that evening rather than disturb the Fiorellis that late.

Chapter 27

Charlie knew Zeke was overkilling the prep, but wouldn't put everyone through it again if he didn't feel it was necessary. He looked at the clock. It was two o'clock Sunday afternoon. This time tomorrow, Team Ben would be assembled in the courthouse waiting room. The jury would have been selected that morning, been sworn, and dismissed for lunch. The prosecution and defense would have made their opening remarks. And one by one, the witnesses would be called.

Ben, Zeke, and Brownie would be at that huge table, the judge ensconced so high they'd get a crick in their necks trying to read his expressions. Having taken Ben to Calendar Call, Charlie could picture the chamber in finite detail. Sunlight would trickle through the parted velvet draperies, splashing rainbows on the polished oak tables, warmly suggesting all was well with the world.

Zeke droned on, reviewing the minutia. "I'm sorry, Zeke. What were you saying?"

"I want everyone in the courthouse by ten a.m. Remind them to review what they must and what they cannot bring past security. Leave the knives and handguns at home." Charlie laughed in spite of hearing that joke again. "Let's go over the ride sheet, and remember, if anyone has car trouble, is sick, or gets backed up in traffic, phone me and my office immediately."

Charlie sighed. "Got it."

"Brownie is picking up Ben at the Fiorelli's house at eight a.m. and bringing him to my office. We'll personally escort him to the courthouse. He's been instructed to dress down—clean and neat, but casual. No coat and tie. We don't want him looking like an adult. I'm sure they'll have Tori dressed in ruffles and lace, ribbons in her pigtails, and Mary Janes with ruffled socks. That's what I'd do."

"Charlie, you'll make the school run at nine a.m. to pick up the students who will testify. The principal, coaches, ophthalmologist, graphic artist, and Burger King manager have promised on their children's heads that they will be there on time. Everyone knows to bring a book or their homework, as this could be a long, boring day."

Charlie said, "After I deliver everyone, I'll pick up Jade and any stragglers who've run into trouble. Old Mr. Greer wants to come too. Any objections?"

"No. He called for my blessing. He wants to be in the courtroom for moral support, as do the Fiorellis who will bring him. I gave permission since I don't need him to testify after all. Bruce Snyder, our polygraph expert, also wants to attend. Bruce might pick up on something Brownie and I miss. A slip of the lip or a contradiction."

"Does everyone know what you'll ask? And how you want them to phrase their answers?"

"Yes and no. I've told them to tell the truth in as few words as possible, to offer nothing extraneous—and I told the adults that I've told the kids where to look, how to sit, and what to do with their hands. We've practiced a dozen ways to say 'he was never at home' without using those words, like he stayed late to help and took extra shifts. I told them, don't guess or speculate. If they don't know the answer, just say I don't know. And they should drop their voice at the end of each sentence, so their testimony doesn't sound like they're asking, *is that right?*"

Charlie was terrified to ask, but needed reassurance.

"What about the hole in the calendar?"

"You let me worry about that. By the time we get to it, the jury should have digested that he was never home and that the accusations don't fit. Rather than clump like-days together, I'll ask the witness about this day. And that. And that. And what they recall about each one. That should get old fast, and the jury will glaze over. And the prosecution's evidence will be in tatters."

"Is Ben going to testify?"

"I'd prefer that he not. That may be a last minute decision."

❧❧❧

Charlie slept fitfully as May seventeenth ticked into May eighteenth. He'd known better than to take a pill. What if he overslept? Or been too groggy to drive responsibly? No, he could sleep for all eternity. Happily, the phone never rang. When the alarm jolted him, he realized he'd only dreamed that he'd stayed awake all night. Funny how that happens sometimes.

While coffee perked, he showered, shaved, and dressed in his most professional-looking attire and spit-shined shoes. Then he retrieved the morning paper, which he had no stomach to read. He tossed it aside. Instead, he studied the day's itinerary and the little piles on the dining room table that he must not forget. He added a water bottle, a small notepad and pen, and the charger for his iPhone.

Breakfast—who knew when he'd have another chance to eat? Jonathan had slept at Alan's house, a rare treat for a Sunday night. Alan's mom would keep Jonathan as long as necessary. In the end, they hadn't needed to fabricate a story. Jonathan, who missed nothing, knew that today the judge would decide who was lying—Ben or the bad little girl—and Jonathan's job was to have faith in the grownups, be a good student, and listen to Alan's mom. A tall order for an almost-seven-year-old. As Charlie cracked eggs into the skillet, he uttered a prayer. *Dear God, let life's disappointments wait a few years for that dear little child.*

Just before ten, Charlie and Jade cleared security and took the stairs, rather than wait with the gaggle of professionals for elevators that appeared to be stalled on upper floors. They were the last to arrive when they opened the conference room door. Dozens of eyes looked up simultaneously. The witnesses sighed, murmured greetings, then returned to their various devices and paperbacks. Everyone flicked glances at the door now and then, an eerie silence having settled over the room. Those who knew each other communicated in whispers. An oversized, industrial clock jerked the seconds with a skinny red hand, reminding Charlie of the polygraph expert's office. Tick. Tick. Tick.

When Zeke strode into the room with Ben and Brownie in tow, the witnesses reacted with a collective gasp and puzzled expressions. Charlie glanced at the clock that read eleven fifty-five.

"It's over!" Zeke thundered. Ben beamed, Brownie grinned, and the room erupted in a jumble of questions.

"What happened?" everyone demanded.

"Last evening they brought Tori into the courtroom for a rehearsal—to try out the chair and the microphone. To hear what the judge's instructions would be. The oath she'd be required to take, to which she would swear to tell the truth. Perjury was explained, and she was asked if she understood the penalty for lying. She broke down in tears, stuttering and sobbing about how sorry she was that she'd lied about 'Benny.'"

Stunned silence followed jubilation, as all the witnesses exploded in unanswered questions. One sentence predominated.

"Did she say why?"

"They didn't pursue it. That's a conversation for another venue. They simply led her out of the courtroom. By that time, it was nine p.m., and the officers of the court had gone home. It was too late to request that the charges be dropped. That, I'm happy to report, just occurred."

Cheers filled the room, as the witnesses processed the extraordinary outcome, until finally one witness asked the obvious. "So—what are we supposed to do now?"

"I suggest we get on with an absolutely, gloriously, ordinary Monday," Zeke said. "Grab some lunch while I wrap up the legalities."

"Wait a minute," the principal asked. "Can she change her mind later? Can the charges be refiled?"

"Not after confessing in front of officers of the court. It's over."

Having collected their personal belongings and substituted plans for a day that would not include courtroom drama, Team Ben exited the conference room. The professionals headed for the elevator to regroup their respective lives. The principal and Ryan, the Burger King manager, divvied up the students for transport to school, while Zeke, Brownie, Bruce Snyder, Ben, and Charlie headed back to the law office.

Charlie sank into the receptionist's guest chair, accepting a small glass of champagne. He sipped. "I can't even remember what I was doing before all this started."

"Did you read the morning paper?" Zeke asked with a wink to Brownie. "You stirred up quite a hornet's nest."

"What are you talking about?"

"Front page news. Section A, above the fold." He handed Charlie the morning edition. He gasped at the photo of Watkins, the orphanage's director, being escorted in handcuffs by a plain-clothes detective and a uniformed officer. He was trying to hide his face with a folder, but Charlie would have recognized him anywhere. The caption read:

Orphanage head T. M. Watkins arrested for embezzling thousands from child protective service agency. Twelve others implicated in the scheme.

"That document and photos you emailed to me corroborated others' complaints about children being used to claim payments to which certain foster parents were not entitled. An undercover investigation had been in progress for some time. According to a police statement in the article, the foster parents claimed a full-month's support of five hundred dollars per child who only stayed with them for a few days. If six families were involved, times six pairs of children, that amounts to six thousand dollars per month tax free, for which they should have received one thousand dollars if two children stayed the entire month. Or they should have been paid a three-day stipend per child. Multiply that times six host families."

"Are more than those six families involved?" Charlie asked.

"The reporter, under whose byline the story is written, says the investigation is ongoing. In other words, stay tuned."

"How did they get away with it?"

"Somebody had to be cooking the books."

"Was the social worker who moved them around involved?"

"Maybe. Maybe not. If she had no knowledge of the financial transactions, and didn't profit from the scheme, it's possible she thought the kids were in witness protection or being sheltered from abuse. They'll put her financials under a microscope. We'll be reading the details for months."

Ben looked up from his Coke. "My parents. What about

them? I can't read print that's so small."

"The addresses I noted that correspond with the home-owners' names don't include your parents. I wonder why."

Ben shrugged. "They never had extra cash to throw around. My dad kept a ledger of every last penny, and the household ran on a strict budget. He's not smart enough to keep complicated bookkeeping straight. I'm guessing that if he was offered money under the table, he'd turn it down. Maybe accept a per diem for the time they actually kept the kids."

"That doesn't sound like those people."

"It does, when you consider that the summer I was seventeen, I threatened to tell Child Protective Services how they treated Oceana. They knew I had eyes on the fosters. They couldn't participate in anything like this until they got rid of me and anything I might observe."

"So they dodged the bullet, having been forced to be honest. They should thank you, Ben. The child is the parent's teacher."

"If someone could give me a ride back to school, I'll get credit for a full-day's attendance. And I have a ton of work to catch up."

Chapter 28

Jade pushed *play* and an angry woman's voice came through the speaker. "I demand that you give me access to my grandson. I'm entitled to equal rights if you're letting my husband see him. You didn't think I'd find out that you were sneaking around behind my back in favor of him, did you! I saw that dear child a year ago at the VA. He couldn't talk, and nobody was treating him. I'm going to report you to Child Protective Services if you don't…" She pushed *stop*.

"How long has this been going on?" Charlie asked Jade.

"That's the third call. I hung up on the previous two then got this device to record her tirades."

"What are you planning on doing with it?"

"I thought I'd try to get a restraining order to prevent her from calling, threatening, demanding access to Jonathan, or stalking us. But when I did the research, my recording amounts to an illegal wire tap."

"But if she's calling your personal phone, doesn't that give you that right?"

"I need an attorney to sort it out. Zeke Geoffrey's partner, Paul—your friend from the VA—isn't he a civil attorney? I thought I'd give him a call."

"What about Jonathan's birthday party? Did you decide to invite his grandfather?"

"I did. He'll come for our family party on his actual birthday, May twenty-fifth. And if monster-in-law shows up, I'll call the police. I didn't invite him to the kids' party. I'd originally thought we'd celebrate on Saturday, the twenty-third. Jonathan wanted to invite a few friends from school, so I'd have him pass out the invitations, but the school's rule is that any invitations distributed at school must include every student in the class. I don't have their mailing addresses, and I certainly couldn't accommodate two dozen first graders here. I panicked.

"Then one of my friends confirmed it was insane to *ever* entertain that many seven-year-olds at home. She suggested I rent a water slide. The company does all set up and tear down. That, I feared, would empty the well and the kids, running all over, would destroy your gardens and overwhelm the bathrooms. She also suggested The Bounce House for two hours on a Saturday afternoon. And that's what I booked. On the invitation, I put in bold-face: NO GIFTS, adding a note *Any presents brought to the party will be donated to charity*."

"What made you decide to add that?"

"If every kid in the class has a party—even a little back-yard get together—that's an imposition for parents who can't afford presents or don't have time to shop. Some kids would have to skip the party. If I'm setting a precedent, that's not my problem."

"And Jonathan's grandfather?"

"He'll come to our family party on Jonathan's actual birthday for Jonathan's favorite dinner and cake."

"It would be my honor to bake it myself," Charlie said. "I'll have all day to create a masterpiece."

"Better arm yourself with antacids. He's sure to want pizza."

"How did your ex-mother-in-law get your number and find out about your meeting her husband?"

"With her resources, she probably hired a private detective to access my personal records. My phone number would be in my college's database, along with my address and other personal information, such as emergency contact names." She patted his arm. "That would be you."

"Well, I certainly hope so."

"If Paul will take me on as a client, I'll have him review my will, durable power of attorney, insurances, and so on. I've got to protect my son. Charlie, may I ask you to be his legal and financial guardian in case something happens to me?"

"I would be honored. And if there's nobody you trust to list as alternates, my daughters would be happy to serve. Jeannette, in Atlanta, has two little boys who love playing with Jonathan, and Suzanne in San Diego is longing for a child."

"About The Bounce House. You want to come watch the fun?"

"Of course. What's involved?"

"Show up, take pictures, eat cake—which they provide—and leave a gaggle of over-stimulated seven-year-olds for their parents to deal with."

⁂

Monday, May twenty-fifth, arrived. It was a school day, but Jonathan didn't mind. "As the birthday boy, I got to bring the treat, wear a fancy crown, and the class sang happy birthday to me. And I didn't even have to wash my hands."

He had surprised Jade by asking for Ben's special spaghetti, meatballs, and red sauce for his birthday dinner. He blew out the candles on Charlie's cake, covered with Hershey's chocolate icing. "Did you make a wish," his mother asked. "Don't tell, if you did, or it won't come true."

"Yeah it will. Everything I wished for is right here."

"Presents!" Jade motioned them into the living room

where the grownups circled the birthday boy. "What do you want to open first?"

"That big box," he said retrieving one wrapped in silver foil and tied with a blue wire-ribbon bow. He opened the card, smiling as he read, then focused on his grandfather. "Thank you."

"Well, open it" he said, leaning in anticipation on his cane. Jonathan lifted the lid and withdrew a large photo album. Balancing in on his outstretched legs, he turned to the first page, which showed a tiny baby in a white shawl. "That was your daddy's first portrait." Jonathan turned awe-struck eyes to the newcomer in his life. "The album is yours to keep. When there's time, I'll tell you all about each picture and what your father was like."

Jonathan set the album gently aside, then gave his grandfather a hug. "Thank you."

"How about the rest of your loot?" he said pointing to the pile of presents. "Go for it!"

"Cowboy boots!" Jonathan exclaimed over Charlie's gift.

"There's more. Look inside." Jonathan withdrew a glossy brochure that showed pictures of horses circling a track. "Since you had such a great time at your friend Callum's farm, I thought you'd enjoy riding lessons." Jonathan beamed.

"Open this one," Ben said, handing him a square package. From its depths he pulled a pair of goggles. "My gift to you is swimming lessons. I've signed us up at the YMCA. You'll be a fish in no time."

Inside a package from his mom was an intricate Lego set. "It may be a little advanced for a seven-year-old."

"But Mom—Now I'm going on eight."

"Hopefully old enough to be street-wise. Open that one," she said pointing to a jumbo-sized gift bag secured at the edges with curly ribbon. He peered inside, then tugged it open.

"Oh boy! A skateboard. Can I ride it in the street?"

"That's from my girls," Charlie said. "They insist it's age appropriate."

Jade rolled her eyes.

When the festivities died down, Charlie ushered the elder Kepley back to his living room upstairs. "I can't find the words to thank you enough for bringing Jade and Jonathan into my life. I'd like to spend a few hours with him, telling him about his father. But I'll tell him, and reassure Jade, that I live far away and won't be dropping in."

"What's next for you?" Charlie asked.

"I'll close up my little home in Upstate New York then take the trans-Canada train to the Pacific Northwest. My late daughter's children live there with their father. I've met his new wife at their wedding, and she's great with the kids. They're close to Jonathan's age and have no memory of their mother who died of cancer shortly after my son disappeared. I'm making a scrapbook for them too. It's the least I can do after all the heartache I've allowed to happen."

"Under the circumstances, I'm not sure there was a lot you could have done."

He shook Charlie's hand. "Thank you for that. And for making this special day happen." He turned to escape.

Charlie smiled. *Two silly old men wiping tears.*

Chapter 29

Tweety-tweet-tweet! June the eighth. With that very first robin, Charlie was wide awake. Four forty-five—Ben's big day had finally arrived. Charlie leapt from his bed and peered around the blackout blind for any trace of dawn breaking. Donning slippers and robe, he strode to the street to retrieve his newspaper while scanning the sky for cloudy mischief that might dampen the occasion.

The agenda was set. After Ben slept as long as he wished, he would shower and dress in new clothes—a pristine white dress shirt, black dress slacks, a tie, spit-shined black shoes, and socks. His mortarboard and tassel lay on Charlie's dining room table, and his robe hung in the hall closet protected in plastic. While the school couldn't demand that the seniors conform to a dress code—after all, receiving their diplomas was a formality whether they attended or not—customs prevailed and families embraced the program, even though a few kids would express their individuality.

At seven, Jonathan and Roxie bounded up the stairs, the child having learned from Roxie how to wiggle through the doggie door. Jade would assume that Jonathan had knocked to be admitted, and Charlie wasn't going to rat him out. If that ever became an issue, then they would discuss it. Charlie gave the little guy a hug and scratched Roxie's ears when she tipped her head in supplication.

"Can we wake him up?" Jonathan asked.

"Not a chance. This is his special day, and it'll be a long one."

"When's Claire coming over?"

"Same time as the last time you asked. Around ten. We'll take lots of pictures, then they'll go to her house for more pictures and something to eat. Then they'll report to the high school to put on their robes, get their final instructions, and line up."

Jonathan giggled with excitement. "Then they'll have this big parade into the stadium and we'll get to watch them throw up their hats."

"With lots of speeches and music in between. Do you think you can sit still that long? Ben's not the only one graduating. Each family and their student's graduation must be respected. Maybe you should take Roxie to run around the yard—even if she's already been—and check out the sky. If it looks like rains…"

"I know. I know. We have to watch from a classroom if there's not enough room in the gym."

Good. He knows what to expect. "If your mom is awake, see if she'd like to have chocolate waffles and bacon with us. Tell her to come as she is."

Jonathan hopped down from the stool and headed outside, Roxie at his heels. Shortly the pair returned. "It's sunny! Oh, boy."

Oh, boy, indeed.

At ten sharp, Claire pulled into Charlie's driveway in her little blue bug. Ben looked unbelievably dignified and older than his eighteen years as he stepped onto the front porch to meet her. They exchanged murmured greetings and a quick kiss, then entered the house beaming.

Claire hugged everyone and then took Jade aside. "What do you think of the dress?" she asked of the short, flared sundress with a little matching short-sleeved sweater. "Is it too short? I never considered sitting on the stage and what people might see."

"It's perfect. And speaking of skirts, the dais where you'll be sitting has one. And when you speak, you'll stand behind the podium. So—relax."

"Thank God, I can use notes. I was terrified I'd go blank."

"You?" Ben circled her shoulder with a hug. "On your worst day, you are articulate."

"Okay, everyone. Pictures. Graduates, if you'll humor us, we'll shoot you in your finery and then in your gowns, both indoors and out, if that's all right. We may not get another chance once the events start unfolding."

෴

Everything should have been perfect—a cloudless June day under a periwinkle sky, the youthful exuberance mingling with parental pride, and so many futures full of promise. Charlie, Jade, and Jonathan sat on a folded army blanket that cushioned the metal bleachers. Ben had suggested the specific area where they could see him and he, them. Old Mr. Greer sat with his buddies in a special section. Not that he needed handicap consideration, he'd said, but he didn't want his friends to feel isolated.

Armed with Nikon binoculars, Charlie scanned the bleachers on the opposite side of the field for Ben's estranged parents. With threats escalating in anticipation of the support hearing just two weeks away, Charlie wouldn't put anything past those terrible people. Ben had seemed unconcerned, eager to graduate and work his butt off to jump start his adult life and pay off his debts. It wasn't lost on Ben that his parents faced mounting legal bills, should they be indicted in the foster care scam. He watched, sharpening the focus. What was the father holding so protectively? A brown satchel that could easily conceal a weapon, and no security measures had been required when they'd entered the vast outdoor arena.

"Whatcha watching, Papa? Can I see?"

"Birds. I think they're barn swallows. And maybe a hawk." He draped the strap around the child's neck and pointed to the sky opposite the sun.

"It's kinda blurry."

"Move this little wheel with your thumb and index finger. See if that brings it into focus."

High on the hill, the sound of musicians warming up drifted toward the families, who turned their collective heads in unison. Shortly the traditional *Pomp and Circumstance* refrain began. Everyone rose as a color guard led school officials toward their places via the track. Row upon row of folding chairs were placed perpendicular to the bleachers, facing the dais for class officers and school officials who would speak, including the president of the school board, the principal, the guest speaker, and a minister who would deliver a politically-correct invocation.

The graduating class followed, two by two, reminiscent of Noah's ark. While maintaining their posture and dignity, students scanned the crowd for their families, grinning broadly and waving to their enthusiastic loved ones. Charlie remembered they'd be in alpha order—his own daughters marching first with a surname that started with *A*. Ben was an *O*. When he finally passed beneath them, he was walking with Claire, who should have led with the class officers. As they passed to the back of the rows, they pivoted, turned right and right again up a center aisle. Ben turned right to follow his leader, while Claire proceeded toward the dais where she joined her fellow class officers.

Charlie frowned. Where was Nicolette? As class secretary, she should be on the dais. For the first time, he wondered how Claire had avoided ugly confrontations with

Nicolette over Ben. "I wonder where she is?" Charlie mused to Jade.

"Who?"

"Nicolette Van Dyke. Maybe she's a junior."

A man behind them answered the question. "She's not graduating with the class. She won't get her diploma until August, assuming she passes summer school. That's why she's not here."

Charlie stole a look at the speaker, who was way too young to be Nicolette's father. He sighed in relief. Since they'd never met in person, that could have been very uncomfortable.

As three-hundred-plus students processed to their places, Charlie scanned the far bleachers again. Ben's parents were gone. He wondered if he should alert security, but to what? The Olingers were as nondescript as they come and would be impossible to pick out of the crowd. Patience, he told himself. And have a little faith. Maybe they just want to see their son graduate and are terribly sorry for what they have done. He sighed. Fat chance of that!

At the appointed time Claire, as class president, was introduced to hoots, whistles, and applause from her fellow classmates. She angled the mike downward and set her notecards on the podium. The top card, Charlie knew, held the names and correct order of the people whom she must acknowledge first, complete with their correct pronunciation, which ended with greeting her classmates.

She began. "We're told that commencement means beginning. A goal, not a final destination. As we stand on the threshold of the rest of our lives, time resembles an elaborate scroll that's been unfurled to the vanishing point, on which we'll write an endless journey of possibilities. The idea of dying is a foreign concept that we cannot imagine, being so young. But." She paused. "There is temptation in that journey to let ourselves die a bit at a time. That should bring us up short. A temptation for which we must be wary."

"We begin to die when we do not stand up against bigotry, intolerance, injustice, and persecution. We begin to die when we fail to honor the dignity of every human being. We begin to die when we ignore the sick, the frail, and those who have not been dealt our lucky hand. We begin to die when we fail to take responsibility for what we should have, but blame others who tried and fell short. We begin to die when we fail to acknowledge our personal failures and don't strive to do better. We begin to die when we say, I am too old to learn something new.

"We leave here today, fortified with hundreds of lessons taught by the best teachers on the planet. When I asked many of you about your personal aspirations, your answers were as varied as your creative selves. I'm reminded of President Kennedy's inaugural comment, 'that to whom much is given, much is expected.' But another realistic person reminded us that 'the Constitution did not say, life, liberty and the pursuit of *excellence*.' Another wise person said 'we should strive for the goodness, not to be great.'"

"It is my personal wish that all of us will stay in touch, help each other along our individual paths, and pay forward the precious gifts we have received in abundance from our families, teachers, youth and faith leaders. Bless you, every one, and thank you for being my friend."

Charlie knew how grateful Claire must have felt, being introduced as representing the graduating class and not as the valedictorian and the class president of which she was both. That, she had argued, would make many uncomfortable because thousandths of points separated the top ten percent and she'd won the class election by a mere handful of votes.

From the moment the announcer started calling the names, and each student approached the chairman and the principal, Charlie had forgotten all about the Olingers. Hearing Benjamin Duanne Olinger called, the three jumped to their feet and applauded, even though they'd been asked to hold their applause until all names were called. Nobody did, so the dignitaries tactfully waited until each family could hear their graduate's name.

Charlie heard a whoop from Old Mr. Greer, seated on the fifty-yard line where honored guests sat in special chairs on the grassy strip between the track and the field. That this school had embraced the Americans with Disabilities Act enthusiastically made Charlie proud.

If the graduates had practiced a stately recession, that plan was scuttled the minute the dignitaries rounded the corner to exit via the track. The class jumped to their feet, whooped, and threw their mortarboards into the air. Ben had told Charlie that the organizers had pleaded with them not to wreck their rented attire, but what the heck. Ben and three hundred of his closest friends let loose, mobbing and regrouping in celebration. Finally, they headed uphill toward the school in a blue-garbed mass.

From their seats, Charlie, Jade, and Jonathan scanned the mass until Ben's outstretched arm waved frantically to them. He pointed uphill as the tide of the graduates swept him along.

As the blue glut headed uphill, Charlie searched the mob for Ben's father. Families, having abandoned the far bleachers, were taking a diagonal shortcut across the football field to intercept their graduates. The Olingers were nowhere in sight. Charlie's worst fear that Leroy Olinger would nail Ben with a rifle hadn't materialized. He swept the crowd's movements as they mixed among the blue gowns to hug their honored sons and daughters.

"Let's go find Ben. Let's go. Now!" Jonathan tugged

Jade's hand impatiently. "We gotta take more pictures. What if he leaves with his friends? Come on."

"What about Mr. Greer?" Jade asked.

"His buddy arranged a driver that also is picking them up in the handicap lot. He said he'd congratulate Ben *back in the hood*."

The trio trudged uphill, slowed by the slug of families and friends, grouping and regrouping in myriad combinations. Ben, Charlie realized as they grew closer, was standing with a group at the top if the hill. Only two wore blue robes—himself and a blonde he immediately recognized by her shiny mane. Charlie stepped to the right around an excited family of twelve and raised his binoculars. He focused. The man having an animated conversation with Ben was his father. His mother stood like a statue, glaring at Ben. Claire was hanging back, holding his hand behind his back.

Ben's father made jabbing motions at Ben's face. Ben, however, didn't move, as if he knew the father would not make a scene in front of this throng. Then he saw her. A little girl who came to her mother's shoulder. Tori. That must be her. Strange, that in the nine months he had known Ben, Charlie had never seen as much as a snapshot of this little girl who had caused so much pain and suffering. He studied her profile. She could be anyone's fifth grader with her pale face, pug nose, straight brown hair and bangs, a sundress, and sandals.

The child was tugging at the sleeve of Ben's robe. At first, he ignored her until Claire appeared to whisper something to him and nod toward the child. Through his binoculars, Charlie could read his lips as he asked, "What? What is it?"

Tori turned her back to her parents and motioned to him. He bent to give her his undivided attention. Even though she was speaking—Charlie could see her lips moving—she was looking at the ground. He said something to her and smiled. Now the mother was talking, motioning over her shoulder in the direction Charlie perceived as their home. Ben said something as his buddies overtook the group. With another brief exchange, he pivoted Claire toward their friends.

Leroy Olinger shifted the canvas bag he was toting from his right to his left shoulder. He zipped it open and withdrew something black. It looked like a handgun. He called after Ben, who turned, his arm draped around Claire's shoulder. Everyone froze as the father extended his arm and aimed something shiny that caught the sun's reflection. He appeared to be shouting, angrily making motions with the object. Nobody moved. Ben's still face showed no emotion.

His father took his shot.

Then dropped what looked like a camera into his bag. Charlie, exhausted, took several deep breaths of relief, having held it for an eternity.

As Charlie rejoined Jade and Jonathan and rendezvoused with Ben and his pack of friends, he realized this was no time to pump him for details. His curiosity would have to wait. Like every other family, they grouped and regrouped for pictures, their friends' parents joining them, many wanting to meet the real Charlie Alderfer who had brought the VA killer to justice.

Ben came to his rescue. "Here's the deal. We'll stop by her house for a bit to see the old folks who couldn't manage the stadium, then we'll bring her parents home with us. Is that okay? There's a party at the high school around eight, over which Claire as a class officer has to preside, then later we'll go out with our friends. Hey! Are you all right?" Ben asked, wiping a tear from Charlie's face with his thumb.

"I'm just overwhelmed with joy and gratitude."

Ben's face became solemn. "Tomorrow, if you have time, I'd like to talk with you about the support hearing. With the trial and graduation, I've managed to forget all about it."

By four, Charlie's house filled with Ben's friends, their families, and those dear to the graduates, enjoying a picture-perfect celebration. Mrs. Fiorelli, over Charlie's objections, brought a huge pan of lasagna and a plate of pizzelles. Mr. Greer brought a salad of every green imaginable in an enormous wooden bowl, and Charlie's dining room table, draped in his Emma's holiday cloth, filled with delicious appetizers. After many stern warnings, Roxie was invited to enjoy the party downstairs in Jade's bedroom.

That morning Jonathan had helped Charlie bake a cake in a huge horseshoe pan, which they bisected at the top and turned half around, reconnecting the cake to resemble a path. They piped flowers around Charlie's message—*May Your Path Be Strewn With Flowers*—just as Emma had done for their daughters' graduations. How he wished his family was here. As soon as his life returned to normal, Charlie vowed to make a swing to Atlanta and on to LA to see them.

Not one to stand on formalities, he set up the bar on the kitchen table and implored their guests to please help themselves. Jade served punch in the living room from wedding crystal that hadn't been out of their boxes in years. After everyone toasted the graduates, they filled Emma's china plates and feasted.

"My present! When can I give Ben my present?" Jonathan pestered as soon as he'd finished his lasagna.

"Let's let everyone finish eating," Jade murmured to him. His face fell.

Ben, overhearing the exchange, teased the child. "But it isn't my birthday."

"But you graduated! Mommy, can I please give him my present now?" She shrugged and nodded consent. "I'll need some help bringing it upstairs."

Charlie set his plate on the hearth. "I'm on it." Five minutes later Jonathan and Charlie emerged from the stairwell, toting the box in which Jade had stored her wedding gown. "Where do you want me to put it?" Charlie asked.

"There. In the middle of the floor." Jonathan beckoned to Ben, bobbing on his toes and clapping like an excited three-year-old. "I made something special, just for you."

Everyone gathered around, intent on the box. Ben lifted the lid, "Aaaah!" Escaping from his smiling face. "Why, it's…"

Jonathan didn't wait for him to figure it out. "It's December, the month you turned into a grownup. See, it *is* a birthday present, sort of."

"Who mounted it?" Charlie asked, as Ben tipped it, revealing the sturdy backing and hanging hooks.

"Our friend Troy," Jade said.

"It's not quite finished," Jonathan said, tapping December eighteenth. "You gotta tell me what goes in there, and I'll draw it for you." Over the guests' heads, Charlie and Jade exchanged expressions that embodied their relief and joy that the impossible had worked.

Jonathan piped up again. "Now can we p-l-e-a-s-e cut the cake?"

Chapter 30

Charlie was surprised to see Ben up so early, or maybe he never went to bed. Dressed in his Burger King shirt, the honored graduate was already reduced to a working stiff.

"Lots to do. I borrowed Steve's car, and after work he's going to help me pick out my new ride. His dad owns a used car lot and has promised to make me a very good deal. The owner of the pizza franchise caved and sent Zeke a check for the entire amount. Zeke had included, in addition to the value of my old car, lost wages for being 'deprived of reliable transportation.' So—it's off to the car lot."

"Please get something practical…"

"I will. But I love to tinker on old cars, and there's a really great junk yard I've hardly tapped." He paused, fingering his cap. "If it's okay and you have time, I'd like to tell you what my parents had to say at graduation. Would this evening be all right? Don't worry about dinner. Mrs. Fiorelli is expecting me for spaghetti, and she has a fresh Ben list."

What the heck. A few more hours won't kill me. "Go! And enjoy your first day of freedom."

Around eight that evening, Charlie heard the distinctive sound of an unhappy muffler. Peering out the window, he saw Ben ease from an elderly Toyota pickup. Great! Not a kid car. He hurried outside to admire Ben's pride and joy.

In the dwindling light, the scents of blossoms stirred his memory. It struck him—it was exactly one year to the day that his aneurysm had ruptured and taken his life in a different trajectory. Months in the hospital, his triumphant graduation from hospice, and the bond formed with Jonathan and Jade into a family.

"What do you think?" Ben asked. "Want to go for a spin?"

"Another day perhaps. Right now we have matters to discuss." Charlie shepherded Ben into his study where they took their customary chairs. Since the recliner was a much better fit for Ben than himself, Charlie decided to give it to him when Ben had a place of his own.

"I have a graduation present for you." He handed Ben a number ten envelope. "I've decided you shouldn't start your future in debt. Go ahead. Open it."

Ben unfolded the notarized documents that Charlie and Ben had signed months ago. Ben looked up, dumbfounded. "This looks like…"

"I'm cancelling your debt. Attached is a list of people to whom you'll want to send thank you notes. Knowing how much a legal defense costs, they contributed, some as little as ten dollars, some fifty, and two people five hundred apiece. Zeke returned two thousand dollars of the retainer and won't charge you for the case for support, at which my friend and fellow vet, Paul, will represent you."

Ben murmured thank you, opened his mouth, but closed it again as if unsure where to begin. Finally, he did. "Mr. A., I have a confession to make. It's about December the eighteenth." He paused until Charlie could barely stand it." He took a breath and resumed. "I *was* at home that evening."

Charlie froze, his mind grappling to comprehend what Ben was saying. "What?" He stammered, staring at Ben. "What are you saying?" That Ben could have fooled everybody all along was not something he was prepared to accept.

"The swim meet was cancelled. I forget why. And a youth group meeting wasn't scheduled. Being so close to Christmas, everyone had conflicts. So I went to Burger King after school to see if Ryan needed help. For once, he was covered. I stayed long enough to grab a burger and a Coke. A guy from the football team, who played with my foster brother, invited me to a party at another teammate's house. I had no plans, so I accepted. The parents weren't home, and everyone was drinking beer. By the volume, I guessed they'd been at it awhile—probably cut afternoon classes. None of my buddies or the swimmers were there.

"To be sociable and not feel so nerdy, I had a beer. It was ice cold and tasted fantastic. I finished it, forgetting about headache triggers. Big mistake. Within the hour, my head was pounding—a full-blown migraine. I went home. It was around six. Tori and one of the little kids were watching a movie. They were dressed for bed. She had on her nightie, no robe or slippers, and was sitting on the floor, knees spread, and panties showing. I yelled at her to cover herself. At ten years old, with young male teens in the house, Mom should have been teaching her to be modest. She glared at me, yanked her gown over her knees, and went back to her movie.

"I went upstairs, took a couple OTC pain pills, and lay down, waiting for relief. I had no sooner dozed off—I was always exhausted back then—when I heard the front door slam. I had no idea how long I had slept. Looking downstairs, I saw my parents enter and take the steps down to the family room. She started yelling at the kids that they were supposed to have been in bed. It dawned on me that nobody else was at home. They'd gone out and left Tori in charge of that six-year-old girl and the little ones asleep in the nursery. Rather than getting into one more fight about neglecting the kids, I grabbed my jacket and split, passing them in the hall."

"What time was that?"

"I have no idea. It was dark, but in December it's dark before five."

"Where did you go?"

"I just drove around. My buddies' cars weren't at their houses. I wasn't welcome at some of them anyway. My friends sneaked around to hang with me as if we were cheating on spouses. There wasn't a basketball game—that would be the following evening—so I stopped by the gym to see if anyone was working out. That's when I noticed the clock—ten p.m. I went straight home, did my homework, and washed the dishes."

"So you didn't see anyone who could verify your time between six and ten," Charlie stated.

Ben shook his head. "A thought popped into my head yesterday. If I arrived home at six and my parents came in the door right after I'd fallen asleep—which was what I assumed—then why was she yelling that they should have been in bed? I must have slept until around nine. That would account for the time. And would have wrecked the alibi defense."

Charlie thought for a moment. "And nobody questioned the other little girl. They probably would have if Tori had specified that specific Wednesday, but she said 'around Christmas.'"

If what Ben said was true, he understood why he had no alibi for the evening of December the eighteenth. "And Tori's story? About you?"

Ben raised his right hand. "I swear to God. She lied. If anything, I tried to protect the kids whenever I saw mistreatment." He studied Charlie's face for a minute. "What would you and Zeke have done differently if you had known?"

"We'll never know. But one thing's for certain—I did not then nor do I now doubt your honesty for a minute." Charlie mulled Ben's revelation. It was possible that the ten-year-old, realizing she'd disobeyed her mother's instructions and angry with Ben for snapping at her, could have fabricated the story to avoid punishment. If Ben's account of how fosters were treated was any example, that could have been harsh.

"I wouldn't say we got away with something," Charlie concluded. "I'd say justice was served. And speaking of which, what did your parents say after graduation? I was afraid your father would shoot you."

"They're all upset about the support hearing. Evidently Paul is suing for a shitload of money. His list is impressive and includes four years of college—tuition, room, and board—for my lost opportunities at athletic scholarships. Remember the swim meet you and Mr. Greer attended when college scouts were present? Brownie researched the colleges, got coaches' names, and got in touch. Evidently, they were very interested in me as long as I graduated and didn't have a criminal record. Having done their due diligence, they saw the false confession I made. The scholarship recipients have been chosen for next years' teams."

"What did your father say? He looked furious."

"That the suit would bankrupt them. Ruin them. How dare I after they'd taken me in and so on. They were all over the planet, offering to buy me a car if I'd drop the suit. A new car at that! Mom said they had presents for me at the house if I'd stop by for a little party 'with the family.' It's strange how I've distanced myself from them. They're just the people who adopted me and the extended family is theirs, not mine. In their minds, I was always one of the fosters, not blood. All I ever wanted was to have a family. Now I feel nothing for them."

"Maybe that's a good thing. You know, the opposite of love isn't hate. It's indifference. Hate is like acid that destroys from within. I'm happy that you figured that out."

"All I ever wanted was to have a family," he repeated.

"And I'm sure you will, that's one of your choosing. You'll always have us. And having had so much experience with foster children, you'll make a great father. I've got to ask. What did Tori say to you? And what did you say to her?"

"She said, 'I'm so sorry I lied about you, Benny.' And I said the only thing that I could. I said, 'I forgive you.'"

Charlie was stunned. Had he ever underestimated the depth of this young man's character, it was never more evident. He could have railed, spitting an angry litany of everything her lies had potentially cost him. His future, his freedom, even his life. But he didn't. And Charlie had no doubt that Ben was sincere.

෬෩෬෩

Charlie and Ben were enjoying a Friday pizza and movie night alone in Charlie's cozy den while distant thunder rumbled. Rain spit at the window. Ben, a child of the tech generation, had helped Charlie analyze his home entertainment needs and choose devices to replace his aging equipment. He had installed, wired, and written cheat sheets for the various remotes that Charlie could not keep straight. Charlie refused to part with his old VCR, having a library of tapes from his daughters' childhoods. But he loved his new flat-screen TV with its sharp digital image that he could enjoy without glasses.

On a rare, frenzy-free June evening, Ben watched a movie with the only real father figure he'd ever known. His band buddies had dispersed for the summer—jobs, college, camp counseling, or travel with family. Ben had taken a full-time job with a thriving new restaurant, his innovative ideas bumping his pay. The owner hadn't asked, nor had Ben volunteered, how long he would stay.

Muting the sound at a commercial, Charlie asked, "What have you decided to do about the support hearing? It's coming up soon. If you don't mind my asking, that is. You don't have to—"

Ben cut him off. "In the first place, I never mind you asking, so you can stop saying that. Ask me anything, and I'll tell you the truth, even if it's not what you want to hear."

"Okay. About that support hearing."

"I'm letting it go. I do not want to commit one more minute of my life to fighting with those people. I'll pay Paul for any expenses that he's incurred. I have a job now. And Mrs. Fiorelli still won't let me pay rent, but I'm painting their interior this summer. They can't believe I can paint ceilings without a ladder."

Charlie grinned, clicking on the sound. With Ben's choices of internet subscriptions, they watched lots of movies, from current releases to old classics that Ben's stunted childhood had missed. They were semi-hypnotic watching *Field Of Dreams* when Ben's muted cell phone vibrated in his pocket. He pulled it out to check caller ID.

He straightened in the recliner and murmured, "Tori?" He clicked it on. His little sister was sobbing, unintelligibly, the sound of wind in the background. Could she be calling from a beach?

"What's up?" he asked, his voice nonchalant, as if communicating with her was an everyday occurrence.

They hadn't spoken, nor had there been any need, since graduation. He hoped she'd get to the point quickly, feeling annoyed by the inappropriate interruption. After all the trouble she'd caused, he didn't want anything to do with her latest drama. "What do you want?"

"They lied to me, Benny. They said if I didn't say—that—about you, that they'd lose all their money. I didn't understand, but they were so upset. They said if I'd say all those things in court, everything would be okay. They wouldn't lose the house and that I could have my own room and they'd take me to Disney World. I didn't care about that, but I was scared about what they would do to me if I didn't obey them. When they get angry, it's awful." She started sobbing again. "I didn't want to live in a shelter."

"Slow down. I can barely hear you." He clicked *speaker*.

"Once they got me into that courtroom with that big high chair and loud microphone that made my voice bounce off the walls, and all these mean-looking people staring at me, I couldn't do it. I couldn't lie about you, Benny. Back home, Dad took his belt to me. Now everyone hates me. I just can't take it any more."

"Tori! Wait! There's got to be someone you can talk to. What about your teacher or your minister?"

Charlie whispered for him to pump up the volume.

"I'm so sorry I lied about you. They made me do it."

"Why? I never did anything to them. I pulled my weight, gave them my wages, cleaned the house—"

"They said you threatened to tell on them. And they'd go to jail, lose all their money, and we'd end up on the street."

"Why didn't you tell someone?"

"They said they'd send me away, like that little girl Oceana. They said nobody will ever find her either."

Charlie and Ben exchanged stricken glances. "What did they do to her? Where did they take her? Where is she now?"

Tori's sobs, backgrounded by the wind, carried her answer away. "Tori? Where are you? Where are the folks?

Tell me, and I'll come get you and we'll talk about it. I'm not afraid of them."

"It's too late. I am so sorry, Benny. I didn't mean to hurt you. I just had to tell you and say goodbye."

"I forgive you, Tori. What's past is past. We need to forget about it." Ben identified sirens in the background, growing louder. "Tori? What's going on?"

"Goodbye, Benny. I love you."

With that, the landline rang, prompting Charlie to leap from his chair. The caller ID identified Old Mr. Greer. "Turn on the TV to the local station. Now! It's that little girl. The one who lied about Ben." Charlie covered the distance from kitchen to study in several fast strides and switched the channel. The wind and rain-lashed view showed the back side of the high school stadium bleachers, emergency lights cutting through the stormy night.

High on the ladder bolted to the light standard clung a little girl, dressed in a sundress and sweater, which they recognized from graduation day. She was clinging to a rung near the top, her one arm crooked to hold something against her chest.

"Tori! Tori, come down! Let the responders help you descend."

The television camera zeroed in on the child, catching the moment when she dropped something that ricocheted off the metal rungs on its way to the ground.

Both men leapt to the laundry room hooks, grabbing slickers en route to the garage. "I'll drive, you navigate," Charlie yanked open his door not waiting for Ben's confirmation. In thirty seconds, they were hydroplaning down the street, displacing walls of water in their wake.

Unimpeded by drivers who had better sense than to be out on such a night, they made record time to the handicap parking lot behind the stadium. Ben was out of the car before Charlie came to a complete stop. He parted onlookers with his outstretched arms as if he were swimming an Olympic race. Even the first responders, who were trying to coax the child with a bullhorn, were too startled by the lunging young man to react. Reaching the bottom of the ladder, he sprang, landing several rungs up, and kept climbing.

Charlie pushed his way to the front of the crowd that appeared to be neighbors, too stunned to do anything but gape. Scanning to the top of the ladder, rain splashing in his eyes, he saw Ben stop just shy of his sister. She clung to the ladder, her back to him, peering over her shoulder at him. Whatever he was saying was lost in the storm.

Finally, he took one more tentative step. Then another. Closing, he enveloped her waist with his left arm. He buried his face near her ear, speaking continually. Finally, she nodded. His communication with her changed its urgency, as he said something, to which she moved her left hand down one rung, then the right. Ben descended another step, instructing her as she followed his lead. In what seemed like forever, they reached the ground. He picked her up, carrying her to a waiting ambulance, and followed her inside.

When a policeman approached the back of the ambulance, Ben hopped out, anger roiling off him. Charlie approached, fearing that Ben was angry enough to slug him. "This is your fault!" He bellowed within everyone's earshot. "If you'd just done your job and given me that damn test, none of this would have happened." A strobe flashed, immortalizing the scene for the reporter who held the mike.

Ben returned to the ambulance, answering the attendants' questions and imploring them to notify Child Protective Services. This little girl, he explained, was in a world of hurt, and her parents were responsible. He hopped into the back as they were closing the doors. A responder thumped them and, with lights flashing and sirens blaring, the ambulance edged from the scene.

Charlie trudged back to his car as the others were dispersing. A reporter who recognized him approached and asked for his reaction to the young man's averting disaster. He shook his head and proceeded to his car, bundling his dripping self behind the wheel.

Chapter 31

Charlie, Ben, Claire, and Brownie gathered around Jade's large oak table. Jonathan was supposed to be sleeping, but Charlie had his doubts. The idea of a family meeting fascinated Jonathan, having heard stories from friends who had large, extended families. They'd talk about things little kids weren't supposed to know, or play cards and games, and sip forbidden drinks.

"What's going to happen to Tori?" Jade asked.

Ben shrugged. "I haven't heard, and I have no way to find out. The court hasn't lifted the restraining order, so technically I was in violation when I came to her rescue. So far, there have been no repercussions."

"That's bullshit. She recanted, then she called you. And you saved her. Are you going to ask Zeke to do something about that order?"

"Nope. And I'm leaving her situation to the professionals. If I fought the restraining order, won, and forced myself into the drama, that could invite trouble all over again."

"Do you even want to get involved?" she asked.

"What I want is to distance myself from the whole sordid mess."

"Speaking of little girls, I have some good news, which is what prompted this family meeting," Brownie said. "This is for you, Ben."

"What is it?" he asked, examining both sides of the

white envelope that bore a Canadian return address and postage. He slipped his Kershaw knife from his pocket and slit the flap. From its depth he withdrew a glossy photo and a folded letter. "Oh my god! It's Oceana!" The group nearly clunked heads to see the picture he laid on the table.

Ben turned the photo over and read: *Rebecca Cohen.* He looked up at Brownie. "Is that her real name? And however did you find her? And are these her parents with her?"

"They are. You gave me two excellent clues to search missing children's databases. Her blanket, which contained her DNA, and a special name that wasn't her name at all."

"Then whose name was it?"

"Nobody's. It was a family password in case the family ever got separated. The family is Canadian, from Quebec to be specific, and they speak French at home, although the parents are multi-lingual."

"So how did she end up in the foster care system in Pennsylvania?" Ben asked.

"Via a convoluted path. Her parents' great grandparents were German Jews, who were in the diamond business. When Hitler came to power in the 1930s, they and their extended families over-reacted, some said, and promptly relocated to France. Thinking they were safe, they re-established their jewelry businesses that prospered until Hitler targeted France, and they heard about the persecution in their homeland.

"They didn't stick around to see what came next. As the story goes, they sewed their inventory into their clothing seams and immigrated to England. Still not feeling safe, they moved to Canada, where several generations still live. Last year the Cohen family embarked on a visit to Germany, hoping to trace descendants of the family who had stayed behind. They found hopeful information that led them to Israel."

"With a small child in tow?"

"No. They'd left Rebecca at home with her nanny. While the nanny and her charge were shopping at a fresh market, there was a distraction—an escaped goat—to everyone's delight. When the nanny glanced down to see Rebecca's reaction, the child had disappeared. The nanny ran in circles, crying and begging for anyone to help find the child. By the time the police got involved and scoured the entire area, she was long gone.

"The parents, who were summoned, took the first flight home and launched a massive hunt, complete with media coverage. A reward was offered, which grew exponentially."

"Wasn't there a ransom call? Was the nanny involved?"

"No call, and the nanny was cleared of any wrong doing."

"So how did she end up in the Pennsylvania foster care system?"

"She was found alone and crying in an amusement park. Evidently, for whatever reason, the kidnapper saw her as a liability and ditched her. Or she ran away. When vendors in the park noticed the child and nobody claiming her, they called security. She didn't match the description of any children separated from their families, kidnapping victims, or lost children, and thus ended up in foster care."

"So!" Ben punctuated the air with his finger. "I was right. She was a smart, loving little girl. She wasn't slow. She only spoke the few words of English that she must have learned recently."

"What's in the letter?" Brownie asked.

Ben unfolded a piece of gold-edged stationery with the mother's name embossed at the top. "She starts with her profound thanks for finding their daughter. That the family is overjoyed about her safe return. And if you ever want or need anything, bla, bla, bla. They'd like to send me the reward that they'd offered." He shook his head. "Not for me. Brownie, you claim it. It was your hard work that re-united this family." He handed the letter back to Brownie but kept the picture and the envelope with the return address. "I'll send them your contact information."

"Ah, no!"

"You can always donate it to a good cause, but I think you deserve a finder's percent. Do something good for your family.

"Gentlemen?" Jade pointed to Jonathan who had crept down the hall. She rose with an admonishing look on her face, but Ben intervened.

"Aw, let him stay up. It's not that late."

Jonathan sidled up to the table and squeezed between Ben and Claire. "Did you tell 'em?" he asked in a stage whisper.

"Not yet."

"Tell us what?" Charlie asked. *Not an engagement. They were barely nineteen with a world of education facing them.*

"I don't know if you're going to like this, but I hope you'll trust me. I've done my homework and thought it out thoroughly. Mr. A. and Brownie, I appreciate, more than I can say, the work you did contacting colleges on my behalf, getting their agreement to take another look at me mid-year while giving me a chance to work out in the pool. Maybe enter some competitions.

"But, in the end, I've decided I'm not ready. I need to get away for a while. I got myself into legal hot water because I was under-educated and lacked maturity. Most important, I need to grow up. So—I decided to enlist in the Navy. They have awesome opportunities for swimmers, and at least I can make land if the ship ever wrecks."

"I don't know what to say," Charlie stammered. "Is it a done deal?"

"I didn't want to tell you until I knew if I qualified. I've graduated from high school and am physically fit—that part was a check mark. I've worked hard on my eye exercises all summer, and my reading proficiency enabled me to pass their written exam. After aggressive treatment of my sinus infections and my nose healed, I'm finally rid of the headaches. I'm ready."

"You've really thought this out. What happens next?"

"I'll be sworn in as an E-1 Seaman Recruit. During basic training, I'll be immersed in the military culture and values and taught the core skills required by the Navy's service component. Boot camp is located at the Great Lakes Naval Training Center on the western shore of Lake Michigan, halfway between Chicago and Milwaukee. After basic, I'll be a Seaman."

"When do you report?"

"In September, which gives me lots of time to paint walls and do whatever else you can dream up."

"Jonathan, did you know about this?" Jade asked.

The child glowed. "He asked me first. He said he wouldn't enlist unless I thought it was okay. He showed me the brochures and all the cool uniforms and ships. Mommy, how old do I have to be before I can join the Navy?"

Jade didn't have a quick answer for that. "See Papa?" Jonathan said. "I can keep a secret."

Ben clasped Claire's hand. "I have no intention of letting this lady go. When I'm discharged from the Navy, I can pay for college and, by the time I finish that, Ms. Claire will be Doctor Claire. In spite of the distance, we'll stay connected."

"Maybe we can go into practice together," Jade said.

"Ben will always be family, right?" Jonathan asked.

"Just like you and Mommy and me."

Charlie smiled. "Ben's like the son I never had. And yes, we'll always be family."

"Then he needs to give you a name, like I gave you, remember? *Indeed Charlie did, at Jonathan's grandpa's funeral. The child had lamented that now he had no grandpa. Charlie had said, you can adopt me, to which Jonathan had agreed and named him Papa.*

All eyes turned to Ben. "Well?" Charlie asked.

"I'd like to call you Dad, if that's okay with you."

"It is indeed!"

⌘

Old Mr. Greer and Charlie sat on Greer's lawn chairs, nursing their eight-ounce cans of Miller Beer. "How do you feel about Ben joining the Navy?"

"To be honest, for so long I hadn't looked beyond his next crisis or the next day. Now I can't imagine not having to worry about him."

"He'll be fine. And just like your girls, you've got to remember our kids are only lent to us. I say, give them roots and give them wings, then let them fly."

Charlie chuckled. "Or swim."

Old Mr. Greer paused, Charlie letting the old gentleman plan the segue to his next point, the pair filling the space with sips of beer as was their custom. "Have you noticed my new fine young man who's mowing my lawn? I mentioned to him that you might need help too. I hope that was all right." *Not a real question.* "He's a hard worker. Earns every dollar. Keeps a killer schedule, with school, a part-time job, wrestling, and soccer practice. Complains about being too short. I told him that's what ladders are for."

"How tall is he?"

"Five eight if that. I told him that as long as his feet

reach the floor, he's tall enough. Did I mention? He doesn't smoke, drink, or do drugs. Comes from a huge family with little money. You'd be doing both him and yourself a favor by hiring him."

Charlie buried a smile in his next sip of beer. *Here we go again.*

✺✺✺

September brought another milestone for Charlie—one year to the day since he *graduated* from hospice. His first homecoming order had been to fire those well-meaning health care workers, having assured them that he was perfectly capable of taking care of himself. He'd practically danced across the lawn to Old Mr. Greer's to resume their old boys' club meetings and discuss the events of the day.

This year, Charlie's blended family waited at Amtrak's Lancaster station for the Philadelphia train that would whisk Ben and Clare to their new lives. Claire would join her freshman roommate for their first semester at Penn while Ben caught the train to Chicago en route to western Michigan and basic training.

They arrived trackside early, having left plenty of time for Old Mr. Greer to amble. He had surprised them, consenting to use a collapsible wheelchair, his excuse to test all those handicap innovations for his *elderly* friends, should they ask his opinion. He gave the elevators, the ramps, and the automatic door plates his approval, even checking out the restroom. Charlie smiled at his dear friend and how little it took to make every day an adventure.

"Hey! I was afraid I'd miss you!" Troy took the steps down to the track two at a time, camera at the ready. "We've got to capture the moment." He stooped to Jonathan's eye level who, as he expected, was trying not to cry.

"Want to try out my camera?" he asked.

Jonathan lit up. "Can I? Oh boy!"

"Now, I gotta warn you. This camera is heavier than yours. Let's see if you can handle it."

"Sure. I'm a big boy."

"Okay. Now we photographers have to protect our equipment, so—here—let's secure the strap around your neck." Troy unclipped the existing strap and hooked a short one in its place. "That's about right. Try shooting Ben and Claire."

"Ah, they're too fuzzy."

"Adjust the focus by squeezing your fingers together like this."

"Where's the trigger?"

"Here. Hold the camera with two hands and press the button with your right forefinger. Now let's see your picture."

"They don't have any heads."

"Try again. What you see is what you'll get. Keep your eyes open." *Click.* "You did it."

"Mr. Troy, will you teach me how to use my new camera? I want to take really good pictures, like the ones my grandfather took of my daddy. I want to start my own book for when I'm a grandfather."

"I'd be happy to."

The distant sound of the approaching train whistle caught everyone's attention. Ben shouldered his duffle bag and tried to snag Claire's suitcase. She gave him a smug look and muscled it herself. As the train slowed, the waiting passengers shifted, aligning themselves to hop aboard. With a flurry of hugs, kisses, goodbyes, and promises to email as soon as they arrived, they boarded. In moments the train disappeared.

Nobody seemed to know what to do next as they sauntered toward the elevator that would take them upstairs to the terminal.

"I'm hungry!" Jonathan punctuated their uncertainty with the prospect of food.

Charlie laughed. "Me too, buddy. And I know just the diner that's family friendly."

"That's us, huh, Papa. We're family."

Epilogue

It's true what they say, Charlie reflected. Your friendship circle grows exponentially when your children's friends' parents become part of your life. With Ben aboard a ship in the Mediterranean, but with years of school ahead for Jonathan, Charlie said yes to pleas for help in community programs that benefited children. This time, it was a bake sale for Ben's high school swim team. The parents club was having a scholarship fundraiser for kids who couldn't afford the travel team. That team was vitally important, especially for low-income families, swim-team mom Ellen Quillen had emphasized whenever she begged Charlie's help. Their travel team attracted college scouts.

Jonathan helped Charlie assemble the ingredients for Brownies for a Crowd, and most of the brownies made it to the sale. Charlie knew they'd sell out quickly as Jonathan beamed at the patrons who lingered at their table, listening to him proudly explain how he had helped make them.

Charlie's mind drifted to that long-ago conversation in the grocery store about the dreadful foster girl who'd lied so egregiously. A scrap of a detail surfaced. Why hadn't it registered before? Had it seemed that irrelevant? One woman had been remarking about a student-athlete who, in spite of being skinny and tall, held a weight lifting record. But Ben was a swimmer. One of his friends called him *string bean*, teasing that he'd never hold a weight-lifting record without cheating.

It dawned on Charlie that, in all the numerous times he'd walked the long corridor that linked the gym with the lobby, he'd checked on the swim team but never the weight-lifting trophies. "Jonathan, can you tend to the brownies with Mrs. Quillen for a minute while I stretch my legs? They're beginning to cramp."

Down the long corridor he passed the trophy cases, crammed with evidence of glory. And years of individual plaques held nameplates immortalizing individual record-holders. Swimmers—yes, there were Ben's records dating to his sophomore year for freestyle, the breaststroke, and diving before he was forced to drop out. Track stars, wrestlers, tennis champions, and on through the hall of honor. Finally he came to weight lifters. Ben held the record for the deadlift that remained to that day.

But how could that be? The family owned no weight-lifting equipment. How does one accomplish such a feat without intense practice? On a whim, he entered the gym where a short, blond coach in a bright blue singlet was spotting a student. When the student rose from the bench and strode toward the exit, Charlie approached the teacher.

"Coach? A Minute? As a taxpayer, I'm delighted that our school district invests in an expansive sports program. I was just admiring the trophies. Do you remember Benjamin Olinger?"

"Of course! One of the best and most honorable kids I ever coached. How he ever found time to work out…" He paused, taking a deep breath. "Awful thing, what happened to him."

"But did he? Work out? When? He was always in class. Or working. And there were no weights at his house or his friends' homes."

"Let me think—it was, um, right before Christmas. From Thanksgiving until we closed for the holidays. He was here every day, squeezing workouts between school and his jobs, sometimes a half hour at a time. If you look at the plaque in the hall, the date of his record-setting competition was Saturday, December twenty-first. His record still stands."

Of course! The day after the snowstorm when he took Jonathan sledding. That's it! One of the two missing times! "Do you still have the attendance records for when he was practicing?"

"No. I turn all that stuff in at the end of each school year. But I can tell you, right to the minute, because I keep my calendars. Have them for my entire coaching career."

Charlie felt elation and regret simultaneously. If only! The coach's records would have accounted for any missing hours for the entire month of December. Stopped the entire prosecution at once. What if he'd gone to prison because of that hole in the alibi because he couldn't account for the entire month? The jury wouldn't take Ben's word over a lying ten-year-old girl.

He had envisioned it, planned it, seen the attorney in his dreams, tapping their homemade calendar with an old-fashioned pointer. It should have gotten old fast. And that little brat would have been exposed to the entire world for the liar she was. But what if…

"Mr. Alderfer?" Charlie jumped back to the present. "Thank God for people like you. If you hadn't come to his rescue—gotten involved—his life would have been ruined. We need more people like you who aren't afraid to stand up for what's right.

"The problem's even bigger than it was years ago. Remember the Vietnam era? 'If I'm old enough to die for my country, I'm old enough to vote!' At the same time school districts decided kids shouldn't enroll unless they were five by September first, not by January thirty-first. And some fathers, who wanted their boys to be standout athletes, held them out even longer. We ended up with eighteen-year-old high school juniors who could sign legal contracts, drop out, refuse medical help, and so on. That includes being questioned by police without parental consent. They may be legal adults, but they lack real-world experience to protect themselves."

Charlie closed his eyes, shaking his head. *I was arrogant. And angry. I took a terrible chance with that young man's life. Playing detective and defense attorney simultaneously. Had the trial proceeded, he could have been convicted, drawn a stiff sentence, and been unemployable. Branded a sexual predator. Maybe died in prison.*

"Papa!" The pair turned toward a beaming Jonathan. "We sold every brownie! We made a whole bunch of money! They kept saying, 'keep the change!'"

The coach stooped to Jonathan's level. "Thank you for helping the swim team. By the way, do you swim?" Jonathan grinned. "If you practice a lot, maybe someday you'll be on the swim team too."

Jonathan beamed. "Ben taught me to swim for my birthday present."

The coach rose and turned to face Charlie, clasping his hand. "For your records, it would be my pleasure to photocopy my calendar pages and see that you have a set for Ben. Just in case. And if you ever need me to testify to expunge his record, I would be honored."

About the Author

Nancy A. Hughes, a native of Key West who grew up in Pittsburgh, lives with her husband in south central Pennsylvania. Following graduation from Penn State where she studied journalism, she spent years as a business writer, specializing in media, community, and public relations for small to midsize businesses.

In recent years, Nancy turned her attention to murdering people—on paper, that is. Her focus is character-driven crime-solving mysteries, her subgenre being amateur sleuth. Her debut mystery novel, *The Dying Hour*, was released in 2016 by Black Opal Books. *A Matter of Trust*, the first in her *Trust* trilogy, followed in 2017, *Redeeming Trust*, also in 2017, and *Vanished* in 2018.

When she isn't writing, she is devoted to shade gardening, volunteering at the VA, and spending time with family and friends. Visit her on her website at hughescribe.com.